"Her Unexpected Catch"

Bulbs, Blossoms and Bouquets #5

By Laura Ann

This is a work of fiction. Similarities to real people, places, or events are entirely coincidental.

HER UNEXPECTED CATCH

First edition. June 3, 2021.

Copyright © 2021 Laura Ann.

Written by Laura Ann.

DEDICATION

To Mr. Brown, my high school English Teacher.
You cultivated my love of literature
and the thousands of other students in your care.
You are a true hero.
Thank you.

ACKNOWLEDGEMENTS

No author works alone. Thank you, Tami.
You make it Christmas every time
I get a new cover. And thank you to my Beta Team.
Truly, your help with my stories is immeasurable.

CHAPTER 1

"Does everyone have their schedules ready?" Hadlee scrolled through her phone, getting to her calendar app. She was nearly giddy with anticipation. They were only a couple of weeks away from heading to the coast so she could start researching the information she needed to finish her last research project.

She'd been looking forward to this for years, and it would be a big milestone for her. Once all was said and done, it would give Hadlee the credentials she needed to go from being an Assistant Professor, to an Associate Professor. Following in her dad's footsteps had become the sole purpose of her life and right now, Hadlee was so close, she could taste it.

"Yep," Chrissy said in her breathy, high soprano. The tiny girl pushed her wide framed glasses back up her nose. They were the same stylish frames most girls only wore in well-planned pictures, but in this case, Chrissy actually needed them. She was legally blind without them.

"On it," Lucas replied, giving Hadlee a chin tilt. The young man was lanky and often loud-mouthed, but smart as a whip and had a good eye for detail, which would be a great asset on this trip.

Joshua grunted. His bulky limbs and dark skin stood out in stark relief against Hadlee's 'Burn-Just-At-The-Thought-Of-The-Sun' skin. He looked like he should be on the football field instead of inside a laboratory, but Hadlee was grateful for his presence. Her TA was perfect for hauling around heavy equipment and his diving certification made him a shoe-in for a position on this research trip.

"Great," Hadlee said, smiling though she wanted to be serious. Kindness always got her farther, even when she didn't feel like being polite. "I just want to double check that we're all on the same page here."

Lucas snickered. "You mean triple check, don't you?"

"More like bajillion-check," Joshua said with a snort.

Hadlee's grin was genuine at this point, if not sheepish. "Sorry," she said. "I just don't want anything to go wrong."

"It's all right," Chrissy said softly. "No one wants a repeat of your last project."

Hadlee held back a wince. She'd tried hard to forget the disaster that had happened last time she'd gone on a research trip. It was a wonder she'd been awarded a grant for this one at all. She knew her father had to have thrown his weight around in order for anyone to trust her again, and normally she wanted to do it all on her own, but in this case...she was grateful for his interference.

"Which is exactly why we're checking to make sure everything is in order," Hadlee said, shoving her embarrassment and shame to the back corner she usually kept them in. *Move on,* she reminded herself. *There's no point in dwelling in the past.* "We leave in two weeks."

"Eight a.m., meet in front of the school, luggage packed the night before," Lucas said dryly. He grinned when Chrissy elbowed him. "Hey...I almost felt it that time," Lucas joked, referring to Chrissy's small size.

Hadlee was five-five and she was a good six inches taller than Chrissy, making her feel like a giant, though compared to the rest of the world, Hadlee was nothing but average. "Lucas, leave her alone," Hadlee said automatically. Her TA's were like siblings after having spent so much time together the last couple of years. Hadlee often felt like a mother as she tried to keep the young college students in line. "Now...we're scheduled to meet our boat captain on the twenty-eighth, but since we're arriving on the twenty-sixth, I'll see if I can wrangle up an earlier meet and greet."

"What's the hurry?" Lucas asked, tilting his head and narrowing his eyes. It was a look Hadlee had grown used to over the last couple years. Lucas was the curious sort and he always looked a little like an overgrown puppy when he wanted to know something. His curiosity made him a good marine biologist, but his persistence made him annoying at times.

Hadlee brushed him off. "Just eager to get going. I know we planned to orient ourselves the first couple of days, but if we're there, what would it hurt to see if we can get started early?"

"Doesn't hurt at all," Chrissy murmured. She was fumbling with a camera as she spoke, fiddling with settings and other things that Hadlee had never been very good at. She was grateful her quiet assistant was willing to come along, though she sincerely hoped Chrissy didn't get seasick. She had once mentioned throwing up on a small boat ride at a family amusement park. That kind of queasy stomach would not be helpful in their limited few months on the boat.

"Are we on the water on the twenty-eighth?" Joshua asked, shifting in his seat, which looked smaller under him than any other person at the table.

Hadlee shook her head. "I'm not sure. I think day one is supposed to be orientation. We go out for sure the next day, unless we can convince the captain otherwise." She sighed and pinched the bridge of her nose, trying to hold back a headache. "I just want everything to run smoothly, guys. Let's be sure our luggage is here on time so the van is ready to go the night before." She looked up, her light brown eyebrows raised high. "Does anyone need help with knowing what to pack?" She specifically looked at Lucas.

Luke scoffed. "Do you really think I don't know how to put some underwear and socks into a suitcase?"

Chrissy made a choking noise. "That's all you're bringing?"

Luke pumped his eyebrows. "It would make for a fun trip, right?"

"Might at least want a wetsuit," Hadlee said wryly. "We're not on the warm ocean side of the country."

"Pity that," Luke grumbled, slumping in his seat and folding his arms over his chest. "It means less girls sitting around in bikinis."

Joshua rolled his eyes. "Man, those girls are too young for you anyway."

"Doesn't mean it hurts to look!" Luke defended himself.

"Um...woman! Right here!" Chrissy scolded. She glared at Luke. "When are you gonna stop treating us like objects?"

"DON'T! Answer that," Hadlee interrupted. She'd heard this argument too many times and the fact that it was happening now made her question why she was bringing this particular group. There were a bunch of TA's in her department to choose from, but these ones had had some of the specific traits she wanted. They'd worked together before and were friends...most of the time. *Maybe they're too good of friends,* she thought warily.

"This is a work trip," Joshua said in his ultra-deep voice. "Better remember that."

Hadlee smiled her thanks. Joshua was the most focused of all the helpers and that would serve him well on this trip, not to mention help Hadlee keep her other workers in line. "He's right," Hadlee reiterated. "This isn't a vacation. We need to gather the information and get it analyzed. Any girl-watching or fun has to happen off the clock."

"Is there actually going to be any off-the-clock time?" Luke argued.

Hadlee nodded. "Yes. I'm not a slave driver, Luke. You'll have your evenings to yourselves, and there will always be days where Mother Nature and weather interfere with our ability to gather information. But..." She pinned him in place with a firm look. "I expect you to be on your best behavior while we're there. You're too old for me to have to be your mother or even older sister. Keep your appointments, stay on top of the information, and I won't have to worry about sending you home early or regretting my choice to bring you along. All right?"

Luke rolled his eyes, but nodded. "I got it. I'm not stupid, I just like to let loose once in awhile."

"Well, do it where the rest of us can't see," Joshua murmured.

Hadlee laughed softly. "Okay, now, let's go over again what exactly we're looking for." She ignored the subsequent groans and opened up her proposal folder. Things were about to get real, and this time...she wouldn't let anybody down.

"YOU NEED HOW MANY FLOWERS?" Felix choked on air and started coughing as he looked at the invoice.

Charli, his sister, rolled her eyes. "Felix. First off, it's not like you're paying for this. I have my own career and I'll take care of it. Second, it's my *wedding*. The only one I'm going to have. I want it to be..." She chewed on her lip. Charli had never been into excessively "feminine" touches, but it appeared that had gone down the drain when it came to her wedding.

"You want it to be a fairy tale," Felix grumbled, quoting something their mother used to say when they were children.

Her grin was sheepish. "Is that wrong?"

He reluctantly shook his head. "No. But I also want to set a few things straight." Felix set down the paper and reached across the table to grab Charli's hands. "You're my sister, Charli. My *only* sister at that. If you think that I'm letting you take on the bill of this wedding yourself...then you're nuts." He held up a hand to stop her argument. "If Mom and Dad were alive, you know darn well they wouldn't care that you have your own career. They would want to help." He smiled warmly. It was a side he didn't show very many people. Felix tended to be fairly serious, but he'd never been able to manage it with his sister. "And since they're gone, I get to. It's my duty and honor."

Charli shook her head, her eyes a little misty. "It's not. I'm too old for you to do that."

Felix raised an eyebrow. "I *want* to, Char." He squeezed her hands again. "I want to."

"Does this mean you'll be the one giving me away?"

Felix straightened and let go of her hands. Who knew such a simple question would bring such strong emotions? He could honestly say that when a car accident took their parents years ago, this was not something that Felix had thought about, but he was pretty sure he knew exactly how his father would feel in his situation. He cleared his throat. "I wouldn't have it any other way," he said. "If you'd asked someone else, I would have pulled out the cement boots."

She rolled her eyes and began to gather all the papers back into her folder. "You're ridiculous."

Felix knocked his knuckles on the table. "I'm ridiculous? You're the one buying enough flowers to fill an entire stadium. AND you're stuffing them inside a church."

Charli shrugged. "It'll smell nice. What's wrong with that?"

He chuckled. "So, it'll cover up Bronson's stench when he sweats?"

Charli huffed and walked around the table to smack the back of his head. "Knock it off. You love Bronson as much as I do."

Felix rubbed the sore spot and glared. "I doubt that. I find I have absolutely no desire to kiss or hug him, which you seem to do in spades."

"He's hot," Charli said nonchalantly as she rifled through the cupboards of the kitchen. "Can you blame me?"

"Yes...yes, I can," Felix retorted. "It's sickening to watch and I have to peer around every corner of the house with a mirror before entering."

Charli laughed. "You're such a dork. If you're so opposed to a little PDA, why don't you go spend more time on your boat?"

At the thought of his fishing charter, Felix scowled. The season was opening up, but he wasn't, and it angered him.

"Hey..." Charli came up behind him and set a glass of water and a sandwich down. "Still mad about that booking you have with the scientist?"

"Marine biologist," Felix grunted. He tore off a bite of the sandwich. "I can't believe I have to spend almost the whole season toting around some chick who only wants to shut us all down anyway."

"How do you know she wants to shut you down?" Charli asked, sitting back down with her own lunch.

Felix shrugged and squished a bit of bread between his fingers. "She's trying to figure out if climate change is messing with our dungeness crab." His dark eyes landed on his sister's. "What else do those crazy environmentalists want? Most of them don't think that humans should even exist."

Charli shook her head. "You're taking this way out of proportion," she scolded. "You have no idea what your charge thinks or what she wants to do. Dungeness crab is a big deal in our state. Maybe her study will help keep the industry going for longer because she's helping make it healthier."

He snorted. "That's what they want you to think."

Charli's phone buzzed and she stopped arguing long enough to look down. When a goofy grin lit her face, Felix knew he'd lost her. Groaning, he finished his sandwich and took his dishes to the sink. He needed to get back out to the boat. He'd been roped into taking this doctor lady around, but that meant that *Morwenna*, his boat, needed to be ready to go and right now, his beauty needed a little facelift.

He walked past his sister, who was still messing with her phone, and kissed the top of her head. "See ya later. Try not to melt into a puddle of goo before I get back, huh?"

"Whatever," Charli brushed him off.

Felix chuckled. If there had ever been any question that she was in love, it would be the fact that she wasn't shooting back quick retorts to Felix's teasing. Bronson, her fiancé, had a way of taking all her attention and Felix had been left behind.

His stride was purposeful and strong as he marched out the door and started down the sidewalk to the docks. It would take several minutes to walk there, but the day was sunny and bright, making Felix crave the fresh, salty air.

She wants me to give her away, huh? The idea of handing his sister off to another man was bittersweet. She'd move out of their shared childhood home and only come back to visit. All the shared dinners, reminiscing, and movie marathons would change.

Truth be told, they had already changed, but mostly they had just added to their numbers. Now, Bronson joined them during their adventures. But after Charli was married, it would be different. Her adventures wouldn't include her brother anymore and that was wonderful and painful all at the same time. He wasn't eager to lose his sister, but there was definitely a part of him that was eager for freedom. And he truly would be free. Even his beloved dog, Hermit, had passed away during the last year from old age. There was absolutely nothing tying him down at all.

Felix had stated more than once that his only love was the ocean and his boat. Other than family and friends, it was the only thing that truly made him happy. There was just something about the freedom of being in the middle of a vast ocean that spoke to him on a level no human could manage.

Expanding his family was great, but he knew it would never come from his side. Bronson was a good guy and he adored Charli, and when they had children, Felix would definitely be the "fun uncle," but that would be the extent of it. After having spent most of his adult life taking care of his sister, not having any immediate responsibilities would be a welcome change.

He took a deep breath through his nose, enjoying the familiar smells of the ocean and the town. Contentment warmed his chest and a small smile played on his lips. When his boat came into view, the smile grew. His first mate and only deck hand were already scurrying around, cleaning out all the winter dirt and dust, and Felix was eager to join them.

This. This is where I belong. And there'll never be room for anything else.

"Captain!"

Felix grinned and gave a playful salute to his crew as he approached. He was right where he wanted to be.

CHAPTER 2

"**Y**ou'll be careful this time?"

Hadlee bit her tongue. She didn't mind her father checking on her, or even reminding her to be safe, but adding "this time" hurt. She hadn't meant for things to go wrong on her last research trip. The storm had come up faster than anyone had foreseen and Hadlee was being blamed for Mother Nature's fickleness. "Yep. I'll be careful."

Her father looked over the tome in his hands and raised an eyebrow. "The ocean is no laughing matter."

Hadlee threw her hands out to the side. "I'm not laughing." She pointed to her face. "Do I look like I'm laughing to you?"

Dr. Caleb Ford sighed and set the large textbook in his lap before pulling off his reading glasses. He was the epitome of a stereotypical college professor. From his gray hair, which curled around his ears, to the leather patches on his sweaters and the bowtie in between, Hadlee had been sure that all the cartoon stereotypes she had watched growing up had been caricatures of her father. "Hadlee," he said with measured patience. "I don't feel like you're taking this seriously."

Hadlee pinched her lips together. "Why? Because I had an accident two years ago?" She held her fingers up in the air. "I've checked, double-checked, and even triple-checked my reservations, my equipment, the rental car, and even that my TA's are still planning to come." She fell into a chair with a plop. "If I try to control any more of this trip, I think my team might rebel."

Her father chuckled. "You can't control everything, dear. Any good scientist knows that."

Then why do people blame me for a storm? Hadlee held back the question. It had been years ago and wasn't worth dredging up yet again. But there were times, like now, that she struggled with the fact that no one seemed to trust her anymore. She knew she'd been lucky that no one had been hurt when a sudden storm had hit their boat, but she wasn't the first person to get caught unawares. Should she have looked deeper into the weather forecast? Yes. Had she learned her lesson? Yes. Should everyone forgive her and let it go? Also, yes.

Unfortunately, no one else seemed to agree with her. She didn't know if it was the fact that she was one of the younger professors at the school, or if it had to do with the fact that she was a woman, but not a single member of her board seemed to be able to let go of her mistake. It was often brought up as a tale of warning, which was fine, but when it only seemed to happen when she was in the meeting, she knew it was more for her own benefit than anyone else's.

"Maybe not, but we can sure try," Hadlee said, forcing a smile on her stiff mouth. She didn't want to argue with her dad, especially since she was leaving for the next few months. She was already worried about him. With her younger sisters all out of the house, her father would have no one there to take care of him while she was gone. "You do plan to control *yourself* while I'm gone, right?" Hadlee gave him a mock scolding stare. "I know you're eager to throw a rager once I'm out, but please try not to ruin any of the furniture."

Her father huffed and put his glasses back on. "Never fear. I only invited a few hundred of my favorite colleagues. Don't be surprised if you come home to an aquarium instead of a house."

Hadlee smiled. It was a joke she and her father had had since she was little. Hadlee had always been as interested in fish and their habitats as her father. When her mother was still alive, she'd joke that her husband and oldest daughter should live inside a tank instead of on land. "I'll look forward to it."

Caleb smirked and went back to his reading.

"But seriously, Dad," Hadlee went on, even knowing she was interrupting him. "You remember you're going to have to fix all your own dinners and lunches?"

He gave her a wry look. "I've been taking care of myself for longer than you've been alive, young lady."

Hadlee laughed as intended, but the words sat heavily. She didn't feel young anymore. Losing her mother at the tender age of ten had robbed Hadlee of her carefree teenage years along with the tender example of womanhood.

Instead, Hadlee had stepped up to become a mother to her three younger sisters and thrown herself into her studies in order to be as little of a burden as possible on her grieving father.

Her years of work had paid off, since Hadlee was now one of the younger Assistant Professors at the same college her father taught for, and her sisters had all been educated and sent out into the workforce. Two had even found their significant others, leaving only the youngest, who was just twenty-one, and Hadlee, who was closing in on her thirtieth birthday, without families of their own.

Celeste, Hadlee's sister, was young enough to enjoy her single state, flitting from man to man and building a resume with her first real career job. Hadlee, on the other hand, hadn't been on a date in years and had nothing but a long list of fish facts to prove herself with.

Which is why her father's words made her feel weighed down. She didn't feel young, or footloose and fancy free. She felt tired...lacking...and weary. All words that definitely shouldn't describe someone still in their twenties.

Sort of still in their twenties anyway, Hadlee reminded herself. She sighed heavily and tucked a piece of her hair behind her ear. She'd never considered herself unfortunate-looking, but it seemed that if you knew more about the mating habits of stingrays than you did what was happening in national politics, you tended to drive off would-be-suitors before you ever had a chance.

"What's the matter?" her father asked, though he didn't look up from his book.

Hadlee shook her head. "Nothing." She forced another smile. "I just need to go to bed early. I've been having trouble sleeping with everything looming in front of me and I'm suffering for it now."

Caleb nodded, still keeping his gaze down. "Can't let yourself get sick before you even leave. It would be a pity if Christian had to take your place."

Hadlee sucked in a quick breath and stiffened. "They would replace me with *him?*" she ground out.

Gray eyes, with the slightest hint of green, so like her own, finally pulled away from the book and stared at her calmly. "They would."

Hadlee huffed and her knee began to bounce. "I can't believe this." Christian had been chasing her heels for years, determined to reach Associate Professor before she did. While Hadlee didn't think the other professor would ever do anything to sabotage her, he did seem to work extra hard to weasel his way into the good graces of the Full or Endowed Professors. There was a word for a man like him, but Hadlee wouldn't let herself use it. She refused to drop to his level and become a petty jerk who enjoyed the failures of others.

"It shouldn't come as a surprise," Caleb said easily, going back to his book. "Christian has proven himself capable and if you couldn't go, he'd be the next logical choice."

Because he's part of the "Good Ole Boys" club.

Hadlee shook away the thoughts. It didn't matter. Christian wasn't here and it wasn't his project. She would do her research, proving she could be trusted with a crew. Then she would write and publish her findings, proving her capabilities as a marine biologist, and voila! She'd be ready to take on the role of being an Associate Professor and there was nothing anyone would be able to do to stop her.

"JULIAN! TOSS ME THAT rope!" Felix turned just in time to see a rope headed toward his face. "Whoa!" He caught it, then scowled, only to break into laughter. "Well, if it isn't Captain Ken." Felix grinned at one of his best friends walking across the deck. "What brings our police captain to my humble dwellings?"

"Shut up," Ken said good-naturedly. His blond hair was being swept around his head by the wind, but nothing could hide his wide smile. "I heard you were getting the old girl prettied up for the season."

Felix growled. "Old?" He petted the railing next to him. "Don't listen to him, *Morwenna*. You're just as beautiful as the day I bought you."

Ken shook his head. "One of these days we ought to have your head checked."

Felix shrugged. "If my worst crime is talking to my boat, then I think I got off pretty easy in life."

Ken chuckled and folded his thick arms over his chest. His hip went against the railing as he lazily relaxed on the gently rocking deck. "It's not. I've given you more speeding tickets than I can count."

Felix rolled his eyes. "I don't understand why being the friend of a cop doesn't have more benefits."

Ken shrugged. "The law's the law, buddy boy. You live by it, you die by it."

"And people wonder why I prefer the ocean." Felix scratched his scruffy chin. "Out here there's far more freedom."

"Keep your freedom," Ken said, tilting his head toward the sun. "I'll keep my order."

"That works."

"Captain?"

Both men turned toward the call and Felix grumbled under his breath. "My boat, Ken. I'm the captain."

Ken's grin was anything but apologetic. "Sorry. Habit."

Felix couldn't seem to help another eye roll. "What is it, Julian?"

"Everything in the galley has been sanitized and put away."

Felix nodded. "Have you restocked the emergency supplies?"

Julian shook his head. "Not yet."

"Let's do that next," Felix said, mentally going over everything left to get ready. "That's definitely not something we want to risk not having on board."

The men were quiet as the first mate disappeared again.

"Why are you worried about emergencies?" Ken asked.

Felix growled. "Remember I told you last year that I'd gotten roped into escorting a biologist around for a research project?"

Ken nodded. "Yeah."

"Well, she's bringing a whole crew with her," Felix continued. "Between all those academic types, we're bound to have a few injuries."

"That's a pretty pessimistic attitude," Ken said with a frown.

Felix straightened and began to coil the rope Ken had thrown him. "I prefer to call it realistic."

Ken was silent for a moment before continuing. "So you're not going to get to do any charters this summer at all?"

Felix sighed. "I could do some in the fall, and I could have done some this spring, but..."

"But it's not peak season and people prefer the warmer weather," Ken finished for him.

Felix nodded. "I've considered staying open year round, but it just doesn't seem to be worth the cost." He pursed his lips and tilted his head. "Although, I've taken her out for my own purposes at times. But usually I leave *Morwenna* docked and bring out the dinghy."

"Paying a crew when you don't have enough customers doesn't quite cover it, does it?" Ken mused.

Felix didn't answer. He didn't need to. He did well enough for himself, but despite his love for the water, he ran a business and that meant he had to treat it as such, or he wouldn't last long. Unless a person was a die-hard fisherman, they wouldn't be found out on the cold winter days trying their luck at pulling up steelhead or rockfish. The water and wind were cold enough to blow through even the best winter gear and the tourist trade was slow during those months.

But from April through September, maybe even October, Felix could make enough of a living to see him through the quiet months. People were willing to pay top dollar to spend a couple of hours on his boat, hoping for "The Big One" to show the guys back home.

The women and wives weren't usually as enthusiastic, if their squeals were anything to go by, but every once in a while, Felix would be surprised by a woman's reaction. If he had ever planned to be married, he knew first thing, she would have to be one of those rare ones that wasn't squeamish and didn't mind getting hit in the face with an ocean spray.

"How goes the wedding?" Ken asked, breaking into Felix's wandering thoughts.

Felix groaned.

"That good, huh?" Ken asked with a laugh. He ran a hand through his hair, but the wind put it right back where it had been. "I don't know if I understand all the hubbub these ladies go through for one day."

Felix eyed his friend. "Are you telling me that when you get married, you're not going to have a big party?"

Ken sobered. "I guess that would depend on the woman I was marrying, wouldn't it?" His voice had gone soft and Felix felt bad for asking such a question. Ken had been holding a torch for a friend of theirs, Rose Ingalls, for several years. The woman had been married before and had a young daughter she protected fiercely.

Felix wasn't sure if Rose's actions were because little Lilly was deaf, or if it had to do with the girl's father, but either way, Rose was not open to Ken's advances at all.

"I think all women want a big celebration," Felix offered, hoping to move past the subject. "Charli has so many flowers ordered that I'm not sure they'll fit in the church."

Ken huffed. "Bet Rose loves that."

Well, that plan didn't work. Rose was the flower shop owner. If Felix was trying to change the subject, flowers hadn't been a good way to do it. He cleared his throat. "I'm sure they all do," he said, referring to the group of women they were friends with. "You remember what Genni's reception looked like?"

Ken grinned and nodded. "It was like a flower garden right in the reception hall."

Felix nodded as well. "Yeah...and now it's Charli's turn." He grew serious. "I'll be honest, I'm not sure I'm quite ready for it."

Ken slapped Felix's shoulder. "I've married off two sisters already, so I hear ya. It always seems weird to watch them become a wife..." He grinned. "And later a mother."

Felix punched Ken's arm. "Not helping."

Ken laughed and moved back with his hands up. "Just telling it like it is."

"Whatever." Felix glanced out at the water and then back to his friend. "I guess I better finish cleaning up here. Who knows what my crew is doing below deck."

"Exactly what you asked them to," Ken said even as he walked to disembark. "For some reason they seem to obey you without question."

"If only I could say the same for my friends!" Felix called after Ken.

Ken laughed and waved over his shoulder as he walked along the dock, checking out the other boats.

Felix sighed and pushed his hair back. Ready or not, the wedding was in only a few more days, and then right after would be the start of his summer-long stint hauling around that scientist and her buddies. He blew out a breath. At least he was getting paid for his cooperation. The fact that it was twice what he normally made might just be enough to make up for the fact that Felix would be stuck with a stuffy academic all summer.

Maybe...

CHAPTER 3

Hadlee thrummed her fingers on the steering wheel. The trip to Seaside Bay hadn't been that long, only a few hours, but she was ready to get out of the van and stretch her legs. Not to mention get away from Luke's constant chatter.

And people think girls are talkative!

"Looks like we're close," Chrissy murmured as she studied the map on her phone. "Main Street should be coming up in, like...two miles."

"Great," Hadlee said with a smile. She looked in the rearview mirror. "Almost there, boys. All the equipment still look good?"

Joshua grunted and Luke twisted in his seat before facing front again. "Yeah. Nothing's moved." He looked out the window. "Not like it had a chance to at your speed," he grumbled just loud enough to be heard.

Hadlee held back a sigh and a retort. "There's no sense in getting a ticket on our first day," she said with forced patience. "In fact, there's no sense in getting a ticket ever." She looked in the mirror again, pinning Luke with a glare. "Don't you agree?"

Luke grinned and put his hands behind his head. "I don't know, Professor Ford. It might be fun to see just how fast this baby can go." He patted the seat next to him. "I've heard to never judge anything by its looks."

Hadlee couldn't help but crack a grin, while Joshua snorted and Chrissy tsked her tongue. "Maybe so, but since this vehicle isn't ours..." She left her words hanging, knowing he was capable of figuring out the rest.

His brown eyes rolled. "Yeah...yeah..."

"How did you ever get into research?" Joshua asked, shifting his bulk in order to get more comfortable. It was almost comical to look at the large man trying to fit into a seat in the van.

"What's wrong with me being in research?" Luke asked, jerking back a little. "Being out on assignments like this is much better than sitting behind a desk all day."

"Maybe so, but research also means long hours in a lab and you just don't fit the mold," Joshua argued.

Hadlee quietly groaned, knowing their argument was going to go on for too long.

"Take the next right," Chrissy said, ignoring the boys, as usual.

At least one person has a maturity level above that of a toddler. "Okay," Hadlee responded. She paused at the stop sign, then turned and slowed her speed.

"I can walk faster than this," Luke complained.

"We're in city limits now," Hadlee said, doing her best to ignore his whining. "Speed limit is slower." She pushed his continued mutterings out of her head and worked her way to the bed and breakfast she and the crew were staying at.

Pulling into the small parking area, Hadlee put the van in park and studied the house. It was stunning and looked like it had been updated recently. It was a mansion by anybody's standards, but the fact that it was old made it fun. A turret came off one side of the house and the bright white gables practically shone in the sunlight.

"Wow," Chrissy said, shoving her glasses up her nose. "It's beautiful."

"This is where we get to stay? Sweet!" Luke said with a laugh. "I thought we'd get stuck in some dumpy motel somewhere."

"It is pretty nice," Hadlee agreed. "Our grant was enough to cover something better than a flea-ridden mattress while we're here." She unbuckled. "So let's be sure to use our time wisely, huh? We don't want to look a gift horse in the mouth."

They all clambered out of the van and began to groan as they stretched stiff muscles and limbs.

"I'm gonna go get us checked in," Hadlee said, reaching back in the van to grab her purse. "Give me a minute." She climbed the front steps and knocked on the door. A few moments went by before a teenage girl answered.

"Yeah?"

"Uh..." Hadlee tried to smile, but she was a little confused. "Is this The Boardwalk Bed and Breakfast?"

The girl nodded and tilted her head.

Hadlee pinched her lips together. *Maybe she's the owner's daughter?* "We..." She waved back at her crew. "Have a reservation."

"Oh, yeah. Genni said she had someone coming by today." The girl opened the door. "Come on in."

"Thanks," Hadlee said softly. She walked in and began to admire the renovation work in front of her. Hardwood floors gleamed and antique furniture filled the large sitting room just off the foyer. The whole place looked like a museum. Hadlee managed to glimpse a couple of full bookcases next to a fainting couch and made a mental note to see what all was available for reading.

"The sign-in book is over here," the girl said as she walked to a small desk in the corner. "I need you to sign a couple of papers and then I'll show you to your rooms."

"Are you the owner's daughter?" Hadlee asked as she looked over the contract before signing her name.

The girl laughed. "No, I'm just covering this afternoon for a few bucks." She took the papers and rolled them up before putting them in her pockets. "Come on. You guys are all upstairs."

Hadlee grabbed her crew and luggage and they followed the girl up the winding staircase. Everywhere she looked, the house was neat, clean, and fully restored. It was going to be a wonderful place to stay.

"Genni and Cooper will be back in a little while," the girl, who still had never offered her name, said. "She'll answer any of your questions."

"Wait!" Hadlee called before the teenager could disappear. "I'm supposed to meet a man named Felix Mendez. Do you know who he is?"

"Uh, yeah?"

"You wouldn't happen to have any idea where I might find him during this time of day?" Hadlee held her breath. She knew she had an appointment with the man in two days, but she was so eager to get started that she figured it wouldn't hurt to at least meet him. Maybe they could get an extra day on the water if he wasn't busy.

The girl grinned. "He's at the church, just like everyone else."

"The church?"

The girl pointed north. "White chapel, maybe a mile down the street. Can't miss it." With that, she turned and headed back down the stairs.

"Friendly little thing, wasn't she?" Joshua asked wryly. They were all standing in the hallways, their doors open, but no one had been able to put anything down yet.

"At least she gave me a direction," Hadlee murmured. "All right, everyone. Into your rooms, and then feel free to take the rest of the day off. Dinner is supposed to be served, but I don't know what time. I'm gonna unpack, then run a couple of errands." She poked her head back out her door. "Anyone need anything while I'm out?"

After mentally making a list of a few groceries, Hadlee quickly threw her luggage on the bed, cleaned herself up in the restroom, and headed back to the van. She wasn't sure why Mr. Mendez, a ship captain, would be at church in the middle of the week, but at least it made him easy to find.

"Off to church we go," she muttered to herself.

FELIX'S MUSCLES WERE growing tired as he stood stiffly in the corner of the reception hall. The wedding had been like a fairy tale, exactly as Charli had wanted, and now they were all mingling. The dinner, followed by dancing, would start soon. However, despite his best efforts to remain aloof, Felix found himself growing soft during the ceremony. At one point, his eyes had even begun to fill with tears and it had about killed him.

Felix wasn't the type to cry...ever. In fact, he wasn't the emotional type at all. No one in his family had ever been and he didn't plan to change. So now he was standing away from the crowds, doing his best not to show his bittersweet feelings, which were too close to the surface for comfort.

"You're gonna hurt Charli's feelings while you brood over here by yourself."

Felix snapped his head to the side and deflated a little. "I know, but I..." He took in a shaky breath and pushed a hand through his hair. He didn't like all this chaos inside of him.

Bennett, another friend, squeezed his shoulder. "Trust me, man. I get it. I just got done doing this with Mel, remember?"

Felix nodded. They'd had several weddings in their friend group lately, including Melody, Bennett's sister. The best part was Mel had married Bennett's best friend, Jensen. But still, Felix now recognized that no matter how good the guy was, giving away a sister was never an easy thing. "It doesn't freak you out to know she's no longer your responsibility?" he asked.

Benny snorted. "Like Charli was ever yours?"

Felix gave him a look, which only made Benny laugh harder. "I know Charli's the independent type, but I'm family. She's always been my responsibility."

"And she always will be," Benny said, his voice unusually serious. "Just because she's married doesn't mean she's no longer family."

Felix nodded. "I get it, I do. But there's something just...unsettling about it. It's just been her and me for quite a few years, ever since our parents died. I was the person she came to when she needed help, or when she needed to talk. Now all of that is gone."

"And now you're afraid you're no longer needed?"

Felix narrowed his eyes. "Since when did you become a psychologist?"

Benny grinned and shrugged. "Just because I hide behind a smile doesn't mean I'm stupid."

Felix grunted and folded his arms over his chest. His suit, however, was too tight, so he had to drop them back down. "Benny, the day you're serious about something is the day the ocean runs dry."

To anyone else the words would have been offensive, but Bennett had always been known for his light-hearted take on life and to their group of friends, he was known as the annoying, but lovable dork who could out-eat a horse. So, it was no surprise to Felix that instead of being upset at his words, Bennett simply laughed...loudly. "All right, you got me." He took a swallow of the punch in his hand. "But still, Charli is gonna notice you're over here and she's gonna end up dragging you into the limelight by your ear if you're not careful."

"Right." Felix threw back his shoulders and straightened his tie. It didn't matter how he was feeling, he shouldn't make a scene on Charli's big day. There would be plenty of time for him to muddle over the hurricane inside of him while she was away on her honeymoon.

Just as he was about to step out of the shadows, a hand on his arm stopped him. Felix looked back to see one of the church secretaries holding onto his suit sleeve. "Yes?"

"Mr. Mendez," the older woman said softly. "There's a visitor at the front desk who wishes to speak to you."

Felix frowned. "A visitor? Now?"

The woman huffed. "I told her you were busy, but she promised it would only take a moment of your time."

Felix looked to Benny, who shrugged. "Her? It's a woman?"

The secretary nodded.

He searched for Charli and found her with her arms wrapped around Bronson as they chatted with friends. A quick glance at the clock told Felix he had about twenty minutes until dinner was served. *Just enough time to get this over with.* "Lead the way." He followed the petite lady out of the hall and toward the front of the chapel. Footsteps at his back let Felix know Benny had followed and it didn't surprise him a bit.

As they came to the front of the church, a woman came into view and Felix tried desperately to place her, but he was positive he'd never seen her before. Thick, medium brown hair was pulled back in a ponytail, though chunks of it fell around her face as if she couldn't be bothered to smooth it back. Large sunglasses were pushed up onto the top of her head, giving her a breezy look, which complimented the casual jeans and T-shirt she was wearing.

She was beautiful in a very natural sort of way and Felix couldn't help but notice. Her figure was decidedly feminine, not too thin but not too thick, exactly the type of figure he was drawn to.

Felix scowled at his thoughts. Hadn't he spent the last few weeks mentally going over how he would never tie himself down the way Charli was? And though he was supposed to be supporting his sister, he didn't want to join her ranks.

"Can I help you?" he asked, probably a bit more gruffly than the situation called for.

The woman was watching him with wide eyes, her jaw slack. "I..." She looked him up and down and Felix wanted to explain why he was in this monkey suit, but he held his tongue. "I'm sorry. I obviously interrupted something," she said in a much more composed tone than she had started with. Folding her hands in front of her, she smiled up at him, startling Felix with the beauty of it. "My father always did say I was too impetuous."

Felix shook his head. "I'm confused. Who are you? And what do you need?" Benny snickered behind him, but Felix ignored his friend.

"Oh, sorry," the woman apologized. She stuck out her hand. "I'm—"

"FELIX!" Charli's voice echoed around the small foyer and Felix winced. He looked back to see his sister frowning as she held her gown up and raced down the hall. "What in the world are you doing?" she asked, giving him a significant look. "It's time for us to eat and you're out here gallivanting around."

Benny's laughter grew.

Felix elbowed his friend, but it made no difference. "Sorry, Char. I was just..." He turned back to the woman, who was looking startled once again, and slightly...dare he say, disappointed? *What the heck is going on here?* "I didn't catch your name?"

The woman blinked and her light eyes caught his attention. Her hair was brown, but her eyes were a light gray, which, now that he was closer, was more alluring than he would have thought. "Oh, yes. I was getting to that, wasn't I?" She cleared her throat. "I'm Professor Hadlee Ford," she said very quickly. "But I obviously came at a bad time." She looked to Charli. "Congratulations." Those eyes drifted back up to Felix. "To both of you." Hadlee ducked her head and dropped Felix's gaze. "I'll get out of here, so you can go back to the ceremony. I'm really sorry. It wasn't...I mean..." She blew out a breath, blowing her hair out of her face. "I'm just gonna go."

Felix stood still as a statue as she practically ran from the church, only to stop at the door and look back tentatively.

"Are we...still good to meet in two days?" Professor Ford looked worried as her eyes went around the group, like she expected Felix to snap at her or break their arrangement for the summer.

"As far as I know," Felix finally managed.

"Thank you, I appreciate it," the professor said, then darted out the door.

Felix felt shellshocked. *THAT'S who I'm taking around this summer? What kind of a joke is this? College professors are supposed to be old and stodgy, not young and...* He couldn't let himself finish that thought. He couldn't let himself admit he thought her attractive. It was going to be miserable enough this summer without throwing in something like that to stir the pot.

"Felix, now!" Charli snapped, grabbing her gown once again and heading back to the reception hall. "Benny, if you have any hope of eating dinner and more importantly, dessert, you'll bring him along with you."

Benny, who had been following Charli, came to a screeching halt and spun, glaring at Felix. "Get that twitterpated look out of your eyes, Felix, and get in here now."

Felix jerked back. "Excuse me?"

"You heard me," Benny said, growling in frustration. "If your jaw was capable of hitting the floor, it would have. And now you're holding up my dinner."

Felix's dark eyebrows shot up high. "First off, I'm not twitterpated. Second, maybe I should stay out here, just to watch you squirm in hunger."

Benny's eyes turned pleading. "You wouldn't do that to a buddy?"

"I would for someone who laughed at me."

Blue eyes rolled toward heaven. "Give me a break. We both know that no matter how pretty she is, the lady won't be able to break through your rough exterior." Benny pumped his eyebrows. "But someone like me? I'm easy to get to know."

Felix snorted as they walked back inside. "Somehow, I don't see you with a professor," he said in an undertone.

"You never know," Benny whispered back. "I can give my kids looks, but someone else might have to give them the book smarts."

Felix chuckled as he punched Benny in the shoulder and shoved thoughts of the lovely professor out of his head. Right now he needed to focus on Charli. Later, he could worry about whether or not those eyes had really been as gray as he'd thought or if her lips were as plush as they appeared.

Or how much people like her are hurting industries like mine, Felix reminded himself. Her looks were irrelevant. In fact, she was probably married, so he had better get his head on straight. And right now that meant getting ready to give a toast to his little sister and her new husband.

CHAPTER 4

Hadlee was sure she was going to curl up in a ball and die. *Who the heck interrupts a man on the day he's getting married?* She slapped her forehead as she drove. "So stupid." It was just like her to jump into something without thinking first. Her excitement and desire to run instead of walk had often led to trouble in her life, but this one took the cake.

Felix Mendez had not been anything like what Hadlee had been expecting. He was about thirty years younger, to start with, and his dark, handsome looks had caught her completely off guard. She'd stood staring at him as if she'd just seen a toothcarp come back to life. Hadlee was pretty darn sure that the resurrection of an extinct fish species was the only other situation where her jaw would fall that far down her chest. *I must have looked like an idiot,* she scolded herself. "And now you have to work with that man all summer, when his first impression of you is you pulling him from his wedding and then fleeing the scene like a common criminal." She shook her head as she pulled into the grocery store parking lot. "Because that's not going to be awkward at all."

The next half-hour was spent trying to set the situation behind her, but it felt as if every single person in the store knew about her faux pas. Though it made absolutely no sense, every time Hadlee caught someone looking her way, she felt her cheeks grow hot, as if that person knew she had not only behaved like a starstruck idiot, but had interrupted the man's wedding day. Her cheeks were going to be permanently red if she didn't find a way to cool off soon.

Once back at the bed and breakfast, Hadlee went to work getting her team settled and tried to lose herself in more research before they all met for dinner, but nothing seemed to be able to take the meeting out of her mind.

She closed her computer with a thump. "Who agrees to take a stranger out on their boat only two days after they get married?" she asked her quiet room. "Isn't he taking a honeymoon?"

Suddenly, Hadlee felt very sorry for Captain Mendez's wife. She might be marrying one of the most handsome men Hadlee had ever seen, but obviously he wasn't much in the personality department if he wasn't even going to spend more than forty-eight hours with his new bride.

A knock on her door caught her attention, and Hadlee looked over to see Chrissy peeking her head through. "Dinner's ready in five. Want to go down?"

Hadlee nodded and forced a smile. "Yep. Sounds good." She followed her assistant out into the hall and downstairs.

"How'd the meeting with Captain Mendez go?" Chrissy asked after grace had been said and they were all filling their plates.

The men watched the girls from across the table and that stupid blush smacked Hadlee once more in the face. "Uh, I didn't really..." She coughed and took a long drink of her water. "I didn't really get to meet with him."

"Oh?" Luke tilted his head, his curiosity tangible. "You didn't see him at all?"

"Oh, I, uh, saw him," Hadlee stammered. "But he was too busy for us to really chat, so we cut it short. I'll just have to wait until our meeting in two days."

The sounds of silverware and glasses dominated the space until Joshua muttered, "It seems kind of rude not to at least be willing to take five minutes to talk to you. The guy must be a jerk."

Hadlee felt a brick land in her stomach as she forced the bite she'd been chewing to go down instead of spitting it out. "He..." She coughed and swallowed more water. "That's not it at all. I...I mean...he was busy, really busy. I'm the one who decided it was best for me to leave." She squirmed in her seat, knowing her face was hot enough to roast a marshmallow on. "He wasn't rude at all, just busy."

"What was he so busy with?" Chrissy asked softly. Her eyes were wide behind her glasses and the question was completely innocent, but Hadlee still felt her whole stomach curl up in a ball of shame.

She pinched her lips together, not wanting to admit her mistake to the group, but all their questions were making it difficult to keep it from them. *Why do researchers have to be so darn curious? Why can't they just accept something at face value?* Even as she asked it, Hadlee knew the question was ridiculous. Curiosity and a desire for the full truth were the best parts about researchers. If they accepted things at face value, they'd never find out more.

Sighing, Hadlee put her fork on the table. "He was getting married."

While Hadlee had choked down her food when she'd been shocked, Lucas, obviously, had no such control and the water he'd been drinking spit across the table.

"Ewww..." Chrissy groaned in her high, quiet tone.

Joshua shook his head and handed his fellow TA a handful of napkins.

Luke gasped for breath, his face red. "The dude was *getting married* and you interrupted him?"

Hadlee pinched the bridge of her nose. What she wouldn't give to be able to melt into a puddle at the moment. Her face was hot enough for it. What would it take to just spontaneously combust? Humans could do that...couldn't they?

"Not quite," she said through a clenched jaw. "No one told me he was getting married. I went to the church and the lady at the front just said he was busy."

"And what?" Luke pressed. "You just marched back there anyway?"

"No!" Hadlee almost shouted, before controlling herself. She worked to rid her shoulders of tension, and calm herself down before she said something she would regret. Taking a calming breath, she sat tall and did her best to own up to her actions. "I simply said it wouldn't take but a moment of his time. The secretary wasn't happy, but she went to get him."

"Should have left well enough alone," Joshua said, his dark eyes full of censure.

"I'm aware it wasn't the right thing, but I didn't know what I didn't know," Hadlee defended. *Who's the person in charge here anyway? Maybe I should be stricter about how I handle my TA's.* "He came out and before I could talk to him, his wife ran out wanting him at the dinner."

Chrissy laughed, covering her mouth with a napkin. "I thought our captain would be an old man. Was he young?"

Hadlee tilted her head back and forth consideringly. "Yeah. Maybe a year or two older than me."

"He's too old for you, Chris," Luke said nonchalantly, having gone back to his dinner as if his explosion had never happened.

Chrissy gasped. "He's married!"

Luke raised an eyebrow. "That doesn't stop some women."

"Lucas," Hadlee said firmly. "That's out of line."

Luke shrugged and went back to his food.

Hadlee knew full well that Chrissy didn't deserve the snap from Luke, but it had also trickled back to her ears that Chrissy had turned down Luke's invitation for a date a few weeks back. *Please don't let this complicate things,* she prayed mentally. *I've already done enough of that myself.*

FELIX SQUINTED UP AT the sun, sighing when he realized he needed to head home and clean up. *Morwenna* was as ready as she was going to get and he had an appointment with Professor Ford.

The woman who interrupted Charli's wedding...

The moment had stuck with Felix, much to his frustration. He couldn't seem to reconcile the fact that he'd been expecting an older, stuffy woman with her hair pulled back in a tight bun and glasses perched on the end of her nose with which she could glare at him over.

A vibrant beauty had definitely not come to mind once since he'd been forced into the contract. "And now you have to meet her for dinner," he grumbled.

"Captain?"

Felix's head shot up. "Yeah?"

"Did you need something?"

He shook his head. "No. I was just talking to myself."

Julian, his first mate, folded his arms over his chest and leaned into the doorway. "What did you do that you're so angry with yourself about?"

Felix chuckled. "Made assumptions."

"Those'll get you every time," Julian said with a laugh. His shoulder-length hair was pulled back in a tie, but a chunk of it was slapping around his face and he tucked it behind his ear. "What else can I do for you today, Cap?"

Felix shook his head. "Nothing. The job starts tomorrow, so you might as well get home to the wife and enjoy what time you've got left before we hit the water."

"You make it sound as if we're going to be away from home on some voyage," Julian said with a groan and then straightened. "Should I wear my wife's colors as well? How about the kids?"

Felix's laugh was stronger this time. He enjoyed his employee. The man was more than a decade older than Felix and his father had been a fisherman, but Julian had decided his love for the sea hadn't extended to long hours and the hazard of sudden storms. Being Felix's first mate had been the perfect solution. They were home every night. They didn't sail in the dark, and they always had a line in the water for their own freezers. "Get out of here," Felix said, waving Julian away. "And take Ethan with you."

"That guppy isn't coming with me!" Julian called over his shoulder. "I've got a teenage daughter. Ethan flirts too much!"

Felix's smile was still wide as he left the boat a few minutes later. Where Julian was settled with a family, Ethan was barely out of high school. He was going to college part time and worked with Felix during the season. It was his second summer on the boat and Felix was glad to have him. The young man could charm anyone he worked with, which was helpful with customers. Yet he pulled his weight around the boat, doing anything asked of him. He was a good kid.

Felix glanced at his watch and muttered a curse. He was going to be late if he didn't hurry, and he hated being late. It made him look unprofessional, which was not the impression he wanted to give Dr. Ford. Felix ran a tight ship and he wanted it to come across that way.

Rushing home, he showered and prettied himself up, ignoring his inner taunting voice about why he wished to look and smell good, and hopped in his truck. "Smelling like fish isn't professional either," he told himself as he drove. "It has nothing to do with the fact that she's young and attractive." The parking lot was full when he arrived and Felix had to drive down the street a little to find a space big enough for his vehicle.

He lengthened his stride, knowing he was cutting it closer than he preferred as he hurried through the glass doors.

"Captain!"

Felix grinned at the hostess. Most of the high-schoolers knew Felix because they took field trips to the docks and he was always willing to show them about operating a boat. "Hey, Miranda. How's it going?"

She grinned at him, her eyes bright. "Good. What brings you here tonight?"

"I'm meeting—"

"Me."

Felix's head snapped to the voice and his breath caught again. It didn't matter how geeky or academically inclined she ended up being. Dr. Ford really was a beautiful woman.

"Don't worry," Dr. Ford said to Miranda. "It's just a business meeting."

Felix frowned. *What's that supposed to mean?* His thoughts startled himself. It was a business meeting, but something about the way Dr. Ford said it made him feel like there was an underlying meaning.

"Right this way," Miranda chirped with a smile. She led them to a quiet booth and slipped the menus down. "Your server will be with you shortly."

"Thanks, Miranda," Felix said as the girl left him alone with his dinner companion. Felix took a moment to look the doctor over. Again, she lacked much in the way of ornamentation, despite the fact that they were here for a business meeting. She wore a simple blouse, very little make-up, and a pair of casual pants that hit her at mid calf. While she didn't look bad, she didn't look like she was trying to impress him either. It made him feel foolish for spending time on his hair and taking the time to shave before he came.

"So…" Dr. Ford said, her eyes darting around the restaurant before coming back to his. "I have to admit that I'm surprised."

Felix's brows pulled together. "About what?"

"That you're here. Wouldn't you rather be home?"

He shook his head, still not catching on to what she was implying. "I'm afraid I'm lost, Dr. Ford." Felix folded his hands on the top of the table. "Why exactly would I be home? I thought we had this meeting planned a long time ago."

She cleared her throat and her cheeks seemed to grow warm. "I'm sorry, you know. I had no idea what I was interrupting when I showed up at the church."

Felix shrugged. "It wasn't a big deal."

Her eyes nearly bugged out of her head. "Are you telling me your wife felt the same way?"

It was Felix's turn to be shocked. "My what?"

"Your wife."

He made a face and leaned back. "I...don't have a wife," Felix said carefully. Then it hit him. When Dr. Ford had shown up at the church, Charli had come out in her gown to gather him, and the doctor must have assumed that he was her groom. "Did you..." He pinched his lips between his teeth to hold back his laughter. "Did you think that was *my* wedding?"

Dr. Ford looked thoroughly confused. "What are you talking about? Wasn't it your wedding? You were in a tux, and the bride came to get you!"

He couldn't hold it in any longer. Laughter burst loudly out of Felix, to the point that he could feel the other patrons looking his way, but his mirth continued. "The bride was my sister," he managed to get out between guffaws.

Dr. Ford huffed and folded her arms over her chest. "Your sister? Well, why didn't you say so?"

"I am saying so," he continued, trying to contain himself. Felix didn't laugh like this very often and now that he'd started, he found it difficult to stop, but the thought of himself walking down the aisle, especially with someone like his sister, was too funny not to let loose about. "Didn't you notice the family resemblance? People say we look alike all the time."

She threw her arms in the air in disgust. "I wasn't looking for that. I was too embarrassed that I'd pulled the groom from his wedding. All I saw was a suit and a wedding dress."

"Two suits, actually. One of my friends was with me."

"Maybe so, but he wasn't in a tux like you."

"I was the best man," Felix admitted.

Dr. Ford put her face in her hands. "Take me now," she moaned. "How many times can a person embarrass themselves before they simply cease to exist?" She peeked through her fingers. "You don't happen to know the temperature it would take for spontaneous combustion, do you?"

He put his hands in the air. "You're the scientist, not me."

Dr. Ford groaned. "I can't believe I'm so stupid."

"While we're on the topic...is there a husband or boyfriend I should know about who might be upset we're meeting tonight?" The words slipped out before Felix could think better of it. *It's a natural question,* he told himself. *She was worried about a jealous wife. I can ask the same.*

Dr. Ford snorted. "Uh...no. Not even close."

Instead of feeling relief, Felix only felt frustration and anger that he'd allowed the words out of his mouth. He didn't care about her social life. This was a business transaction, nothing else.

CHAPTER 5

*W*hy *did I say that? Why can't I keep my mouth shut?* The heat that had already been infusing her cheeks grew to epic proportions as the implication of her words hit home. *Nothing like showing him how pathetic I am at our first meeting, and now I've just confirmed it by talking about my love life...or lack of love life.* "Sorry," Hadlee said, her face still covered with her hands. "I need to just shut up and stop talking. Obviously, I can't be trusted with anything at the moment."

Another deep laugh met her ears and the shiver that had rocked Hadlee during the first one started back up again, causing her stomach to flip. She felt like a young girl with her first crush. It was slightly foreign to Hadlee, as it had been so long since she'd considered anything outside her work.

She finally dropped her hands and studied his face. Laughter took several years off Captain Mendez. His resting face seemed to be slightly on the broody side and it made him look intense and a bit intimidating.

He took in a breath. "I had no idea this is what I signed up for this summer."

Hadlee gave him a sheepish grin. Deciding that the best thing she could do right now was to start over, she held out her hand. "Hadlee Ford."

Captain Mendez gave her a funny look, but shook her head. "Felix Mendez."

"Do you prefer to be called Captain Mendez? Or maybe Captain Felix?"

He shrugged. "Do I need to call you Dr. Ford all summer?"

She waved her hands through the air. "No way. Hadlee is fine. Or Haddie. Or Lee. People call me all sorts of things." She pinched her lips together. *Stop talking. Right! Now!*

He chuckled and gave her a little smirk. "Captain, Cap, or Felix all work for me."

She nodded. "So noted." Hadlee was beyond grateful that their waitress showed up at that moment, giving her time to get herself back under control. Once their orders had been given, they were once again left alone. Hadlee was determined to be quieter now that she had already spilled all her embarrassing secrets, so she waited for Felix to speak first, but he must have been of a similar mindset, because neither spoke for a couple of minutes.

Things quickly grew awkward and Hadlee began to fidget with her napkins.

"So..." Felix leaned forward, interlacing his hands on top of the table. "This...project you're doing?" He raised an eyebrow, obviously waiting for Hadlee to start speaking.

She nodded., putting a pleasant smile on her face.

Felix's brows pulled together. "Did you want to tell me about it? So, I know what all to expect?"

"Oh, yeah." A stiff laugh broke through Hadlee's lips. She tried to give herself a mental shake. Things had started off weird with Felix and she was still trying to find her footing. "So...I'm studying the effects of the ocean's acidity on baby dungeness crab." She looked up, expecting to see the same easy-going expression he'd had since her mess-up and was shocked to be met with a scowl.

"And what exactly do you hope to do with those findings?"

Hadlee slowly sat back in the seat, suddenly feeling like she was sitting with a predator. She wasn't sure why Felix was so angry with her, but she didn't like it. He was already large enough to be intimidating, but his anger made everything worse. "Publish my findings.

This is the last publication I need to be advanced to an Associate Professor at my college." She could see his jaw grind.

"And ultimately? Are you hoping to shut down the crab trade in Oregon?"

"What? No!" Hadlee said, shaking her head adamantly. "While I can't guarantee what environmentalists will do with the information, that's not my purpose." She leaned forward, hoping to ease his anger. "I'm simply worried about the crabs. Environmental changes are causing our oceans to become more acidic than they've ever been before. It's believed that the change in the water might be affecting the ocean wildlife, of course. I'm just here to figure out what it's doing to the crabs, if it's doing anything at all."

He didn't look appeased. "And what's going to happen to the fishermen? It's one of Oregon's biggest industries. What happens when they get shut down and thousands are put out of work?"

Hadlee found herself scowling right back at him. "While I already told you that I'm not here to shut anyone down, I feel that I need to clarify a couple of things. Would you really be willing to just keep collecting crab even if you knew they were sick and dying? What if the population wasn't able to reproduce as much as normal because of the changes? Don't you think it's important to take care of our oceans?"

Felix's eyebrow was the only response she got as the waitress set their meals down and checked to see if they needed anything else.

"I think we're good, thank you," Hadlee said politely when Felix refused to speak. *He's looking less like a handsome warrior and more like the jerk Joshua thought he was,* she thought. Acting as if his behavior wasn't affecting her at all, Hadlee picked up her fork and began to eat. "This is very good," she said, getting the nerve to look him in the eye.

"Glad you're enjoying yourself," he snapped. "It's good to know that people like you can sleep at night."

"People like me?" Hadlee shook her head. "Are you serious?" She realized her voice was getting a little loud, so she pulled it back and leaned over the table as far as she could to keep the conversation between them. "There is nothing wrong with wanting to take care of nature," she hissed.

Felix's nearly black eyes were flashing as he met her pose. "There is when it comes at the expense of people's lives."

"So what? We should just let humans ruin the world?"

Felix gave his head a hard shake. "No. But if we would simply back off, nature has a way of taking care of her own. Scientists like you can't seem to leave good enough alone." He sat back. "I'll warn you right now that locals aren't going to be happy about why you're here. If I were you, I'd keep my mouth shut."

Hadlee's mouth flapped open and closed a few times. She had the thought that he'd threatened her...sort of. Finally deciding that cool politeness was going to be the only response she had, she sat back as well. Leaning forward had been a mistake anyway. He smelled delectable, and being so close had sucked the air from her lungs, making the restaurant disappear until only Felix's handsome face had been in her vision. "Thank you for your concern," she said in her most patient voice. "I appreciate your warning, but I'm sure it won't be necessary. I'm not here to cause trouble. I'm simply trying to answer a concern in the marine biology community." She took a bite of her dinner and gave him a look, hoping he could see she would not be frightened off by his words.

Scientists the world over met with resistance all the time, but it was mostly because people didn't understand what they were trying to accomplish. She wasn't trying to hurt Seaside Bay or anyone else in Oregon. She was just trying to protect a species that might be having a hard time. Surely anyone who was interested would understand that.

Hadlee glanced up to see Felix's face had not changed. *Or maybe they won't. Anyway, they won't stop me from my work. I need this project, and it won't do anything to hurt their precious industry.*

FELIX WASN'T SURE WHAT to make of this woman. On one hand, she had been completely clueless and fumbling when it came to the misunderstanding about his wedding, or lack thereof, but now she was standing firmly in front of him, acting exactly like the scientist he had expected in the first place. Unyielding and assuming she was always right.

"Don't say I didn't warn you." Felix grunted. He went back to his dinner, the conversation having stalled. This wasn't going to make their time together easy on the boat, but maybe that was for the best.

Despite preparing himself, Hadlee's looks had once again thrown Felix off his game. When she'd grown embarrassed and her smooth skin had turned bright pink, he'd had the crazy urge to run his fingers along her cheek, just to feel the heat. He was old enough to have had his share of dates and even a couple of girlfriends, though none had been serious. All of this meant that Felix was neither inexperienced or naive, and he'd come out of that time content in his bachelorhood. Which is part of why he was so thrown by the fact that Hadlee was tugging on his attention without even trying.

He wasn't looking for a new relationship, or any relationship at all, yet here he was, imagining what it would be like to touch Hadlee's face.

He mentally smacked himself and threw his attention into his dinner. The fish was well prepared and Felix had always enjoyed this restaurant. He knew he should probably spend more time getting to know Hadlee and about her project, but he was completely put off by her unwillingness to see how her actions might affect thousands of people. While he believed her when she said that she wasn't trying to put anyone out of business, the results of her study, in the right hands, could.

"Do you ever tire of it?"

Felix's head snapped up. He hadn't been ready for her to break their silence. "What?"

Those light eyes darted down to his plate, then back up. "Fish? As someone who captains a boat, I'll bet you fish a ton. And yet here you are eating fish at a restaurant." A small smile tugged on her lips. "So I wondered if you ever get tired of eating fish?"

A laughing snort broke free from Felix's lips. "No."

She raised her eyebrows and turned her head to the side just slightly, obviously waiting for more. When Felix didn't offer it, she continued. "No? Never?"

"Nope." Felix went back to his plate, but his dinner companion wasn't content with that.

"Do you not eat it at home, then?"

Felix sighed and looked up at her. "I like fish. A lot. I eat it all the time. If you asked my sister, the one who just got married," he gave Hadlee a smirk at the reminder of her mistake, "she'd tell you that I'm going to turn into a fish at any moment. The only time I get tired of it is when it's not cooked well." He raised his eyebrows. "Any more questions?"

Hadlee looked slightly taken aback at his abruptness, but Felix refused to feel bad about it. This woman was not his friend. She was a chore, and no matter how attractive she was or how tempting her flushed skin was, he refused to look at her as anything else.

"Wow," she said dryly. "That was a very thorough explanation. Thanks."

Felix huffed and moved to finish his dinner.

"After you're done, would you like to come meet the team?"

He held back a growl. *Why can't I just eat in peace?* "If that's what you want."

She wiped her mouth with her napkin and set it softly back in her lap. "I think it might be good for you to meet everyone. Since I'm so offensive to you, maybe it'll help soften your opinion of researchers who are only trying to help take care of the very place you call home."

He sat back slowly, wanting to clap at her performance. He couldn't say the set-down wasn't deserved. He wasn't exactly being open and friendly, but it appeared that Hadlee was the type to fight with words, not fierce looks or cold shoulders. After studying her, he gave one hard nod. "Sure. I'll meet them. But the very nature of what you're doing is bad for my business, so don't expect miracles."

He held back a chuckle when she mumbled, "I wouldn't dare," under her breath.

The meal quickly finished and Felix walked just behind her as they left the restaurant.

"Captain!"

Felix stopped in the parking lot and turned to see George Herman shuffling his direction. Felix smiled and doffed an imaginary cap at the older fisherman. "George."

George was grinning, despite his slightly hunched stature. "It's midweek, Captain. Has Charli's marriage sent you out of the house in search of dinner?" He cackled and Felix laughed with him.

"Nothing so desperate," Felix assured him. "Besides, I know how to cook, you know that. Every good fisherman does."

George nodded. "Indeed. But most of us can't cook more than the fish we pull in." He reached out to nudge Felix's shoulder. "At least learn how to add a few potatoes to the mix or something."

Felix grinned and shrugged. "Why? Fish is all you need."

"Until you get scurvy."

Both men turned to look at Hadlee who was standing with her hands folded in front of her. She was the picture of innocence, but

Felix knew better. The woman was slowly showing that she had a backbone of steel.

George whistled low. "So, that's what got you out of the house, huh?" He grinned and reached out to Hadlee. "George Herman." He shook her head. "I'm retired now, but I'm the one who taught pups like this," George threw a thumb in Felix's direction, "all they know."

Hadlee laughed as intended. "Dr. Hadlee Ford," she said in return. "I'm glad to see Captain Felix had such a wonderful mentor."

Felix held back an eye roll and didn't bother to correct George's assumption that he was on a date. It wasn't worth the argument or the embarrassment.

"Doctor, huh?" George narrowed his gaze and the playfulness in his demeanor disappeared. His wrinkled face turned to Felix. "Is she the one coming about the crabs?"

Felix hesitated, then decided it was going to get out anyway, and nodded.

George's already thin lips pretty much disappeared as he turned back to Hadlee, who was looking confused. "You have no business here," George snapped.

Hadlee jerked back. "Excuse me? I don't think you understand—"

"I understand plenty," George said harshly. "I understand that you environment people can't just leave things alone. You'd be happiest if all of us starved to death as long as the animals survived."

Hadlee shook her head, her confusion turning to alarm. "No! That's not it at all."

George backed away, shaking his head. "We don't need your kind here." He glanced at Felix. "I've always respected you, son, but you need to be careful with this one." Without another word, he disappeared into the evening, slowly shuffling further down the sidewalk.

Hadlee's eyes were suspiciously wet as she looked at Felix. A deep urge inside of him wanted to give her a hug and assure her it would all be okay, but he held back. That wasn't the kind of relationship he had with her, nor would it ever be the kind between him and Dr. Ford. Instead, Felix shrugged. "I warned you."

She blinked, the moisture disappearing, and her shoulders straightened. "You did," she said in a very calm voice. "But if you think I'm going to tuck tail and run, you don't know me well. This project is important to me and your fear is unfounded. No one is trying to hurt anybody or their industry." Spinning on her heel, Hadlee began walking away from him. "I think we'll save that introduction for the morning. See you at the boat."

Felix didn't move, watching her get in a van and pull away, his head a whirlwind of emotions, most of which he wanted nothing to do with. While he wasn't happy about what she was doing here, he couldn't help but be impressed by her strength. Nothing about her easy beauty and casual appearance would tell a person that a strong will lay beneath her polite words. And dang, if that wasn't intriguing to someone who tended to be stubborn himself.

Between her looks and determination, Felix found his attraction pulsing stronger and stronger, and that just wouldn't do. He growled at himself and headed down the street to his truck. He couldn't go back on his commitment, but between tonight and the morning, he needed to get his priorities under control. He had a plan for his life and it didn't include a woman who had the ability to hurt him and his friends.

CHAPTER 6

Morning came too soon for Hadlee, which was unusual for her. She was an early riser, but her night had been difficult with very little sleep. Images of Felix and his scolding, along with the angry, older man they'd met outside the restaurant, kept running through her head.

She shook her head as she tied her sneakers. She couldn't understand why anyone would be so upset about her project. Yes, she could see why they might initially be worried, but not being willing to listen to her reassurances made no sense. Hadlee was trying to help save the crab population, not shut down the fishing industry.

People respond like this when they've been burned before.

She paused at the thought, her shoelaces hanging from her fingers. Sighing, Hadlee put herself back into motion. The thought had merit. And if that's what had happened, she couldn't blame them. Just like in every profession, there were the good guys and the bad guys.

Unfortunately, the extremists within her community weren't even usually the actual scientists. They were people who took their information, twisted it to meet their own needs, and then put together a campaign that was more about making money than making a difference.

Grumbling under her breath about the shadows those people cast over her profession, Hadlee grabbed her backpack and headed out into the hall. "Everyone ready?" she asked as she came down the stairs. She'd grabbed a few bites of breakfast earlier and then gone upstairs to get ready. Most of her group liked to do the opposite, so she found them in the dining room.

"You must be Dr. Ford," a beautiful woman around Hadlee's age said, rising from her seat. She walked across the room, with her hand outstretched. "I'm Genni James. My husband Cooper and I own the bed and breakfast."

Hadlee put on her best smile. *Hopefully the local attitude toward scientists doesn't extend this far.* "Hadlee," she said. "No need with the formalities."

Genni smiled kindly. "Hadlee, then." She looked around the room at the other guests. "I think I finally met your whole group this morning." Her brown eyes came back to Hadlee. "I'm sorry I missed you when you arrived. We were at a friend's wedding."

Hadlee's cheeks once again heated up, but she wasn't about to share her mistake.

"And yesterday, I must have just missed you all day. You must have been in and out."

Hadlee's smile was shaking a little, but she kept it in place. "Yeah, sorry about that. I had a bunch of errands to do around town yesterday. We head out on the boat today and I was doing all the last-minute things."

Genni laughed softly. "I completely understand. No matter how much we plan for something, it seems that we're always running around like crazy right before it happens."

Hadlee found herself relaxing. Genni was proving to be quite friendly and didn't seem to know about any of Hadlee's mistakes since she arrived in town. "I haven't seen any other guests," she ventured.

Genni nodded. "We only have one other room available, and decided it was best to keep it open for now. Your group will probably be more comfortable if you have free reign, especially since I was made to understand you might work at odd hours of the day."

Hadlee shrugged. "Sort of. We'll want to get samples at different times and we're subject to Mother Nature a bit, but overall, we shouldn't be too crazy with our comings and goings."

"Great." Genni smiled again. "Well, if you need anything, you're welcome to let our desk clerk know, or you can find me personally out in the barn in the back of the property. We have an apartment inside there."

"I appreciate it, thank you," Hadlee said sincerely. She liked Genni. Hopefully her husband was just as welcoming.

The room had emptied as they'd chatted, and they walked together out of the dining room and toward the front door. Footsteps on the stairs caught Hadlee's attention and she turned to see Chrissy and the boys emerging from their rooms.

"Everyone ready?" Hadlee asked. When everyone gave her the affirmative, she gave Genni a polite goodbye and they walked outside. "Buckle up," Hadlee reminded her passengers as she started the van. Just as she was ready to back out, her phone rang. Glancing at it quickly, she noted it was her father. "Chrissy, can you grab that?"

Chrissy answered her phone and began chatting with Professor Ford.

A few of the things Chrissy said made Hadlee frown, but she was driving and unable to do anything about it. Luckily, the dock was only a couple of miles down the road and soon enough they were parked. Hadlee held out her hand for the phone.

"She's available now, Doctor," Chrissy said, handing the phone over. Her face was sympathetic and Hadlee's heart began to beat a furious rhythm.

"Hi, Dad," Hadlee said warily.

"Hadlee," he said in a low tone. "The department has been talking."

Hadlee held her breath. She already knew that they'd been of mixed feelings in letting her come, but she was already here. Surely they couldn't do anything to stop her now. "Yes?"

"Dr. Matheson thinks you might not be able to handle your assignment."

Her jaw clenched. "Dad. I'm not some untrained newbie who's never done research before. I'm almost an Associate Professor. I know what I'm doing."

"I understand that, sweetheart, but the results of this project could have lasting effects on other research projects, not to mention the entire scientific community."

She pushed out a harsh breath and pinched the bridge of her nose. "I'm fully aware of that." *And so are the locals, which is why they already hate me.*

"There's talk of sending Dr. Summers out to help you."

Hadlee wasn't given to sudden fits of temper—in fact, she considered herself a fairly calm person, despite her propensity for leaping before looking—but right now she was seeing red. "This is not his project," she said in as even a voice as she could manage. "He has no more experience or expertise than I do. What could he possibly add to the situation that would make it better?"

Her father sighed and Hadlee knew what he wanted to say. *He's a man.* It didn't seem to matter how hard women had worked to prove themselves in the workforce, or how instrumental they were in new findings or developing solutions to problems, there was just something about the male population that couldn't seem to let go of the idea that men should rule in the scientific world.

"I was given permission for this trip," Hadlee said, doing her best to keep from letting her father hear the tremor in her tone. "The grant was given to *me*. Christian Summers has no business being here, and I will not take him out on the boat should he show up."

"Now, Haddie, listen—"

"No, Dad, you listen. I know I've made mistakes in the past, but none of you are perfect either, and it's not fair to hold it against me. I've proven myself over and over again and I shouldn't have to keep doing it. You can tell your friends that they don't have the right to interfere. I'm here and I will do what I set out to do. When I'm done and have analyzed my findings, I'll let you all know...through the proper channels."

She stuck her chin in the air despite the fact that no one was around to see her. She's never spoken to her father this way, but Hadlee had enough problems on her hands without having to deal with those that were several hours away. *I wonder if Syliva Earle ever had to deal with problems like this.*

Her father still hadn't responded to her ultimatum, probably in shock from her forceful words, but Hadlee refused to care at the moment. "I'll talk to you soon. Tell Emmy that I love her the next time you speak to her."

Without another word, she hung up, then slowly lowered her head to the steering wheel. She was shaking too hard to leave the van and deal with another female-slash-scientist hater at the moment. As soon as she could breathe properly, Hadlee would once again try to take on the world, but first she needed a break.

FELIX WATCHED HIS CREW and Hadlee's interact as they went through introductions. They seemed pleasant enough and even better, the only other female didn't even come close to creating the rioting sensations inside his chest that Hadlee did. The only downside to that realization was that he wasn't just companion starved. It was Hadlee herself that was drawing his attention.

Where is she? He told himself his curiosity was from a professional perspective, but it was more than that. He wanted to see if she was still upset about their confrontation last night. Since they'd showed up at all, he knew she wasn't backing down, but would she give him the cool aloofness she did last night, or would she act as if nothing had happened?

"They seem like a nice bunch," Julian said as he entered the wheelhouse. The room wasn't large and two good-sized men made it crowded.

Felix grunted.

"Care to tell me why you're hiding out in here?"

Felix scowled over his shoulder. "I'm not hiding out."

Julian raised his eyebrows. "Could have fooled me."

Felix shook his head and faced forward again. "Have all the introductions been made?"

Julian snorted. "Yeah. The youngest guy, Lucas? He sounds like a barrel of fun."

Felix grinned. "You mean he's young enough to be annoying, but old enough we can't do much about it?"

"About sums it up," Julian answered with his own smile. "Hopefully his professor can keep him in line." Julian straightened. "Speaking of which...do we know where she is?"

Felix squinted through his sunglasses back to the parking lot. He found the van he'd seen last night and watched it closely. "There." The door opened and that soft brown hair, which called to his fingers, flashed in the sunlight. Shorts, a T-shirt, and sneakers made up her outfit, which was more attractive to Felix than a woman in a formal dress. He was casual himself, in almost every part of life, so a woman who appeared the same way definitely caught his attention. Julian snickered and Felix spun. "Something funny?"

Julian put on a fake innocent face. "I don't know what you're talking about."

Felix shook his head. "Whatever. Let's go down and I'll introduce you." He practically slid down the steep steps to the deck. Standing tall, he walked nonchalantly around to the front of the boat. Ethan and the scientist crew were chatting and laughing as if they were old friends.

"Captain," Ethan said as he snapped to attention and saluted.

Felix bit back a grin when Hadlee's helpers all looked at each other, as if unsure whether or not they should follow suit. "Carry on," Felix said in a lofty tone.

"Sir, yes, sir!" Ethan yelled, before moving into an "at ease" position.

"Uh…" Lucas was looking from person to person, trying to figure out what he should do.

"This isn't the military!" Hadlee shouted from the dock.

Felix looked over and gave her a smirk. "Doesn't mean the captain doesn't get respect."

Hadlee put her hands on her hips. "So does a doctor, but I thought we weren't being formal with each other."

He shrugged. "Maybe I changed my mind." He could feel her eye roll behind her sunglasses.

"Then in the spirit of being formal…permission to come aboard, Captain Mendez," she said with an exaggerated tone.

Felix pursed his lips and pretended to think about it. "Permission granted, but only if you promise to swab the deck."

"I thought that was this guy's job?" Lucas inserted, jabbing his thumb at Ethan.

Ethan groaned. "How can they tell?" he moaned.

Felix chuckled. "Peon is tattooed on your forehead."

"I knew it," Ethan muttered.

"Oh!"

Felix snapped over to Hadlee, who was standing still with her arms out. She was crossing the gangplank, but a wave had shifted it and she had stumbled. Without thinking about the consequences, Felix hurried and jumped onto the end and held out his hand. "Come on. I've got you."

Hadlee glanced up and their eyes met, or that's how it felt. It was difficult to see her eyes through the sunglasses, but the pull was too strong to be anything else. She didn't speak, but her hand reached out and landed in his.

Felix studiously ignored the jolt he felt from her touch. It was much stronger than it had been last night and he didn't want to consider why his reaction was growing. "Careful," he murmured as she walked toward him on unsteady legs. The boat was still rocking slightly more than normal, so Felix didn't let go of her hand until she was safely on deck. "Better?"

Hadlee nodded. "Yeah, thanks," she said breathlessly, letting go of him and wiping her hair out of her face. "I'm not quite sure what happened. I'm not usually so unsteady."

"Have you ever been on a boat before?" He felt foolish as soon as he asked the question, but it was out now and there was no taking it back.

Hadlee gave him a small smile. "I'm a marine biologist," she whispered, as if trying to help keep his mistake to themselves.

"Yeah..." Felix rubbed the back of his overheated neck. "I spoke before thinking."

Her smile was everything that was good in the world. "No worries. I thought you got married, so..."

He chuckled. "I guess we're even."

"Cap?"

Felix suddenly realized they had an audience and the heat in his neck grew. "Julian, Ethan, this is Dr. Hadlee Ford, professor of Marine Biology."

Hadlee was sweet and charming as she greeted his crew. Ethan seemed overly eager to show her around the boat and immediately began giving a tour. Hadlee's helpers followed them as they began to walk around.

"So that's why you were waiting in the wheelhouse," Julian murmured as they watched everyone walk away.

Felix pinched his lips together. "I don't know what you're talking about."

Julian snorted. "Yeah...we'll go with that...for now." He winked and then hurried after the group, throwing out a few bits of information as he grew closer.

Felix grimaced and scratched at the stubble on his chin. He couldn't let it go on like this. Hadlee was pretty... Okay, she was beautiful. But she was also a visitor and a threat to his area. Felix was a grown man and fully capable of controlling himself and any emotions that tried to rise unbidden inside of him. This was a job. Nothing more...nothing less. He couldn't let it be.

CHAPTER 7

Hadlee squinted into the sun and tried to ignore the tingles in her fingers from Felix's touch. Although she'd been on lots of boats during her time as a marine biologist, she'd been caught off guard by the moving bridge. It was ridiculous really, but she couldn't find it within herself to argue with the results.

Felix had come running to her rescue, offering a strong hand and a touch that made her stomach flutter. Playing the damsel in distress had never been Hadlee's idea of a good time, but right now she was seriously considering it again, if only to see if the moment between her and Felix had been a fluke.

"When do we sail?" Hadlee asked her guide, trying to force her mind away from an attraction she knew could go nowhere.

Felix glanced at his watch. "In about an hour. That'll give us time to get the traps set up just before slack water." His dark eyes met hers and Hadlee nodded.

"Got it. That's smart. The crabs will be more active then." She put her hands on her hips and took a deep, salty breath of air. "What are we using for bait?"

"Some heads and tails from a recent fishing trip."

"Are they fresh?" Hadlee turned back to him. "They always seem to work better if they're fresh."

Felix pulled a pair of sunglasses out of his back pocket and slapped them on his face. "They've been in my freezer, so they'll be fine."

Her nose scrunched up involuntarily. "You keep fish heads in your freezer?"

Twin dark eyebrows went high on his dark forehead. "I'm a fisherman, Hadlee. Are you telling me that as a scientist, you've never kept weird things in the freezer?"

She laughed awkwardly and tucked a chunk of hair behind her ear. "Uh, maybe I should plead the fifth and stop putting my foot in my mouth."

His chuckle was low and seemed to resonate in her own chest. "I suppose we both keep doing that. Probably something we should fix if we're going to be stuck together for the next couple of months."

Stuck together... Hadlee forced her face to stay neutral. Those weren't the words she would have used. Felix was handsome, if a little broody, and despite the fact that he wasn't thrilled about her work, she thought they could get along well when he finally realized she wasn't a threat. That, obviously, was not how he felt, if he was using words like "stuck." She nodded, glad her sunglasses hid her eyes, which probably showed disappointment. "Right."

"Ahoy, Captain!"

They both turned to see a man standing on the docks. Hadlee put her hand over her eyes, trying to see him better, but it was no use. She didn't know anyone in this town, so it wasn't like she was going to recognize him. However, his hat and vest let her know he was more than likely a man who frequented boats just like the one she was standing on right now.

"Harry!" Felix waved and grinned, then walked quickly over to the bridge and walked down to speak to his friend.

Hadlee tried not to stare, but it was difficult. Felix wasn't the tallest man she'd ever met, though he had a few inches on her, but his shoulders and chest were broad and thick, which made watching him a little too enjoyable. Especially when he folded his arms over his chest, as he was doing right now. Despite the view, Hadlee didn't want to come across as a creeper, so she turned her body around and began to walk around the boat. It was a very nice size and she was grateful to her friend for hooking her up with Felix. They would have no problem taking care of all her tracking and measuring the crabs she hoped to gather.

She walked around the opposite side of the boat from the dock, but came to a halt when she heard shouting. Frowning, she paused and tried to determine where it was coming from. Her helpers and the ship's hands were all still below deck, which left...

She peeked carefully around the corner to see the stranger, the one Felix had called Harry, shouting and waving at the boat. Felix, for his part, was standing tall and unmoving, though the frown on his face let her know he wasn't happy with whatever was going on. *At least he's not screaming back,* she thought.

"I'll talk to her myself!" Harry yelled, marching toward the gangplank.

"Don't do it," Felix warned. His voice was low and barely audible to Hadlee, but she was still pretty sure of what he said.

A sinking feeling in her stomach formed when she realized she was the *her* Harry was talking about. *What is with people hating me before they've even met me? Between the professors back home and the strangers here, I've never had so many enemies!*

Hadlee considered herself the type of person who got along with almost everyone. She would never be the popular, beautiful, or charismatic type, but she didn't think she was terrible either. She wasn't shy, even if she was a bit of an introverted nerd, and fashion might not be a way of life, but she wasn't completely out of touch either. She was intelligent and not hot-tempered, so really, she was mostly the forgettable type. Very few things stood out to make anyone pay attention to what she was doing or who she was. Yet in the last couple of days, she seemed to have become the topic of heated conversation both here and at home.

It was definitely not something she was enjoying.

Swallowing hard, Hadlee straightened her shoulders and stepped around the side of the cabin, coming into full view of Harry as he ignored Felix and stormed the deck. "Are you looking for me, sir?"

Harry's face was pinched as he stared her down. "Are you the doctor lady who's come to study our crabs?"

She nodded and put on a smile, praying it didn't look at brittle as it felt. "Yes." Putting out a hand, she walked forward. "I'm Dr. Hadlee Ford. What can I do for you?" When he ignored her greeting, Hadlee let her hand fall, instead clasping them at her waist. It would keep him from noticing how she was trembling. Not being shy didn't mean she enjoyed confrontation.

"You can go back to your college, where you belong."

Hadlee blinked. "I'm sorry?"

His finger shook in her face. "We don't need you coming in here to ruin an industry that's been supporting families since before you were born," Harry said in a dark tone.

"Are you saying you're not interested in keeping the crab population healthy?" Hadlee asked, hoping she could make him pause just long enough to help him see her side. She splayed her hands to the side. "All I'm here to do is check on the young crabs. I'm not here to blame anyone for anything or cause a fuss. I promise—"

"You're here to cause trouble!" Harry yelled, interrupting her. "You science people come in here, thinking you know more than anyone else. That all your books give you an advantage over those of us who have lived here our whole lives." He put a fist to his chest. "I grew up on these waters, as did my father and my grandfather." His finger nearly jabbed out her eye with its force. "Nothing you can read about or concoct in that overactive brain of yours gives you the right to take away a man's livelihood." His glare could have melted steel. "We won't let you," he growled.

Hadlee stepped back, her worries slowly morphing into true fear. This man wasn't just upset, he was threatening her. Words, she could work with. Physical violence was another matter.

"ALL RIGHT, HARRY," Felix said, putting a hand on the older man's shoulder. "That's enough."

Harry spun, his anger not abating at all. "Just because you don't make your living from the crabs doesn't mean her work won't affect you," he said tightly. Shaking off Felix's hold, he glared once more at Hadlee, then hurried back to the gangplank and stomped down the dock toward the parking lot.

Felix waited a few heartbeats before turning back to Hadlee. Truth was, he didn't blame Harry or George, or any of the other fishermen in the area who were afraid of what her study would do to their jobs, but he also didn't believe threats were the answer. "Are you okay?" he asked.

Hadlee's cheeks were red and her breathing was heavy, but otherwise she appeared whole. "Fine," she rasped, stepping back from Felix as if afraid of him.

A sting of shame hit his chest, but Felix kept his face steady. He had nothing to be ashamed about. This whole trip was because he owed a buddy a favor, not because he actually wanted to be here. He was starting to feel like he was stuck in the middle, however. Locals were mad that he was taking her onto his boat, though if Felix hadn't taken her, someone else would have. There were plenty of ships that wouldn't have a problem with what Hadlee was doing, especially the bigger fishing companies. When game was scarce, it was the smaller fishermen that went belly up, not those with corporations based in other cities.

Despite all of that, however, Felix would never be okay with the idea of hurting a woman, and that's where his friends seemed to be headed. If Harry had gotten any closer to Hadlee, Felix would have physically stepped between them. He didn't like the idea of friends of his ganging up on a scientist, especially a woman scientist, who was only doing her job. Last night he'd said his piece and that was enough. Harry, on the other hand, hadn't seemed content with words.

Felix wasn't naive enough to believe that Hadlee was the sole reason this might hurt their local fishermen She was one person. It was the information she was gathering that might cause a ruckus, depending on whose hands it ended up in.

"Should we get going?" Hadlee turned away from him and the stiffness of her shoulders only added fuel to the fire inside Felix's chest.

He didn't like her being upset. At all. *Why the heck do I care? I barely know her.* He shook his head. "Yep." He walked the opposite direction in order to go find both of their crews. "JULIAN!"

The sound of heavy steps came closer as his first mate rushed up the stairs. "Yes, Captain?"

"It's time to go," Felix said without preamble.

"Aye, aye, Captain." Julian called down to Ethan and the deckhand appeared within moments.

Without waiting to see if Hadlee's people also came upstairs, Felix went to the ladder leading to the wheelhouse. He would simply keep to himself and then he wouldn't have to deal with all the conflicting sensations that always seemed to rise to the surface when he was around Hadlee. He was an older brother. That was the only reason he was feeling protective of her. If someone cornered Charli the same way Harry had come after Hadlee, there was no way that Felix would have sat back and not interfered.

He took a deep breath as he stood in front of his station. *Of course, Charli would have taken Harry out before I got there,* Felix mused, his mouth twitching into a smile. His sister wasn't one to be pushed around and he loved that about her, but a small voice in the back of his head whispered that he was glad Hadlee wasn't as outspoken. He found her desire for kindness just another thing that reeled him in.

Nope. No being reeled in. I'm just the captain. Nothing more.

It took a few minutes, but soon the boat was out of the harbor and moving smoothly through the water toward their first destination. Felix had mapped the best places for them to put down traps up and down the coastline. He knew he'd eventually need to go over it all with Hadlee, to make sure they were covering all the areas she wanted, but right now, his first few stops were fine.

"Captain?"

He would never admit how her soft voice made his ears perk up, but his whole body seemed to come to attention when she came up behind him. "Yes?" Felix didn't let himself turn around. If she had a question, fine. Otherwise, he didn't need the distraction.

"May I come in?"

He clenched his jaw. So much for keeping his distance. "How can I help you, Dr. Ford?" He could hear her shuffling inside the wheelhouse, but even her footsteps were hesitant, and it brought that shame back to a boil in his belly.

"I wanted to apologize."

He turned around with a frown before he could stop himself. "Excuse me?"

Hadlee sighed and pushed her glasses up onto her head. "I wanted to apologize that I've obviously caused so much trouble among your buddies." She held out her hands. "I've never had so many people hate me before actually meeting me and I'm not sure how to convince you that I really am here just for research. No one is trying to take away their jobs or mess with your ecosystems." She scrunched up her nose, which made her look younger and kind of adorable, causing Felix to stiffen his grip on the wheel. "I'm just trying to finish my last publication to become an Associate Professor. The question of rising acidity along our coasts has come up quite a few times lately, and wondering how that affects the local wildlife is a natural question."

Her words were knocking softly on Felix's wall, but he wasn't one to be easily cowed. "Understood," he answered crisply. "But Harry's behavior is his own. It's not your fault." Deciding the conversation needed to be over before he started to feel sorry for her again, or those pesky protective feelings rose to the surface once more, he turned back to the front. "We'll drop the first trap in about a half-mile."

There was silence behind him, followed by another sigh, though this one was quieter and sounded disappointed. "Of course. Thank you, Captain."

He nodded, still keeping his eyes on the ocean. "Of course. It's what I'm here for." *And nothing else. Not even to be your friend. I'm just the captain and you're the passenger.*

The next few minutes were fairly quiet and Felix appreciated the time to think. He'd been harsher than he needed to be with Hadlee. She had come, trying to make amends, and he'd sent her away like a scolded child. But what else was he supposed to do? She stirred feelings inside of him he didn't want to acknowledge and was afraid that spending too much time with her would make it difficult to keep his distance.

No...it's better this way.

Responding to her kindness would only hurt them both in the end. They were on opposite sides of the spectrum when it came to her work, plus they didn't even live in the same city. And how many times did he have to remind himself he didn't want a relationship? He was just now getting to experience a free life and wanted to explore that further, no matter how many of his friends paired off.

If hurting Hadlee's feelings meant he was able to resist her al-lure...then he'd simply have to hurt her feelings. Hopefully she'd take the hint quickly enough that he wouldn't have to do it too many times. The sharp point of pain in his chest wasn't pleasant and Felix didn't want to cause any more grief than he needed to.

She's smart. I'm sure she's already received the message. It should be smooth sailing from here on out.

CHAPTER 8

“I’m gonna gain ten pounds if we stay here much longer,” Luke groaned, lying back in his seat.

“Might be more like fifty,” Joshua said dryly, “since we only got here a few days ago.”

Luke moaned again, rubbing his stomach.

Hadlee shook her head, but smiled. “Maybe try cutting back on the amount you eat, huh?” she said, knowing it would make no difference. Not only would Luke not listen to her advice, but he wouldn’t gain any weight either. The man was almost too slender and could eat enough to put a body out of business if he really wanted to.

“I’m still a growing boy,” Luke said with a grin. “I need my energy.”

“Rolling you around like Violet Beauregarde is going to take all my energy.” Joshua grunted.

“I’ll help you,” Chrissy said, adjusting her glasses. “I’ve been working out.”

Hadlee pinched her lips between her teeth. While Chrissy was probably telling the truth, her tiny, delicate frame did not show any signs of strength or athleticism. In fact, she was the type of woman who looked like a good breeze would knock her flat. Hadlee often felt like the Jolly Green Giant in Chrissy’s company, despite the fact that she was very average in size.

“Someone get me a magnifying glass,” Luke said, sitting up straight.

“What for?” Chrissy tilted her head to the side, looking like a curious little bird.

He squinted. "I'm trying to see the muscles you're talking about." He laughed when Joshua punched his shoulder.

Time to get away from the table. Hadlee began to stand when Genni came back into the dining room.

"Is there anything else I can get you?" she asked politely.

"Our compliments to your chef," Hadlee said with a smile. "We're all overeating at every meal."

Gennis laughed softly. "That's what we like to hear, but I'll share that with Mrs. Hall. She's not a certified chef, but she loves the kitchen and has been cooking for people her entire life."

"Shoot," Luke said with a pout. "I was hoping she wasn't married, so I could take her home with me."

"She might take you up on that," Cooper said, coming in behind his wife. His crooked grin made Hadlee smile back automatically. His edgy, but stunning looks had to have been in his favor when Genni fell for him. "She's a widow," Cooper continued in answer to Luke's comment.

Joshua raised an eyebrow as he turned to Luke. "She's probably old enough to be your grandmother."

"Who cares?" Luke shrugged. "As long as I'm fat and happy, I can overlook anything else."

"Did anyone want dessert?" Genni inserted.

"Actually," Hadlee hurried to say before any of her group could respond, "I was hoping for us to take a walk. Any suggestions on where to go?"

Luke leaned forward. "Somewhere where we could get dessert along the way?"

"I thought you were too full?" Chrissy asked.

Luke winked at her. "There's always room for dessert."

"There's a great chocolate shop on Main," Cooper offered, throwing an arm around his wife's shoulders. "Or you could hit the cookie truck down at the beach."

"Those both sound wonderful," Hadlee said. She raised her eyebrow at her helpers. At their nods, she turned back to her hosts. "How about the cookie truck tonight? We'll grab chocolates another time."

Genni nodded. "Sounds good. Just walk along the beach and about a mile down, you'll see a parking lot. Can't miss the truck. It's called 'Cookies Up!'"

"Perfect. Thank you." Hadlee pushed her chair in and grabbed her dirty dishes.

"No, no, no," Genni said, stepping in to grab the plates. "I told you already, let us take these."

"We're going to be here a long time," Hadlee argued, "and I'm not a fan of letting us get lazy in taking care of ourselves."

"You can—" Luke started.

Hadlee gave him a look and he ducked his head.

"We got it," he said before grabbing Chrissy's plate as well as his own.

"Such a gentleman," Hadlee teased, smiling at Luke as he rolled his eyes. She turned her smile to Genni and Cooper, nodding a thank you as they walked out of the dining room and into the kitchen.

It was several more minutes before they headed outside, having got caught up in saying thank you to Mrs. Hall, but once they were outside, Hadlee breathed a sigh of relief. Being outside was one of her favorite things. She loved the sea breeze and the salty fragrance of the coastal town. There was something so cleansing about being in nature, and nature that included the ocean was her absolute favorite.

Hadlee had an ulterior motive for getting dessert in town. She wanted to be seen around the area. After having two very unpleasant run-ins with the local fishermen, she decided that the best thing she could do was be out and about, which would hopefully allow people to get to know her aside from her research, and if she managed to make friends with anyone, she would be able to defend her work to ears that might actually listen.

Killing them with kindness was the best ammunition she had and Hadlee was going to use it to her advantage. She knew these people were simply afraid, but if she could get them to stop for just a moment, she would be able to help them understand that she wasn't a threat.

"Everyone ready?" Hadlee asked as they walked down the porch steps.

"I might need you to do that rolling," Luke whispered to Joshua.

"Don't count on it," Joshua said in his low tone. Without a backward glance, he pulled on his sunglasses and marched away from the house.

Hadlee, along with everyone else, had to speed up in order to keep up with his long legs. "Pull it back, Josh," she called. "Not all of us are as tall as you."

"You mean not all of us have tree trunks for legs," Luke muttered.

"Don't be jealous," Chrissy said sweetly.

Luke scoffed. "I'm not jealous. The guy's huge!"

"Which means he's big enough to fold you into a tiny, little ball," Hadlee said, giving Luke a look. "I wouldn't tease him too much." She held back a chuckle when Luke continued to mutter under his breath. She knew full well that Luke would never back off. It wasn't in his nature. If you were going to work with him, you simply had to learn to handle his enthusiasm. Although, even Hadlee had days when she was ready for him to shut it off.

As they reached the heavy sand, Hadlee took a moment to take off her shoes. She wanted to feel the grains between her toes. Right now was a pleasure moment and she wanted to savor it. So much of her life revolved around her work, but just because she was at the beach to document the crabs didn't mean she couldn't take time to feel the sand between her toes.

Tugging the rubberband out of her hair, she shook it out in the breeze, feeling free and easy. Hope was bubbling inside of her and she knew that everything was going to work out just fine. She would get to know the locals, they'd figure out she wasn't anything to worry about, and she'd come out of this an Associate Professor. Everything was going to be wonderful.

FELIX SCRUBBED AT HIS wet head with a towel as he followed the sound of his phone to the family room. Just as he came into the room, the ringing stopped, but he grabbed the phone anyway. Before he could see who had been calling, it started up again. "Hello?"

"Felix! It's Jack," the voice on the other side said.

"Hey, what's up man?" Felix asked. He liked the cookie food truck owner. Jack had come into town a few months ago and was dating Caro, the chocolate shop owner and a friend of Felix and Charli.

"There's trouble."

Felix paused. "What?"

"That doctor lady that you're taking around on your boat? Uh, Haily or something?"

"Hadlee?" Felix began walking to his room to grab his shoes. He had a feeling he wasn't going to be relaxing in front of the TV tonight.

"Yeah. Well, she and her friends just came by and got cookies, but I think something's wrong."

"Tell me exactly what happened," Felix demanded.

Jack blew out a breath. "Sorry, I'm just worried, but I've got a line a mile long and can't really leave the truck."

"It's okay, I'm on my way," Felix assured him, "But I need to know what's going on."

"Right. Sorry. Anyway, Hadlee and a few others were here getting some cookies and Hadlee was walking around introducing herself to everybody who's hanging around."

Felix pinched his lips together and squeezed his eyes shut. *Why can't she just stay in the background?*

"She's really cute and all, but a few of the older men didn't seem to like whatever she was saying."

Even though Jack couldn't see him, Felix was nodding. "Yeah, that's an understatement."

"Anyway, Hadlee was trying to be friendly, but they kind of shut her down. But that wasn't the crazy part." Jack took a breath. "Hadlee and her people left, but I happened to see that the younger three people with her headed toward town and Hadlee is headed back down the beach toward the bed and breakfast. A few minutes later, Harry and a couple of his buddies took off in his truck, headed in her direction, which as you know, is opposite of where he lives."

"Crap, crap, crap," Felix muttered. He shoved his shoes on and sprinted for the truck. "Thanks, Jack. I'm on it." Felix didn't wait around for Jack to answer. Instead, he shut off his phone, grabbed the keys to his truck and rushed out the door.

It took him a moment to decide who to go after first. The group in town was probably in just as much trouble as Hadlee, but she was on her own and Felix found himself pulled to her first. Hopefully the other three could take care of themselves if a situation arose.

He slammed the truck into gear and spun out of his driveway, not paying any attention to the speed limit as he pulled into traffic and gunned it.

It only took seconds for lights to be flashing in his rearview mirror and Felix threw out enough curses to have any sailor raising their eyebrows. Knowing there was little he could do at the moment, he pulled over and thrummed his fingers on the steering wheel.

"Where's the fire?" Ken asked as he walked up to Felix's window. He put one hand on the top of Felix's door and leaned in with a smirk. "How many times do I have to give you a ticket before you slow down?"

Felix growled. "I don't have time for this," he said through his clenched jaw. "Hadlee could be in trouble."

The smile fell off Ken's face. "Who's Hadlee and why is she in trouble?"

Felix pinched the bridge of his nose. A headache was pulsing behind his eyes. "Hadlee is the scientist I'm helping this summer. Some of the local fisherman have decided she's here to shut down their crabbing businesses with her research and have already approached her a couple of times. Jack just called and said she's walking by herself and Harry and a couple of others followed her."

Ken tapped the top of the truck. "I'll write you up later. Let's go." He started to walk away. "Where is she?"

"I don't know. She was walking back to the bed and breakfast."

"You head that way. I'll go down Main."

Felix nodded, grateful he had friends in high places, and pulled back into traffic. Knowing Ken was going to be in town meant he could take care of any altercations with the other three scientists as well eased his mind. Felix blasted past the parking lot with the food truck and went about a half-mile down the road before he saw Harry's truck on the side of the road.

Felix hit the brakes and pulled over, jumping out of the truck before the engine had truly shut all the way off. Gripping his keys, he raced into the weeds and up the hill that separated him from the beach. Once he was at the top, his heart almost stopped.

Hadlee was standing by herself, backing toward the water as three grown men crowded her from the front. As he watched, her calves were hit from behind by a wave and Hadlee stumbled, giving the men a chance to close the distance between them. She was running out of space and Felix wasn't sure just how far the men would go in order to get their point across.

Gritting his teeth, he took off once again, pounding the sand with his boots, and praying that the men he had always thought of as friends weren't going to ruin their relationship.

Felix had grown up in Seaside Bay and had always looked up to Harry and the other fishermen. They'd done nothing but support him in his journey to becoming a ship captain and going against them felt wrong, but watching them attack a woman was worse.

"Hey!" Felix shouted as he grew closer.

The men turned around and Felix's ears picked up a sob of relief from Hadlee, which only served to spur him on.

He reached the group a few seconds later and immediately moved between them, facing the men. "What do you think you're doing, Harry?"

"Get out of the way, son," Harry said. "We need to talk to the girl."

Felix slowly shook his head. "She's not a girl, Harry. She's a grown woman and a doctor at that. Surely any problems you have can be talked out without threats."

"Her research will shut us down!" Cole shouted from Harry's left.

Felix held up a hand. "You don't know that."

"You also don't know that it won't," Harry argued. "Are you willing to take the chance that she'll ruin everything we've worked for?"

"I'm not trying to shut anyone down!" Hadlee shouted from behind him.

Please just be quiet, Felix prayed, but Hadlee apparently didn't know how to read minds, or she just didn't care, because she wasn't done yet.

CHAPTER 9

"I've told you that my study isn't what you think it is," Hadlee argued, feeling slightly bolder now that Felix's large body was between her and the men. Her legs were shaking to the point that she was struggling to stand. The cold from the water and the fear at being cornered by three men had her trembling from head to toe. "I'm only here to check on the health of young crabs. It has nothing to do with your factories or your fishing."

Felix held out a hand behind him and Hadlee grabbed hold, feeling immediately better at his strength and warmth. He stiffened at her touch, then gave her hand a squeeze.

"Gentlemen, this isn't how to handle all this. You heard her. Her work isn't about your jobs. Now let's just leave it alone."

The tallest of the men, who was thin and wiry, shook his head. "We can't do that. You know how much our whole state depends on the crabbing industry. We'll be doing all fishermen a disservice if we let this go on."

Hadlee stepped closer to Felix's back, still holding his hand, and gripped the back of his shirt with her other hand. "Please," she said softly. "What will it take for you to believe me?"

"Harry! Cole! Vincent!"

Hadlee jumped nearly out of the water at the new voice. She hadn't seen the new man approaching, but the fact that he was in a policeman's uniform was the best thing she'd seen all day. Felix relaxing at the man's approach was an added bonus.

The large man came up behind three, now sheepish, bullies. "What's going on down here?" the officer asked. He glanced at Felix, then Hadlee, before going back to the men.

"Nothing, Captain," Harry said with a sigh. He rubbed the top of his head. "We just wanted to talk to the girl."

"Backing her into the ocean at night isn't just talking," Felix said in a low tone.

"No one forced her into the water," Harry shot back.

"If you were new to town and three men, who were both bigger and stronger, came at you, do you really think she felt like she had a choice?" Felix started to step forward, but Hadlee's hold kept him back.

She was tempted to let him go and let him handle the men, but she didn't want any violence. She didn't know why the men were so angry. She'd explained her work and it had nothing to do with shutting down the fishing industry, so it made no sense that they continued to disbelieve what she told them.

The men had no answer to Felix's question and the police officer clapped Harry on the shoulder. "Somehow I doubt a lady as educated as she is would be stupid enough to get wet at this time of night unless she felt threatened." His eyes went to Hadlee. "Did you feel threatened by these men?" he asked in a much softer tone than he'd been speaking to the men in.

Hadlee swallowed hard. She had definitely been frightened by the men, but she also wasn't interested in them being arrested or in causing any type of trouble at all.

"Hadlee," Felix said in an undertone, his tone urging her to answer.

"I..." Her grip on Felix's shirt tightened and she could feel her hand in his growing sweaty. Her mouth was dry and her mind jumped back and forth as to what the right choice was.

"Hadlee!" Felix said more urgently, glancing a little over his shoulder.

Finally, she shook her head. She couldn't do it. She wanted to be left alone, but she didn't want to send these men to the police station. "Yes, they frightened me, but I don't want to press any charges."

"What?" Felix turned fully this time.

Hadlee stumbled a little as his shirt was jerked out of her hand and their fingers twisted apart. She felt immediately colder at the loss.

"They're just going to do this again," Felix hissed in her ear.

Hadlee stood straight, forcing herself to not pay attention to the desire pulsing through her to have him touch her again. She ignored Felix for the moment and turned back to the policeman. "I just want them to leave me alone."

The policeman sighed and scratched his chin. "Looks like it's your lucky night, gentlemen." He stepped in front of them and ushered them back toward the road. "But I think it's time for you to go home."

As Hadlee watched the police officer walk them away, her legs finally gave out and she fell to her knees.

"Hey, hey, hey," Felix said. The anger from his earlier words was gone and his low voice was full of concern. He dropped her hand and wrapped his arms around her waist, pulling her out of the water.

Hadlee was shaking so hard, her teeth felt like they were going to break against each other. "Thank you," she forced out.

"We need to get you warm," Felix growled. He shifted her in his arms and then next thing Hadlee knew, she was being swept into his arms.

"Oh!" she squeaked, automatically wrapping her arms around his neck. "Felix, you don't have to carry me."

He stopped and looked at her intensely. "Can you walk?"

She opened her mouth, then paused. "I...don't know."

Felix nodded, his usual scowl in place as he began walking again.

The anger emanating off his person was enough to heat Hadlee all the way to her core. She wanted to ask why he was so angry with her—it wasn't like she had been the person in the wrong—but despite the heat, she was still shaking and her teeth chattering, so she clenched her jaw together and stayed silent.

It took a few minutes to arrive at his truck and Felix tucked her, surprisingly gently, into the passenger seat before shutting the door and walking around to the other side.

"I'm staying at the bed and breakfast," Hadlee whispered into the quiet cab.

Felix nodded. "I know." His actions didn't match his words, however, as he pulled onto the road in the opposite direction.

"Wait!" Hadlee said, panic making her trembling worse. "It's the other way."

"I'm aware," Felix said darkly. "But first we need to warm you up."

Hadlee eyed him warily. She wasn't sure what he was planning to do. She had access to dry clothes and a shower back at the bed and breakfast, so she couldn't figure out what he thought he was doing by taking her somewhere else.

His phone buzzed, distracting her from her worries.

Felix grabbed it and gave it a quick glance before shoving it toward Hadlee. "Can you text?"

She clenched her muscles to try and slow down the shaking in her hands as she took the phone. "Yeah."

"Just answer the new text and say 'my place.'"

Hadlee's thumbs froze. "Excuse me?"

His eyes were dark and filled with anger when they shot to her before going back to the road. "I said…'my place.'"

Confusion didn't begin to cover the emotions going through Hadlee at the moment. She was wet, cold, scared, and probably in shock, yet it was Felix saying he was taking her back to his home that had her heart pumping so hard she could barely breathe.

Turning back to the small screen, she typed the response and waited while a thumbs up emoji came in return. Setting the phone on the dash, she folded her still trembling hands together and kept quiet. Right now there was too much going on for her to compartmentalize it all. All she could do was watch and wait.

FELIX PACED THE FLOOR of his sitting room. Hadlee still hadn't emerged from the bathroom where he'd put her with some of Charli's old clothes and a towel. Then he'd changed his own pants, which had been covered in water and sand, and come out front to wait for Ken.

"What's taking him so long?" he muttered, running a hand through his hair. He didn't know whom he was more upset at. Harry for instigating such a stupid situation, or Hadlee for not pressing charges so that they could be sure this wouldn't happen again.

A door opened down the hall and Felix paused to watch the room entrance. He clenched his hands into fists when Hadlee appeared, obviously wary.

"Thank you for the clothes," she whispered, picking at the shirt that didn't quite fit, but was good enough for the moment. Charli was more athletically built than Hadlee, so her clothes were a little tight on Hadlee's curvier frame, making Felix's muscles clench even tighter.

He squeezed his eyes closed to try and shove the appealing image out of his brain, but it wasn't about to move. "Have a seat," he bit out, going back to pacing in order to keep from reaching for her and making sure every part of her was still okay after her frightening encounter.

His protective instincts had gone completely haywire when she'd taken his hand. He'd reached back, trying to signal to her to be quiet, hoping he could diffuse the situation if she would only stop talking, but instead, Hadlee had grabbed hold and not let go. Then, when her other hand had gone to his back, Felix had felt a hurricane of unwelcome emotions. He could feel her trembling, her hands cold and clammy, and it made him want to slay every demon she faced, all while fighting the urge to turn around and see if her kiss would cause the same pulsing warmth that her hand did.

No other woman had ever rocked his world so hard, and Felix wasn't even dating her. They hadn't even gone on a date, yet she had him so discombobulated, he wasn't sure where to turn, and that made his normal broodiness stronger than ever.

"Why are you so mad at me?"

Felix paused and turned slowly to her timid voice. She looked so forlorn and confused that he felt a sympathetic tug in his gut. His shoulders deflated and he let out a beleaguered sigh, pinching the bridge of his nose. "I'm not...mad at you."

"Felix," she said a little more strongly. "I'm not stupid. I *know* you're mad."

He forced himself to meet her light-colored eyes. Something about her darker hair and lighter eyes was so intriguing, especially compared to his own dark coloring, which he had always felt left him looking monotone. "Doesn't mean I'm mad at you."

She rolled her eyes, letting him know she was starting to recover from her experience. A small part of him pouted that she obviously didn't need him to hold her again, but the bigger part of him cursed that voice back to oblivion. "You growled at me, Captain Mendez. What part of that means you aren't mad at me?"

He shrugged. "I growl at everybody."

A small smile spread across her face. "So, you're just a bear to every person you meet?"

He pushed a hand through his windblown hair and chuckled darkly. "I suppose that's an apt description."

"Well…" Hadlee slapped her knees and stood. "Thank you so much for your help tonight. I was caught off guard and didn't know if those men would hurt me or not." She gave him a look that felt a little too close to hero worship. "Thank you for stepping in."

Felix shook off her thanks. "It should have never happened to begin with."

She nodded and tucked a piece of hair behind her ear. "I know, but for some reason, no one in this town will believe me when I say this has nothing to do with the fishing industry."

Felix also found that odd, though he understood their initial worry. "You promise this isn't about trying to shut down the crabbing jobs?"

"Are you kidding me?" Hadlee shook her head and her lips pinched into a tight, white line. She marched up to him and poked Felix in the chest. "What is it gonna take to get this through your thick, bear skull?" she asked, sorrow filling her tone. "I'm here to earn my Associate Professor accreditation. I don't want to hurt anyone, I don't want to shut down jobs, I don't even want to put limits on what you're doing. I've lived in Oregon my whole life and I love the fact that our state relies on natural resources to support its people. I. Don't. Want. To. Stop. That." She backed up a little, her brows drooping. "I just want to move up as a teacher. Absolutely no hidden agenda. Is that too much to ask?"

Felix slowly shook his head. His hands came up without conscious thought and rested on her upper arms. "There's nothing wrong with that," he said, his voice having dropped. He rubbed her exposed skin with his palms, noting that she had goosebumps. "Are you still cold?"

Hadlee visibly shivered, then shook her head. "No."

His eyes locked with hers and Felix found himself shuffling slightly forward, his fingers lightly gripping her arms. "You're shivering."

She nodded. "I know."

Felix couldn't seem to make himself look away. She'd almost been hurt tonight. He was almost too late. The thought of her being hurt made him nauseous. His whole, carefree life was looming in front of him, but right now he couldn't even remember why he wanted to stay away from women.

The air between them seemed to vibrate and Felix came forward even more. They were standing toe to toe, simply staring into each other's eyes. The pulse at the base of her throat was beating rapidly and it took Felix only a moment to realize his was doing the same.

His hold on her arms tightened and his head slowly lowered. Her eyes fluttered shut as his forehead touched hers, and Felix followed suit. With his vision gone, he breathed her in. The smell of the ocean and a distinctly floral, feminine fragrance overwhelmed his senses. He knew he would never walk into a flower shop again without thinking of Hadlee.

"Felix," she whispered. Her tone was husky and Felix almost jolted at the pleading undertone.

Does she want this as much as I do? He'd never been so nervous about a kiss before. The anticipation was going to give him a heart attack before he ever touched her lips. A tug caught his attention, and he realized she was fisting the front of his T-shirt, the same way she had back at the beach.

That was it. The signal he needed to know that she didn't want him to back off. Fortifying himself for what was to come, Felix tilted his head and started to close the distance between their lips...

"Ahem."

Hadlee squealed and jumped away from him, scrambling backward so fast that Felix was worried she would fall on her backside.

He stood watching her for a moment, feeling completely unsatisfied and in shock at the loss of her touch.

"Sorry to interrupt." Ken's tone held an undertone of laughter, letting Felix know his friend wasn't sorry at all.

Shifting back into his usual scowl, Felix turned and raised an eyebrow at the police captain. "What took you so long?"

Ken smirked. "Had to deliver a scolding to three ornery old men. Excuse my tardiness." His eyes went to Hadlee and Felix followed.

She was on the couch, folded into herself, looking much more like the frightened woman he'd brought into his house a half-hour before.

"Dr. Ford, I'm Captain Ken Wamsley."

She nodded. "Nice to meet you. And thank you for your help."

Ken nodded, then went back to Felix. "Let's have a seat and get this figured out, huh?"

Felix nodded in return, trying to pretend he hadn't just been caught in an intimate situation. He forced himself to not look at Hadlee. Now that his head was clearing, he was far too aware of how much of a mistake it would have been to give into the attraction between them. And looking at her would only bring that desire back to the surface, something he couldn't afford to have happen.

CHAPTER 10

Hadlee's trembling had absolutely nothing to do with the cold. Her stomach wouldn't stop quivering and her heart was having a hard time slowing down from her near-kiss with Felix. She hadn't expected to have such a moment with him, and now she was feeling bereft that it had never happened.

His hands had been so warm and soothing on her skin, and when his forehead dropped to hers, she had felt like melting into a puddle, but was afraid if she did, she would miss something amazing.

She had managed not to melt, but with the addition of Captain Wamsley, she was positive she *had* missed something amazing. It almost made her want to adopt Felix's signature scowl, but she kept herself from mimicking him.

Captain Wamsley sat down in a seat and leaned forward, his elbows resting on his knees. "I know you said you didn't want to press charges, but could you tell me what exactly happened tonight?"

Hadlee found herself relaxing at the soft tone in his voice. It was no wonder he was an officer. He obviously made everyone feel safe, though she didn't find herself wanting to burrow herself in his chest the way she had with Felix. Blowing out a breath, Hadlee tucked the same strand of hair behind her ear again. It seemed determined to be in her way tonight. "My TA's and I went to get cookies at that food truck down by the beach."

Captain Wamsley nodded.

She shrugged and put her hands out to the side. "I was trying to introduce myself to the locals a little, since there seems to be some misinformation about what I'm doing here." She glanced at Felix, who was studying the carpet as if it held the answers to the universe. "I've had a couple of men confront me and tell me to go home."

The officer pulled out his phone and started typing away. "Do you know who they were?"

She pinched her lips and glanced at Felix again, hurt that he was stepping back and refusing to speak. "Harry was one, the same guy who was there tonight."

"There was more than one instance?"

She nodded. "Yeah..." She tucked her legs beneath her, trying to get comfortable. "I also met George Herman."

"And they threatened you?" the captain clarified.

"No." Hadlee shook her head. "No one threatened me...exactly, they just...made it clear they didn't want me here."

"Felix?"

The scowling man finally turned and acknowledged there were other people in the room.

"Were you with her during these instances?"

She almost missed his dark eyes meeting hers before turning back to his friend.

"Yeah."

"Was she threatened?"

Felix huffed and leaned back in his seat to fold his arms over his chest. "Not exactly, but she's right. They both made it clear she wasn't welcome in town."

The officer nodded and went back to Hadlee. "So...you decided to change their minds?"

Hadlee nodded. "Yes. Everyone seems to think I'm trying to shut them down, but it's not true. I'm just studying the crabs. Nothing else."

"So, you approached the men?" Captain Wamsley asked with a frown.

Hadlee scrunched her nose up. "That sounds really stupid when put like that, but I was just trying to show everyone I wasn't a threat."

"But they didn't believe you."

She shook her head. "No. When I left, my TA's all wanted to go into town and see what kind of night life you have around here, but I wanted to head back to the bed and breakfast." She picked at a loose thread in her borrowed shirt. It was a little tighter than she was used to, but she couldn't help but be grateful that Felix had offered her something dry to change into. She'd be in her own clothes soon enough.

"And...?" he pushed.

"And apparently, they followed me," Hadlee continued, her voice more of a whisper, but as she recounted the story, the fear from before came flooding back into her system. She squeezed her eyes shut. "They surrounded me, making claims that I was trying to single-handedly ruin the crabbing industry and take down their grand traditions of crabbing." She brought her legs to her chest and rested her forehead on her knees, trying to keep from gasping for breath. "I don't know them well enough to know if they would hurt me or not, so I started backing away from them when they wouldn't let me defend myself."

"And that's how you ended up in the water."

It wasn't a question, but Hadlee nodded anyway. It had been her only way of escape. She was a scientist, not an athlete, though tonight's experience made her want to take a self-defense class, if only to never be afraid like this again.

"Did the men threaten physical violence at that point?" Captain Wamsley's voice was soft again, as if speaking to a wild animal he was trying to tame.

"Not explicitly. They just kept saying I didn't belong here and they wouldn't let me ruin their lives." She could hear more typing and assumed the policeman was making more notes. Forcing herself to look up, Hadlee ignored Felix's statue act in the corner and faced the officer. "I know I probably could have accused them of something, but I don't want trouble. I just want them to leave me alone to do my work. I don't know why everyone thinks my study is going to hurt them, but it's not. I promise. I'm not trying to make any enemies."

The officer's eyes were still on his phone, though he nodded as he kept typing. Finally he looked up. "I understand. But I think we need to make a plan going forward. Harry, George, and some of the other men are older and set in their ways. I don't know where they got their information from, but I think we can assume that they're not going to back off if they truly think you're going to shut them down."

Hadlee deflated, resting her head against the back of the couch. "What do you suggest? Just not going into town while we're here?"

Captain Wamsley ticked his head back and forth. "As helpful as that might be, it doesn't seem very feasible." His golden brown eyes went to Felix, but he continued speaking to Hadlee. "I was hoping we could do something a little more helpful."

When the men kept having a staredown, but no one bothered to say anything more, Hadlee had to ask. "So what exactly are we talking here?"

Felix's jaw tightened and a pulsing vein was visible.

"I think we might need to get you some protection," Captain Wamsley said, not looking away from his friend.

Hadlee frowned. "You mean like a bodyguard?" She looked back and forth between the two men, but no one answered her. Jumping to her feet, Hadlee headed toward the door. Truth was, she wouldn't mind Felix acting as her bodyguard, but not when he obviously wanted nothing to do with her. He might have been the one to initiate their small bit of contact earlier, but it was clear he had found her wanting. There was no other way to interpret the nearly tangible angry vibes pulsing from his person. "Thanks, but no thanks," Hadlee said quickly, grabbing her shoes and forcing them on her feet. She put her hand on the doorknob, turning back enough to see both men watching her cautiously. "I can tell when I'm not wanted, gentlemen, and I'm not usually one to force myself anywhere I'm not welcome. I'll just be more careful in the future."

With her head high and her self-respect in tatters, she opened the door and marched into the night.

"GO GET HER, YOU IDIOT," Ken hissed, giving Felix a fierce look. "You totally brushed her off and now she's leaving, in the dark, I might add, when we were just discussing how she needs someone to keep her safe."

Felix rose from his chair, giving into his urges to protect her, but he forced himself to stop. "I can't," he said, locking his knees.

"Are you kidding me?" Ken huffed. He shook his head and stood up. "Felix, I've always been proud to call you my friend, but right now I'm totally ashamed of you."

"You don't get it," Felix shot back. He clenched his jaw when Ken gave him a look. "I don't plan to get involved with anyone...ever. I'm finally free to run my own schedule, to fish whenever I want, and go out on the boat without any strings. Why would I ruin such a good thing by starting a relationship with a woman who doesn't even live here?"

Ken slowly shook his head again. "Do you really think that I wouldn't give anything to have the woman I'm interested in pay attention to me? I can barely get her to look at me," Ken said in a low tone. Their entire friend group knew that Ken wanted to date Rose, but she kept a distance between them, though no one knew why. "From the way I found you two when I walked in, I don't think she's opposed to exploring this with you." He pointed his finger toward the door. "The woman you're interested in is walking home. Alone.

In the dark. On the same night that three men tried to attack her, all because you're a coward."

A muscle jumped in Felix's jaw at the accusation, but he couldn't argue, because Ken was right. Taking a chance with Hadlee meant changing everything Felix had planned for his life.

"Keeping her safe doesn't mean you have to marry her," Ken said, turning his back and walking toward the door. "I'll find her and take her home. If you'll send me your schedule, I'll provide an officer to keep an eye on the docks more than usual. Who knows…maybe I'll send one of the younger ones." Ken smirked over his shoulder. "It's not like she isn't available."

"Stop." Felix wasn't sure what part of Ken's speech had caused him to react, but he couldn't do it. It didn't matter that his heart was about to leap out of his throat and that a cold sweat had broken out on the back of his neck. The idea of somebody else spending time with Hadlee and being close to her, even in the spirit of protection, brought an irrational rage that could only be described as a green-eyed monster choking the very breath out of Felix's lungs.

Ken paused. "Every moment I wait is another moment she's by herself."

Felix glared at his friend. Ken knew too well how to press Felix's buttons. *Probably because they're the same buttons that would drive him crazy.* "I'm going."

Ken stepped away from the door and waved an arm toward it. "Go get 'em, Tiger."

"If you were off duty, I'd punch you," Felix muttered as he marched out the door.

"You could try," Ken said easily, not the least bit upset by the threat.

Ignoring the taunt, Felix headed into the dark and tried to figure out which way Hadlee had headed. He knew which would take her back to town, but he didn't know if Hadlee knew which direction to go. "Hadlee?" He stilled and listened, but she didn't answer. Now his heart was pounding for a different reason. *I waited too long.*

Felix rushed to the end of the driveway. "Hadlee!" He spun around, looking up and down each side of the road. Luck was on his side when a car drove down the street, the headlights creating a beam that lit a dark silhouette in the distance. He took off running to catch up with her, not wanting Hadlee to get any farther down the road than she already was.

"Hey," Felix panted as he caught up with her. "Hold on."

Hadlee glanced his way, but Felix couldn't read her expression in the dark. "It's late," she said curtly. "I'll see you in the morning."

"Hadlee." Felix grabbed her arm, but Hadlee jerked away. He couldn't explain why that action hurt so much. He still wasn't sure what to do about their attraction, but her rejection still stung. "Sorry," he said, putting his hands in the air. "But could you stop for a minute?"

"I've got a long walk," she said, still facing forward. "So, now's not a good time to chat."

Felix held in a sigh. This was his fault and Ken was right. He was a coward. "Hadlee, please."

His pleading must have broken through her ice wall because her footsteps faltered.

Taking a chance, Felix reached out, but instead of trying to stop her by grabbing her arm, he took her hand and slowed them down until they were standing still on the side of the road. "What do you want, Felix?" she asked in a tired tone. She wasn't quite holding his hand back, but she wasn't pulling away.

Felix pushed his free hand through his hair. He might not know what to do with her, but he didn't want to hurt her. "Let me drive you home," he said, keeping his tone low and soothing. Right now was not the time to let his usual surliness come through.

"I'm capable of walking," she said, starting to pull away.

"Look, Hadlee, I'm sorry."

She stopped.

"I didn't mean for things to get out of hand, but I was..." Felix cursed in his mind. He did *not* like having a discussion like this. "I'm attracted to you, okay?" he all but shouted. "I got caught up in the moment and wanted to kiss you."

Even in the dark he could see her eyes were wide, having obviously not expected his outburst. "Do you just go around kissing any woman you're attracted to who crosses your path?" she asked bluntly.

He took a minute to answer, but eventually shook his head. "No. In fact, I don't really...date...at all."

"Oh." She pulled her hand away and Felix let her go, despite his inner voice saying to hold on. "Well...I guess that settles that?" Her voice went up at the end as if it was a question, but Felix wasn't sure how to answer. Hadlee cleared her throat and looked around while rubbing her upper arms.

"Let me drive you home," Felix said, waving his arm back toward his house. "It's not safe for you out here."

She scoffed. "You really think your sleepy little town is unsafe?"

"Were you not there earlier tonight?" he asked sarcastically. "Plus, we might roll up the road at ten, but let me assure you, the wildlife doesn't." That got her attention and she began eyeing the forest behind her. "I'm sure your team is worried about you," Felix said softly. "Let's get you back and then we can forget today ever happened." *Well...you can forget, but I'll keep wondering what it would have felt like to actually kiss you.*

She nodded. "I appreciate it. Thank you."

Tension slid off his shoulders at her capitulation and Felix found himself doubly grateful she hadn't given him grief about his no dating rule. He'd spent a lot of years taking care of his younger sister and while he didn't regret it, for the first time ever, Felix was free. Was it wrong to want to enjoy that? He didn't think so... Then why did

Hadlee mess with his emotions so much? He needed to get control of himself, and soon.

CHAPTER 11

Hadlee knew that if someone took the time to look up *awkward* in the dictionary, they would surely find her picture there. The entire morning, she had been dropping things, tripping over nothing on the boat deck, and generally making a fool out of herself. She couldn't seem to get the intense moment with Felix out of her head, despite the fact that it had happened almost two weeks ago. The heat coming off of his body, the tension sizzling through the air, the anticipation thrumming through her at the thought of his touch and kiss.

After her little tantrum that night, which was embarrassing enough in and of itself, she'd had to have a *talk* with Felix, only to learn that she'd stood up for herself for nothing. *He doesn't date. But the question is...does he not date at all, or is it simply me?*

She didn't have an answer to her question and she wasn't about to ask. Things were weird enough as is. Hadlee felt like every time she turned around, Felix was standing in her line of sight looking like some kind of ocean god. He was wearing a baseball hat today and his hair stuck out the back in a haphazard fashion, while the curve of the cap accentuated the strong line of his jaw. His thick shoulders and chest kept distracting her from her work now that she knew what the muscles felt like under her palms. And the aloof air he had perfected made her feel like an unschooled teenager fangirling over some kind of celebrity.

It was beyond ridiculous.

You're almost thirty years old, she scolded herself internally. *Get over it and get back to work.*

"What about this one, boss?" Luke asked, holding up a smallish crab from the bucket he was searching through.

"Did you measure it?" Hadlee asked. They were specifically looking for the effect on young crabs, which meant the crabs had to fit within certain size requirements to be considered young enough.

Luke shrugged.

Hadlee gave him a look. "You have a ruler right next to you. Measure before you offer them up for observation, please."

Luke muttered under his breath, but did as she asked.

"You ready for another basket?" Ethan, the deck hand, asked over his shoulder.

Hadlee looked up. "Already?"

Ethan grinned, his boyish good looks giving him a mischievous air. "The Cap is moving a little faster than you guys are."

Hadlee huffed, irritation helping curb her out-of-control hormones. "Bring it on, Eeks," she joked, using the nickname he'd given her when they'd been introduced.

"Anything you say, beautiful," Ethan said as he turned back to watch the water.

Hadlee grinned. *At least someone is willing to flirt with me,* she mused. She steadied herself as the boat slowed down, cruising up alongside a buoy that marked their crab trap.

"Ooh," Ethan said after pulling the trap onto the deck. "Looks like we've got slow pickings today." He dumped a single crab into Hadlee's bucket.

"Huh," Hadlee murmured. "It is normal for us to get so few? I thought crabs were big business around here?"

Ethan nodded. "They are. But everything has its off day." He shrugged and began coiling the rope from the trap. "Looks like the crabs just aren't hungry today."

Hadlee squished her lips to one side. "Well, it's a good thing we've got plenty of time out here, huh?"

"Yep." Ethan put the rolled rope and trap off to the side. "Cap is gonna hold still for a few before going after the last trap."

"Sounds good," Hadlee muttered, putting her focus back on her bucket of crabs. If Ethan was willing to play "go-between," then she was all for it. Felix might be good at acting like nothing had ever happened between them, but Hadlee wasn't quite so strong. She dug her gloved hands through the bucket. "Too big," she said, dumping the crab into another bowl. Noticing her discard bowl was getting full, she grabbed it and spun around in order to dump it overboard. "Oh!" Hadlee stumbled, the bowl falling to the ground, spilling crabs all over the deck.

"What the—" Felix growled, stepping back, his eyes on the scrambling crabs.

"You scared me," Hadlee scolded, letting her anger slip into her words. She knew blaming Felix was childish, but his cold shoulder was more painful to endure than she would have expected.

"Do you throw crabs at everyone who catches you off guard?" he asked, a slight smile on his enticing lips. He bent over and grabbed a crab that was kicking its legs in the air before throwing it easily over the railing.

"Ah!"

Hadlee groaned and hung her head. "Sorry, Chrissy," she offered, recognizing her TA's screech.

"It's okay, Dr. Ford," Chrissy said, her voice higher than normal. The tiny woman was dancing around the deck, trying not to step on any of the crabs rushing across the wood.

"Just toss them over," Hadlee said, getting down on her knees to grab the ones closest to her. Her heart nearly stopped when Felix did the same just a couple of feet from her. *Oh my gosh! Knock it off!* It was going to be a very long summer if she couldn't get her emotions under control.

"Are you finding the crabs you need?"

It took Hadlee a moment to realize Felix was talking to her. "What?"

His grin grew and even under the bill of his cap, Hadlee could see his dark eyes snapping with humor. "The catch has been low today. I was wondering if you've been finding enough specimens to study."

"Oh...right." Hadlee nodded and tucked a piece of hair behind her ear. "Um...we've found a few, but you're right, the catch had been light today." A pressure on her finger had her snapping her head down. "Ouch," she muttered, pulling a crab off her finger. Her thick rubber gloves helped keep the pinch from really hurting her or breaking the skin, but the pressure was still enough to create a bit of pain.

Felix snatched the crab from her hand and tossed it over his shoulder before leaning closer to look at her hand. "Are you okay?"

Hadlee sat frozen stiff with wide eyes as he tore off her glove and inspected her finger. His hands were warm and his fingers were just like the rest of him, a little thicker than the normal man.

Those same pleasurable tingles from the other night came rushing back into her bloodstream with a vengeance and she couldn't find it within herself to answer his question. Her tongue was stuck to the roof of her dry mouth and refused to budge, no matter how much she cursed it to high heaven.

"What happened?" Joshua's deep voice broke the moment between them and Hadlee jerked her hand back, feeling guilty, though there was nothing to be guilty about.

"Crab caught my finger," she grumbled, her eyes on the deck. "But my glove was on. I'm fine."

Joshua's eyes went back and forth between Felix and Hadlee multiple times before he nodded. "I'm gonna make sure no more escaped," he said, walking away without asking any more questions.

Hadlee squeezed her eyes shut and let out a long breath. When she opened them, she was shocked, yet again, to see Felix staring at her as if trying to figure out a puzzle with a missing piece. "I..." She swallowed hard. "What?"

I'M SORRY. The words were on the edge of Felix's tongue, but he couldn't quite get them to come out. Things between him and Hadlee hadn't felt normal since that night at his home two weeks previous. Their words and actions were stiff and jerky, making it clear to anyone who bothered to pay attention that something weird had happened between them.

"Are you sure you're okay?" Felix forced himself to ask. While she probably deserved an apology for his whiplashing, he was afraid that saying those words would break down the tentative wall he'd built between their almost kiss and now. It would take almost nothing to burst through the barrier he'd erected, especially since he didn't actually want it there.

He knew it was best to keep a distance, but everything he'd felt when holding her was calling to him, and Felix was fighting the craving to not only experience it again, but to take it a step farther and make sure they weren't interrupted this time.

Hadlee rolled her eyes and blew a stubborn piece of hair out of her face. "I'm fine. It really didn't hurt. I only said ouch as a reaction, not out of real pain." She dumped a couple more crabs in the bowl, then began to climb to her feet.

Grabbing her elbows to steady her was an automatic reaction, Felix told himself. It was exactly what a gentleman would do and had nothing to do with the desire to touch her.

"Thank you," she snipped, stepping away from him and walking toward the railing before dumping the crabs into the water.

Trying to distract himself, Felix stepped up to her work station. A few crabs climbed over each other in a bucket, while two sat in a small bowl. "Tell me what you're doing," Felix said softly, keeping his hands clasped behind him.

Hadlee gave him a look, but shrugged and pointed to the bucket. "I still need to measure these." Her finger went to the smaller bowl. "These ones are small enough that I can do some tests on their shells."

He nodded. "And you're hoping to find...?"

"I'm not hoping to find anything," Hadlee responded. "In fact, if my theories are incorrect, it would be better for everyone, but I'm looking to see if there's a difference between the shells of the younger crabs who are being born and raised while the acidity levels are higher, and the shells of older crabs we've studied in the past when acidity levels are lower."

Felix pursed his lips. "So if you find a difference, what are you hoping to do about it?"

Hadlee scrunched her nose, drawing his attention to the few freckles that trickled across the bridge of it. "The truth? I don't know. I'm not really sure if there is anything we *can* do. The acidity levels are a part of climate change, and trying to change them requires more power than myself or any of my colleagues possess."

"So, why study it, then?" Felix tilted his head. He found himself fascinated by her answers. Her eyes, which had been wary before, were now sparkling with intelligence and eagerness. The more he listened to her, the more he realized she was telling the truth about not wanting to mess with the crabbing industry. Nothing she'd said hinted at all that she was hoping to create some kind of change in business.

"So we know," she said quickly. "The more we know, the better armed we are if there comes a problem we can correct. If the young crab shells are being affected, then we can start studies on what happens when they're older. Does it change their growth patterns? Do they taste different? Will our supply be tainted by this situation? And of course, is there something we should do to shift the tide so we don't lose the species altogether?"

"So, your life is just one big why?"

Hadlee laughed softly, the sound resonating in Felix's chest. "I suppose so. I've always been on the curious side."

She finished measuring the last crab and dumped it in the appropriate bowl. "Here, let me." Felix grabbed the discards and took the few steps necessary to put the unwanted ones back in the ocean. *You need to walk away. Spending time with her isn't going to keep a distance between you.* "Anything else I can help you with?" His mental self slapped his forehead.

"No, I think I've got it," Hadlee murmured, her focus on a crab she was holding.

"Is that a good specimen?" Felix asked, not quite ready to walk away from her, despite knowing he should.

She blinked and finally looked at him. "What?"

Felix chuckled. "Nevermind." He slapped the table a couple times. "I'll take us over to the last trap. You get the specs you need, huh?"

"Right." Her focus was gone again and he couldn't help but smile as he walked away. Seeing Hadlee so enthralled with her work was fascinating, though a small part of him was pouting that he wasn't the reason she was distracted.

Calling himself every name in the book, he climbed the stairs back to the wheelhouse. "Let's grab that last trap and then we'll call it for the day," Felix said to Julian, who was standing near the entrance to the space.

"Aye, aye, Captain," Julian said with a grin. He stepped aside to let Felix take the wheel.

Felix began to get ready to head out when he realized Julian was still standing in the doorway. He frowned and turned around. "Did you need something?"

Julian's grin was pure mischief. "Just wondering how long it's going to take you to make a move."

Felix raised an eyebrow. "Excuse me?"

Julian put his hands up in surrender and took a step back. "Come on, Captain. We both know I haven't seen you speak to a woman except your sister's friends for ages." He pumped his eyebrows. "And now you've got your very own marine biologist aboard and suddenly you're running errands like a little puppy dog."

"Julian..." Felix growled. "If we weren't friends, I'd throw you overboard."

Julian laughed. "And that, ladies and gentlemen, is all I needed to know." Still laughing, Julian quickly climbed down the stairs and left Felix to his traitorous thoughts.

Grumbling under his breath, Felix went back to moving *Morwenna* toward their last trap. It only took a few minutes to navigate the waters and arrive at their destination, but this time, he stayed in the wheelhouse, unwilling to show more of his hand. If Julian was already cracking jokes about Felix's interest, then it was a sure bet that the others were noticing things as well.

His resolve to stay away from the beautiful researcher was crumbling, but Felix was determined not to lose. His freedom was too recent and too precious to let go of right now, no matter how much he enjoyed her smile and her passion.

As he steered, a reminder of why he hadn't been staying away from her came rushing back and Felix groaned. *You still have to keep her safe,* he reminded himself. He'd told Ken he would stay close and act as her personal bodyguard, though he'd been doing it mostly under the radar, so Hadlee didn't really know it was happening. *But how the heck am I going to do that and not touch her?*

His fingers tightened on the wheel. This summer was supposed to be boring. He was going to go crazy not being able to fish or enjoy his boat on his own schedule, but it seemed that every time he turned around, something popped up that shifted the view in front of him.

First, his client was an entirely too alluring scientist who drew his attention like no other woman before her. And to top it off, she had to go get herself in trouble with the locals to the point where Felix needed to protect her.

Boring my foot, he snorted, slowing the boat to a crawl as his marker came into view. "I'll be lucky if I survive, let alone worry about having nothing to do."

CHAPTER 12

They pulled into the dock a few hours later and Hadlee couldn't help but be a little discouraged. The haul had been small today and that meant she hadn't gathered enough information to be very useful. *You've got plenty of time,* she reminded herself. *This is exactly why you're here for a couple of months, rather than a few days.*

She held onto the railing as she watched Ethan scramble over the edge and onto the dock, pulling the ropes to help guide the boat into place. "Hang on a sec and I'll grab the ladder," he called to the waiting passengers.

"Man...I'm ready for a nap," Luke said with a yawn.

Hadlee frowned. "It's almost dinner time," she said. "If I napped this late, I wouldn't be able to sleep tonight."

He shrugged. "I'll be fine."

"Well, it's going to have to wait anyways because we should help clean up," Hadlee pointed out, her tone brooking no argument. "I've been letting us leave, but it's really started to bother me. I'd like us to stay. It would be the polite thing to do."

"Crud." Luke took his hat off and scratched his head before slapping the cap back on.

"Don't worry about it," Julian offered as he walked by. He winked at Hadlee. "We've got cleaning this thing down to a science."

Chrissy giggled. "I think our definition of science might be a little different."

"True enough." Julian nodded. "But it's still fine. Truth be told, we'll probably be done faster without your help."

"I'm good with that!" Luke answered loudly.

"Luke," Hadlee scolded. "We really should stay."

"Let him go," Felix said from behind her shoulder.

Hadlee squeaked and spun, putting a hand to her heart. "You scared me." She scowled at Felix's smirk.

"You seem to frighten easily," he said with a chuckle, then suddenly grew serious.

Hadlee figured his words brought to mind her situation with Harry and his cronies the same way it had for her. She straightened her shoulders. "Well, if you weren't some kind of ninja sea captain, I don't think we'd have this problem." She refused to think about the other situation. She'd spent the whole day on the ocean. She didn't want to spoil it with thoughts of cranky old men who refuse to listen to reason.

Ethan snickered behind a fist. "Ninja sea captain? Cap couldn't sneak up on someone if his life depended on it." The young man began stomping around the deck. "He walks like his boots are made of lead."

Hadlee laughed when Felix lunged for his deckhand and put him into a headlock.

"What was that?" Felix asked, giving Ethan a little shake.

"Uncle! Uncle!" Ethan's hands were in the air as he laughed.

Instead of doing so, Felix bent his head down. "I write your paycheck."

Ethan sighed. "Fine. You don't stomp like your boots are made of lead."

"That's what I thought." Felix led Ethan go and gave him a playful push.

Ethan scrambled his thin body up onto the walkway, then paused and grinned. "Let me correct that. You walk like Sasquatch." With a holler, he leapt onto the dock when Felix lunged for him.

"Considering that no one has ever been able to find Sasquatch, I think he just gave you a compliment," Hadlee said with a grin, feeling some of her awkwardness from the day slip away. She'd managed to survive the day despite the weirdness floating through the air, and now that she was watching Felix joke with his crew, it helped Hadlee feel like she could relax.

Felix scratched his scruffy chin. "I see your point, but I'm still not sure I appreciate being compared to a large, hairy, ape-like creature."

She pinched her lips together, trying not to laugh, but Hadlee lost the battle and it slipped from her mouth. "Sorry," she said through her chuckles. "I just...the image you created was funny."

Felix gave her a wry look. "So, you're saying that you find me to be big and hairy?"

She shook her head. "Nope. No way. I just..." She shrugged. "It was just funny." Clearing her throat, Hadlee looked around. "How can I help?" she asked, trying to change the subject. "And I'm sorry we've haven't been helping before now. It was an oversight on my part."

Felix rubbed the back of his neck. "Julian was telling the truth that we can probably do it faster without you."

She ignored the sharp prick of pain those words sent through her chest. It felt like yet another rejection from the captain who had already toyed with her, only to cut her loose. *Just another reason to keep your heart to yourself,* she told herself. *Now if he'd quit teasing his crew and being so helpful during my research, I might be able to manage just that.*

"But if you want to swab the deck, I'm not gonna stop you."

Hadlee thrust her chin in the air. "You think I won't do it." It wasn't a question, it was a statement. Felix was smirking at her, as if he thought the fact that she wanted to help was funny. He didn't believe that she would really stick around and it only made Hadlee more determined to prove him wrong. She might be socially awkward and maybe a bit clumsy, but she knew how to work. She wouldn't be one of the youngest professors at her college if she wasn't. "Where's the mop?"

"This way, Doctor," Julian said, waving an arm toward the door that led downstairs.

Giving Felix a firm nod, she followed Julian and was soon cleaning up all the salt and dirt that had caked onto the deck during their excursion for the day. She hummed to herself as she worked, doing her best to ignore Felix and his crew as they worked around her. The deck was large enough that it took her a while to finish her job and by the time she'd put the mop and bucket away, Felix, Julian, and Ethan were done with their work as well.

"Thanks, Doc," Ethan said with a salute. "That's usually my job and I'm happy to hand it off."

Felix huffed and folded his arms over his chest. "It'll be your job again soon enough," he said with a glare.

Ethan grinned unrepentantly. "I'll take any break I can get, Sassy."

Hadlee made a face. "Sassy?"

Ethan put a hand to the side of his mouth and mock-whispered, "He's Sasquatch, remember?"

"Ah... gotcha." Hadlee smiled and shook her head. The young man reminded her of Luke. By the time she and her TA's left for the summer, she might have to pry the two men apart. *Speaking of...* She looked around. "Where did everyone go?" she asked.

"You were the only one determined to get your hands dirty," Felix said, stuffing his hands in his pockets. "They headed to dinner."

"Right." Hadlee rubbed her hands on her shorts. "I guess I better head out, then." She gave a polite nod to everyone. "Thank you for taking us out today. We'll see you tomorrow." She climbed the steps to the gangplank and held onto the rail while she went to the dock. At the bottom of the plank was a handsome blond man who looked familiar to Hadlee, though she wasn't sure why. "Hello," she murmured when their eyes met, just before she turned to walk down the dock.

"Hello, Doctor," the man said with an easy grin.

Hadlee paused and turned back to him. "I'm sorry, have we met?"

He held out his hand, blue eyes laughing. "Nope. Not officially anyway." Hadlee shook his hand. "I'm Bennett Frasier." He held onto her hand and leaned in. "I was with Felix at the wedding."

Heat instantly infused her cheeks. "Oh." Hadlee ducked her head at the reminder of her embarrassing situation. "I shouldn't have..." She made a face. "Sorry. I'm Hadlee Ford. No doctor necessary."

Bennett tucked her hand into his elbow. "I've never been one to turn down a chance to get closer to a beautiful woman like yourself."

Bennett's flirting helped soothe the rejections Hadlee had received from Felix lately, but she couldn't deny the fact that the cute blond didn't even come close to creating the riot of sensations that the dark, brooding sea captain of the *Morwenna* did. Still...she wasn't one to turn down a friend, especially in a town full of enemies. "I do believe you're a flirt, Mr. Frasier."

"Benny," he said with a wink. "No mister necessary."

Laughter bubbled from her lips until a throat cleared behind her, drawing Hadlee's attention.

TRAITOR. Felix raised an eyebrow at one of his best friends, and held back the word he wanted to use, but just barely.

Bennett's smile grew. "Why, Captain Mendez. Whatever are you doing here?"

Felix scowled. "Hands off, Frasier."

Bennett looked down at Hadlee, who was staring wide-eyed at the two men. "I don't know... She doesn't look like she wants me to let go."

"Benny..."

"Do you mind?" Bennett asked Hadlee. "I suppose it really should be the arm of your bodyguard that you hold onto."

Hadlee's jaw dropped before closing with a snap. "Bodyguard?" she squeaked. Dropping Bennett's arm, she backed up. "I don't have a bodyguard."

Felix huffed. "Come on, Hadlee. We already talked about this."

Her hands clenched into fists. "And I already turned you down. I don't need protection."

"Oh?" Felix walked toward her. "So you're completely comfortable walking past all the fishermen here at the dock? By yourself? The whole way home?"

"It's not like it's that far to the van," she shot back. "And I've been doing that since we got here."

He raised an eyebrow again. "Your TA's left, remember? They took the van. You were always in a group before. Now you're alone."

"How?" Hadlee grunted in realization. "I forgot that Chrissy had an extra key." She glared at the parking lot as if it had personally offended her.

Felix couldn't stop his chuckle, though he did try to keep it quiet, but when she turned her narrowed eyes on him, he knew he hadn't done a very good job. "Come on," he said, gently taking her elbow. "Let's get going."

Hadlee grumbled, but did as he asked.

After a few steps, Felix stopped and looked at Benny, who was following them. "Did you need something, man?"

Benny opened his blue eyes wide in an innocent face that Felix knew too well. It was the one that said he was up to something.

"What? I don't know what you're talking about. I'm just walking. Starving...but walking."

Felix snorted. "Really? That's how you're going to ask me to let you mooch dinner off of me?"

Benny shook his head and shrugged. "I didn't ask to mooch. I just said I was hungry." He scratched his chin. "Can I help it if you have a freezer full of fish?"

Muffled laughter brought Felix's gaze down to Hadlee, who had a fist over her mouth, but she couldn't contain her mirth. He turned back to Benny, feeling more charitable after experiencing Hadlee's smile. *I will not examine WHY that is, however.* "Come on. I'm sure we can wrangle something up that'll fill that bottomless pit of yours."

Benny whistled cheerily behind them as Felix walked Hadlee to his truck. After getting her settled in the passenger side, he closed the door and began to walk around. "You're not riding with me," he shot at Benny.

Benny smirked. "Don't worry. I brought my own ride." He gave Felix a knowing look. "If you don't show up at your house for a while...I'll get it."

Felix rolled his eyes. "It's not like that."

"Of course not!" Benny tsked his tongue and shook his head. "Never said it was." His signature grin in place, Benny ducked into his SUV and revved the engine.

Felix ignored his friend's innuendo and went around to the driver's side. He wasn't fooling anyone. Both Benny and Julian had noticed easily that Felix's attention was stuck on the scientist and Felix wasn't sure what to do about it. No matter how many times he cussed himself out or scolded himself for not being able to leave her alone, he couldn't quite do it.

He could lie to himself and claim it was all just to keep her safe. After all, Harry had been eyeing them from his own boat not too far down the dock, but the weight of the lie sat heavily in Felix's stomach and he didn't like it.

I like her.

There was no way to deny it. He liked Hadlee. He'd been attracted to her looks first, but then he'd started to get to know her and things only got worse. She had a kindness that was unusual in today's world. She had a passion for her work that spoke to him as a man who lived and breathed his job. He'd seen her work with her TA's in an authoritative, but gentle manner, and the fact that Luke was comfortable enough to tease and Joshua cared enough to act protective said a lot about their relationships. And now to top it all off, she'd stayed behind, determined to help clean up a mess she helped create, though none of it was truly her responsibility.

Every single thing he'd seen only made Hadlee burrow a little deeper under Felix's skin, which made his determination to stay away too difficult to follow through with. He wanted to bask in her goodness and let it ease the loneliness he hadn't known he was feeling.

"Why did you bring me here?"

Felix blinked and realized they'd arrived at his house without him remembering driving, having been so caught up in his thoughts. He put the truck in park. "We're having dinner," he said casually, as if she should have known that, even though he hadn't asked if she wanted to come.

"Ummm..." Hadlee pinched her lips together and scrunched the adorably freckled nose. "I think you were having dinner with Bennett. You should just drop me off at the bed and breakfast. I'm sure Genni is waiting for me."

"You can send her a text," Felix said, slipping out the door. He walked around and helped her down.

Hadlee glared at him. "You're awfully high-handed. You know that, right?"

Felix smirked. "It comes with being a captain."

She rolled her eyes. "Maybe it's time someone cut you down to size."

"Please tell me that someone is you," Benny's excited voice said from behind them.

Felix took in a long breath to keep from losing his temper. He was already regretting inviting his buddy. "Hadlee...would you please join us for dinner?" Felix asked, his voice tighter than he wanted it to be, but with Benny listening to everything they said, he couldn't quite bring himself to calm back down.

"Dude...that was pathetic." Benny's hand came down on Felix's shoulder. "A little sugar goes a long way," he teased.

Felix stepped back and put his hands on his hips. "Fine." He waved a hand toward Hadlee. "Show me how it's done." Benny never took anything seriously, which probably didn't appeal to someone like Hadlee, who was fairly serious. He was looking forward to seeing his friend strike out.

Benny tugged on a pretend lapel and straightened an imaginary tie. "Mademoiselle Hadlee," he said in a too-smooth tone.

Felix snorted, then smiled when Hadlee shot him a look.

"Your beauty is beyond compare this evening. Would you do me the honor of joining me for dinner?" Benny bowed, but kept his face up in order to see Hadlee's face. "Our chef will be preparing a scrumptious meal of fish and...fish."

Felix looked down to see how Hadlee was handling his friend's stupid invitation and his jaw dropped when she graced Benny with a stunning smile. "You're so sweet," she cooed. "I'd love to have dinner with you. Thank you for asking." After giving Felix a pointed look, she stepped forward and slipped her arm into Benny's elbow.

"Oh, sure! You don't give him any trouble!"

Benny looked back at Felix and pumped his eyebrows. "Sucks to be you!"

Felix growled and folded his arms over his chest as he watched them walk into his house. Shaking his head, Felix slammed the truck door and followed them. If Benny really thought he was going to get away with stealing Hadlee...he had another thing coming.

CHAPTER 13

Deep inside, Hadlee knew she shouldn't poke the bear that was Felix Mendez, but a small, rebellious part of her enjoyed seeing his shock. After all, he'd been the one to shut *her* out. It wasn't like she needed to keep her time and attention for just him.

"Have a seat, m'lady," Bennett said in a dramatic tone.

Hadlee lost her composure and began to laugh softly. "Does this kind of behavior actually get you any female attention?"

"Nah," Bennett said, breaking character and slouching next to her on the couch. He grinned. "But it's fun because it ticks Felix off."

Her eyes darted to the doorway where Felix was coming in, grumbling under his breath. "It does that," she murmured.

Bennett made a show of sighing and leaned back, stretching his arms along the back of the couch. Right behind Hadlee. She pinched her lips, but ultimately had to turn away to hide her amusement. Apparently, Bennett had taken it upon himself to make Felix jealous. Her smile faded. *Too bad Bennett doesn't understand that Felix won't be jealous. He'd have to be interested to be jealous.*

"Lay off, Benny," Felix snapped as he walked past them farther into the house. "Don't make me pull out the fishing wire!"

Bennett made an "O" with his mouth. "Oooh, he just threatened me." His lips went back to his ever present smile. "Guess that means he's serious."

Hadlee huffed. "Uh...I don't think so."

Bennett tilted his head to the side. "You're not interested?"

"I..." Hadlee felt her eyes widen and she leaned back. Did this guy have no boundaries? "Um..."

He laughed. "Say no more. I'm on board." He pumped his eyebrows. "Get it? Ship? On board?"

Hadlee nodded. "Got it."

"Don't worry," Bennett hissed as he stood up, beckoning her to follow. "There's more where that comes from." He walked ahead of her, then paused in the doorway. "And the best part is...Felix *hates* puns."

"Oh, dear," she whispered. Tonight was shaping up to be a night of revelations and Hadlee wasn't sure she wanted to be stuck in the middle. Still, she stood up and followed.

"Whatcha fixin'?" Bennett asked as they walked into Felix's kitchen.

Hadlee paused in the doorway and let her eyes wander. She hadn't seen this part of the house the other night when Felix had saved her from her attackers. It matched the rest of the residence, though the stack of dirty dishes was a good sign of a bachelor in residence. "Can I help?" she asked, turning her gaze to the man standing at the stove.

Felix shrugged. "I'm good." His alluring dark eyes went to Bennett. "You asked for the fish in my freezer and that's what I'm serving."

Bennett slid into a wooden chair at a small dining table before looking over his shoulder at Hadlee. "If you want any of the girly stuff, you know...veggies and whatnot, you better take that over. Old Felix has no idea how to fix anything but the fish."

"You're welcome to cook," Felix snapped. "Nobody asked you to come."

"Hey, man...it's okay to admit you like having me here," Bennett teased, putting a hand on his chest. "Our sisters have married and left us behind, so it's no wonder we're both having abandonment issues."

Hadlee kept her laughter quiet while Felix continued to grumble. Bennett was a hoot, but she had a feeling that enough time in his presence would tire her out. As long as his teasing was directed at Felix, however, she could probably handle him a little better. Warily, she went into the kitchen and stood at Felix's side. He was in the process of dipping fillets into a homemade batter. The hot oil he had on the stove sizzled and popped every time he dropped a piece in. "What can I do?" she asked, eyeing how his fingers were covered in batter.

Felix turned his head just slightly to look at her. "Despite being the caveman that Benny implies, I actually do have some lettuce in the fridge. Would you like to chop it up for a salad?"

She nodded. Having something to do made Hadlee feel much more at ease and here she knew she wouldn't hold anyone back by being slow. Within minutes, she was chopping the green leaves and putting them into a bowl. "Carrots?" she asked.

Felix shook his head. "Hate 'em. But I think there's some cherry tomatoes and cucumbers in there."

Back to the fridge she went, finishing out the salad with a few more items she found in the near empty fridge. "Would you like me to set the table?"

"Setting a table? Sounds fancy," Bennett offered from his spot at the table.

Hadlee looked over to see the man relaxing with a mischievous grin on his face. While it fit his personality, it immediately sent up a red flag. He definitely seemed like the kind of guy who would pull out all the stops if he wanted to accomplish something. *But what is he planning right now?* she wondered.

"How's the fish coming?" Bennett asked.

Felix frowned over his shoulder. "Fine. I'm almost done."

Bennett pursed his lips and nodded. "Maybe you'd like to share the *tail* of how you came to be a fisherman."

Hadlee frowned and looked back and forth between the two men.

"Careful," Felix said tightly. "He's just warming up."

"You know…just for the halibut."

"Oh no," Hadlee said, stifling laughter.

Felix snorted and set the last of the fillets on the paper towel.

"I'll bet she'll be hooked from the beginning."

She covered her smile with fingers. "Does he do this often?"

Felix gave her a wry look. "Let's eat. Maybe if his mouth is full, he'll stop talking."

Hadlee grabbed the salad and brought it over to the table. "Hungry?" she asked, hoping to get Bennett off his pun kick.

Bennett jumped from his seat and brought back some plates from the cupboard. "Yeah…this should *tide* me over for a while."

"Wow," Hadlee said, shaking her head slowly. "I'm impressed."

"Enough," Felix said in that low, growly tone.

Bennett simply grinned, obviously not listening to his friend, though the puns stopped long enough for them to say grace and dish up their plates.

"So, Dr. Ford," Bennett started. "What exactly brings you to Seaside Bay?" He took a bite of fish while waiting for her answer.

Hadlee held up a finger, since she was still chewing. When finished, she turned first to Felix. "This is amazing," she gushed. The fish was tender and flaky and the batter had a better flavor than anything she'd ever had in a restaurant. "Thank you so much."

"Didn't know he was such a catch, did ya?" Bennett inserted.

Felix threw his head back and groaned. "I'm this far from throwing you out of here," he said in a tight voice, making a small distance with his fingers.

"What's the matter? Was I too small? Or is it a catch and release situation?"

Felix jumped to his feet and Bennett put his hands in the air, the universal sign for surrender.

"I'll stop, I'll stop," he hurried to say, though the laughter in his eyes made Hadlee wary that he meant it.

FELIX FELT AS IF HIS nerves would snap at any moment. He was wound so tightly, he could barely talk in a normal tone, and Benny's jokes were only making it worse.

There was something decidedly domestic about having Hadlee in his home and the brief stint of contentment he'd felt when they'd worked around each other in the kitchen had an addictive quality to it. Staying aloof had been difficult... Now Felix found himself regretting the distance. With everything she said and did, Hadlee proved she was exactly the type of woman he wanted. She was kind, she wasn't pushy though she knew when to stand her ground, she was intelligent, and she had an appreciation for his work. None of those qualities even had anything to do with her looks, which were the first thing that had drawn his eye. Instead, her beauty had become the cherry on top of a very desired cake.

He still spent time thinking about their unfulfilled kiss, and his hope for such a connection was growing stronger than his desire to stay single.

Dangerous thoughts...

"Are you going to answer my question?" Benny sent the conversation back Hadlee's way.

Hadlee smiled and nodded. "Sorry about that. I'm here studying the effects of the heightened acidity of the Pacific on young dungeness crabs."

Benny was completely still except for his eyes, which blinked several times. "Wow. Okay. Just a word of advice. If you think that's the perfect line...you're wrong. Dead wrong."

"Benny." Felix groaned. "Will you stop?"

Hadlee laughed. "I don't know how you do it. I'm completely lost. How do so many puns reside in one mind?"

"I think you mean…you're lost at sea over my gleaming vernacular."

Felix rolled his eyes. "Do you even know what vernacular means?"

Benny gave him a look. "I'm playful, not stupid."

"Sometimes it's the same thing," Felix said with a look.

Hadlee shook her head. "You two are something else."

Felix turned her way, his eyes meeting hers. Right now her face was fairly glowing with amusement and Felix found it hard to look away. It wasn't until Benny cleared his throat that Felix was able to bring his face back to his plate.

"Oh, man…" Benny stretched and made a show of yawning. "I feel a sudden wave of sleepiness coming on."

Felix would have growled if Hadlee's laughter hadn't been so distracting. "Finally full, are you?"

Benny nodded. "If I eat any more, I think I might get a little green behind the gills."

Hadlee groaned through her laughter. "Oh my gosh, Bennett."

He pushed himself up from the table. "It's probably time for me to sail home before I begin floundering around like an idiot."

"Too late," Felix muttered. His words must have added to Hadlee's amusement, since her laughter grew and Felix found himself smiling against his will.

"Careful," Benny said as he backed out of the room. "Felix here throws out a lot of lines, but you're too smart to take the bait."

"Good night, Benny!" Felix said loudly, trying to send a hint to his friend. Despite the fact that Benny had come, mooched dinner, and was now skipping out before helping clean up, Felix was ready for him to be gone. Best friend or not, Bennett had worked hard to overstay his welcome.

"Throw him back if he gets too fresh!" Benny hollered before slamming the front door.

Hadlee slowly shook her head and whistled low. "I've never seen anything like it," she said, the awe evident in her tone.

"You get used to him...unfortunately," Felix said with a chuckle.

Those light eyes caught his attention once more. "It must be nice to have a friend you know so well. I mean..." She looked around the table. "He came and ate your food, only to skip out before having to help with anything. Only a really close relationship would let someone get away with that."

Felix laughed. Loudly. "That's Benny for you," he finally managed to answer. "He does it to everyone, and despite how annoying it is, we all get a kick out of him too much to be mad about it." His mirth trickled to a manageable level. "Not to mention that no one will have your back like Benny. He might come across as a total dork with no manners, but he's one of the first people to jump in when there's a problem."

A flash of sadness ran through Hadlee's soft eyes and Felix found himself curious about it. "It doesn't seem like you have much family around, but it looks like you created your own."

He shrugged and poked at his dinner. "I suppose you could say that." He looked up from under his lashes. "Do you live around family?"

She hesitated before nodding. "My father is a professor at the same college I am." Her fork made a small clanking noise as she set in on the table. "I have three younger sisters, and since my mother is gone, I spent a lot of time taking over her role while we were all teenagers."

"I'm sorry," Felix said softly. "My parents are gone too."

"Do you have any other siblings besides your sister who just got married?" Her cheeks turned pink, as if recalling their first meeting, and that unbidden smile came back onto Felix's face.

"No. Just her." He started to reach out, but hesitated. Those flushed cheeks were so enticing, but he had no right to touch her, so his hand hung mid-air instead, leaving an awkward silence in its wake.

Hadlee looked back and forth between his hand and his eyes before reaching out and holding onto his fingers. Slowly, as if she was afraid she would spook him, she brought his palm up to her cheek and set it on her skin.

Felix watched the movement of her throat as she swallowed hard, then his attention was caught on her slightly parted lips. Her breathing was heavier than normal and the warmth coming from her cheek to his arm was undeniable. He flexed his fingers, sliding his hand into her hair and around her ear so he could pull her forward.

The moment felt like it lasted an eternity as he pulled her head towards his own. Neither of them spoke, though the air between them vibrated, giving an anticipation to their actions that needed no words.

He paused as their lips grew close, still struggling with vague thoughts of how this was not a good idea, but he knew he was too deep to stop now. After a fortifying breath that filled his nose with her sweet scent, his reservations melted and Felix left a soft kiss on her upper lip.

The light gasp pushed him forward and he moved to the corner of her mouth, again touching her just enough to feel the sizzling chemistry between them.

"Please..." she whispered, breaking Felix's last bit of control.

Hoping the first touches were enough to warm her up, he tilted his head, slanting his mouth over hers, and took her mouth the way he'd wanted to from the start. Her sigh and subsequent leaning into his kiss only spurred him on. His grip on her head tightened and he soaked up the small noises she made as he deepened the contact.

Forcing himself to pull back before he completely lost his head, Felix allowed his thumb to softly rub against her red and slightly swollen bottom lip. "I shouldn't have done that," he admitted softly. "But if I'm being honest..." He paused, unsure how to admit his next words, but knowing they were the absolute truth. "I'm not sure how to stop."

Her hand gripped his wrist. "Please don't."

With a sheepish smile, he obeyed and pulled her back to him. Warning bells that he would regret this were ringing through his head, but he shoved them aside. He hadn't felt this content and at ease in a long time, and he wasn't quite ready to give up the sensation. *Maybe later...but not right now. Right now is just me and her and visions of a future that I can't give into.*

CHAPTER 14

The next week passed in a flurry of research and stolen glances. Hadlee had no idea where she and Felix stood exactly, but she couldn't deny that something had definitely changed between them. Last week's kiss still haunted her dreams and there were mornings that Hadlee didn't want to get out of bed.

Footsteps behind her had Hadlee glancing over her shoulder and her heart skipped a beat when the familiar, bulky outline of *Morwenna's* captain came into view.

"Water?"

Hadlee took the cold bottle. "Thanks," she said softly. She watched Felix as he settled himself next to her on the bench. She could feel him even without looking his way. Her senses were always heightened in his presence.

Felix replaced the cap on his own bottle. "They've been down there for a while," he said, glancing at his watch. "How much oxygen did they have?"

Hadlee nodded. "They should be back up in the next ten minutes or so." She shrugged. "Their job shouldn't have taken that long. They're just gathering samples and doing some visual research of the area."

He nodded before shifting his body a little closer to hers.

Hadlee wanted to grin at the not so subtle move. She felt the same pull, and after giving into the attraction once already, it had made her restless for more. Their work had them in the same vicinity, but since they were both in charge of other people, they didn't always get to be close to each other. Deciding to show a little response back, she put her right hand out on her leg, thrumming her fingers against her thigh.

It only took moments for Felix to respond, entwining her fingers with his.

This time the grin was too strong to deny and Hadlee sighed as a joyful peace zipped through her. She allowed her body to lean sideways and rested some of her weight against his shoulder. His answering squeeze to her hand let her know he didn't mind the contact at all.

"You haven't shared much of your findings," he said in his normal gruff tone.

She shrugged as best she could. "I don't have enough information to say much yet, but I think it's possible that our worries are founded."

He turned to her, but his sunglasses hid the deep allure of his gaze. "So the crabs are being affected?"

She squished her lips to the side. "It looks like it...maybe. I'm finding that some of their shells are softer than they should be, but really...I need a bigger sample before I can say so for sure."

Felix sighed. "Perfect."

Frowning, Hadlee looked up. "What do you mean?"

"Things have been so quiet with Harry and the guys that I was hoping we were past the problems. If word of your findings gets around though, you'll probably become a target again."

"I don't know how they'd know," she said warily. "The only person I talk to outside of you and the people on this boat is my dad."

Felix nodded. "Maybe we'll get lucky."

"They're here!" Chrissy called from the stern.

Hadlee jumped to her feet, secretly excited when Felix rose with her and kept a hold of her hand. They hadn't been open about their budding relationship at all in front of the crew, so a small part of her was worried someone would be upset, but she wasn't willing to let go of him just yet.

Julian and Ethan were leaning over the edge, helping Luke climb up the ladder while Joshua bobbed in the water. Five minutes later, the men were on deck and pulling off their gear.

"Did you get the samples?" Hadlee asked, helping set aside the oxygen tanks.

"Yep," Luke said breathlessly. He slumped on the deck and let his head fall backwards. "I'm out of shape."

Hadlee laughed softly. "Thanks for going down," she said.

"See anything interesting?" Ethan asked. He rolled one of the tanks off to the side in order to tie it off, then came back for the second one.

"It was surprisingly clear down there," Luke said. "I thought it would be murky."

"I'm gonna have to come back," Joshua muttered. "You guys have some cool stuff down there."

"You'll have to check out some of the shipwrecks," Julian offered. "There's several hundred out there."

"Why is Oregon so dangerous?" Luke asked, climbing to his feet. He handed over a couple of vials to Hadlee.

She took them gratefully and left the men to their chat while she headed back to her gear to put the samples away. Although she and Felix were no longer holding hands, he followed, staying close, especially when she ducked into the shade and her lab set-up.

"Do you have the stuff to test that here?" he asked in her ear.

Hadlee shivered and glanced over her shoulder in what she hoped was a coy manner. "No, but I'll label them and be able to do it back at the lab." Following through with what she had said, she grabbed some stickers and a marker to put down the location and date of the samples.

"Ready to head back, then?"

She turned around fully, sucking in a breath when realizing that he was so close and tilting her head back to see him more clearly. "Yeah."

His answering grin made her warmer than the overhead sun. "Want to come skipper with me?"

Hadlee raised her eyebrows. "The boat? You want me to steer?"

Felix took her hand and spun toward the stairs, pulling her with him. "I'll teach you."

Feeling giddier than any almost thirty-year-old had a right to, Hadlee happily followed. In no time at all, she found herself standing with her back to his front and his arms wrapped around her as he guided her toward the harbor. It was like something out of a romance novel and Hadlee loved every second of it. "Is this where I spread my arms to the side and say I'm king of the world?" she joked.

Felix chuckled, his chest bumping into her back. "I think that's my line." He bent down and brought his lips to her ear. "I suppose you could be the queen."

She froze, unsure how to take his comment. Did he mean it literally? Or was it just she was a girl and he was a guy? Deciding it was best to laugh her way out of the situation, she said, "If you think I'm gonna walk one step behind you and pander to your ego, you better think again."

His laughter was louder this time and Hadlee smiled with him, grateful he hadn't taken offense. A soft kiss on the side of her head nearly had her knees buckling.

"What if we just walked side by side?" His question was soft and a little cautious, as if afraid of her answer.

Slowly, Hadlee looked back, wishing she could see past his glasses. This question didn't feel like a joke. Her heart was pounding so hard against her ribcage she was sure he could hear the frantic rhythm. Deciding it was time to lay her cards on the table, she gave him the most honest answer she could. "I think I'd like that," she answered just as softly.

One side of his mouth pulled into a grin. "I was hoping you'd say that," he muttered just before bringing their mouths together for a firm but short kiss. "I better keep my eye on the controls or we might end up on the dock instead of next to it."

Hadlee allowed herself to study his strong profile for a moment before she also turned back to the stretch of water in front of them, though a permanent smile sat on her face. It wasn't going anywhere for a while.

I COULD GET USED TO this.

Hadlee in his arms, the wind on his face, and the ocean in front of him. Felix knew he was playing a dangerous game. He hadn't made a move during the last week after their kiss, and it had been mostly on purpose. The kiss had been a bold way to declare there was something between them, and he hadn't wanted to rush into something either of them would regret. But after dinner last week, there was no way to completely shut down the fact that they were interested in each other.

The scolding voice in the back of his head had finally dropped to a quiet murmur, and after Hadlee had so generously made her hand available for the taking, it had gone into radio silence. The more he stayed close, the more he didn't want to separate from her at all, and it had nothing to do with keeping her safe from the other fishermen.

"There it is," she said, referring to the harbor that was coming into view.

Felix grinned. He was sure he detected a hint of disappointment in her tone. It was a feeling he reciprocated. "Do you have plans for dinner tonight?"

She didn't answer right away and he grew slightly concerned, but a look down at her grinning lips relaxed his tense muscles. "No…"

He bent his head down, close to her ear. "Would you like to have dinner with me?"

"Are you asking me on a date, Captain Mendez?"

"Would you say yes if I was?"

Hadlee looked over her shoulder, forcing Felix to back up a bit, but the sultry look on her face made it worth it. "I would."

"Then that's definitely what I'm asking," he hurried to say.

Hadlee laughed softly and turned back around to the front. The pier was getting closer and as if feeling that their time in the wheelhouse was quickly coming to an end, she leaned back fully into his chest, sending a quick jolt through Felix's body.

He kissed the top of her head, enjoying the fresh scent of ocean and the ever present flowery tone she carried. It only took a few minutes for them to maneuver into their slip and then they were climbing down from the control room.

"Looks like you've got company," Julian offered as Felix and Hadlee came onto the deck.

Felix frowned and walked around until he could see the dock. "Charli!" His smile grew and he climbed up the side, leaping to the wood before they'd bothered to put the bridge up. Grabbing his sister in his arms, he gave her a tight hug. "I didn't think you guys would be home for another week." Felix kept a hold of her arms and pushed her back so he could take a good look at her. "You look good. Marriage must agree with you."

Charli laughed and stepped in to hug him again. "It's been three weeks already," she said. "I said that was how long we would be gone."

Heat infused his neck and Felix was grateful for his darker skin. "I guess I lost track of time," he said sheepishly. Heavy steps came down the dock and Felix turned to smile at his new brother-in-law.

"Bronson." They played their usual "who can squeeze the hand harder" greeting before breaking into laughter.

"I'm not sure I've met someone with hands as strong as yours," Bronson said, flexing his fingers. His arm moved to grab Charli around the waist, tucking her into his side like it was the most natural thing in the world.

I suppose it is when you're married, Felix admitted to himself. Most people seemed to thrive on finding a life partner. In fact, he was the only person he knew who had declared he would never marry. And yet, in only a few weeks' time, things had changed drastically.

"Captain!"

Felix turned around at Ethan's call and helped set up the walkway from the boat to the dock, then fortified himself for the next thing to come. "Hadlee?" he called, waving her over.

Hadlee walked slowly, looking slightly unsure and a little embarrassed as well.

"Isn't that the woman who was talking to you at our wedding?" Charli asked from behind Felix.

Felix looked back for a second. "Yeah. Hang on." He held out his hand as Hadlee stepped down on the dock and she gripped it as if it were the only thing keeping her on her feet.

"Hello," she said softly. "I'm Dr. Hadlee Ford."

Felix dared to look at his sister, who was visibly shocked. Her dark eyes went from their entwined hands to Felix and back, over and over again.

"Hello, Dr. Ford," Bronson said easily. He reached out a hand. "Bronson Ramsay. This is my wife, Charli."

Hadlee shook his hand then turned to Felix's sister. "Nice to meet you, Charli. Congratulations on your wedding."

"Thanks," Charli said weakly. She gave a tenuous smile. "Uh, are you the scientist who hired Felix for the summer?"

Hadlee nodded and looked up at him. "Yeah. Captain Mendez has been nice enough to help me get all the information I need for my project."

Felix's grin fell when Charli folded her arms over her chest. "I see." She looked at them consideringly and Felix pleaded with his eyes that she would wait until they were alone to say anything brash. "Is that all he's helping you with?"

"Charli," Felix growled, his eyebrows furrowing together.

"No, it's okay," Hadlee said with a small smile. "I get it."

Felix blew out a breath through his nose. "We've hung out a couple of times," he clarified, not wanting Charli to jump to any other conclusions.

Her eyebrows shot up. "I never thought I'd see the day."

Felix groaned and hung his head, while Bronson tried to cover his snort with a cough.

"Has he introduced you to everyone?"

Felix's head came back up quickly. He wasn't quite ready for that. Things between him and Hadlee were moving slow and still very tentative. Introducing her to the group was a completely other level.

"No," Hadlee answered. "At least I don't think so." She scrunched her nose. "I met Bennett."

"Good heavens, that's not the way to start," Charli said with a shake of her head. "Well...if Bennett didn't scare you off, then no one else will." She smiled at Felix. "There's a bonfire tonight. You should bring her."

You declaring that in front of her gives me no choice. Felix wasn't amused that his sister had backed him into a corner. The sly grin she was wearing and raised eyebrow told him she knew exactly what she'd done. He'd never liked being told what to do, so pasting on a smile when he wanted to scowl was harder than it should have been. "I was planning on it," he fibbed, putting his arm around Hadlee's waist.

"A bonfire?" she asked. "Do I need to bring anything?"

Charli shook her head. "Nah. We've always got it covered." Charli stepped back, taking Bronson with her. "You just make sure that my lug of a brother gets you there on time. Everyone will be so happy to meet you."

"Okay," Hadlee responded, though the confusion in her tone was strong. She obviously didn't quite know why Charli was being so weird.

But Felix knew. His sister was enjoying this a little too much, and he had no course of revenge. He hadn't thought about the consequences of introducing the two women. It looked like Hadlee was about to become a topic of conversation, though this time in a good way...he hoped.

CHAPTER 15

Hadlee was positive that somehow today she'd swallowed a bed of electric eels which were currently shocking her relentlessly, making her knees shake and sweat trickle down the back of her neck. Her leg bounced as Felix drove them back to the beach for the bonfire Charli had invited her to.

Hadlee wasn't certain if she should be excited or scared out of her wits. There had been something a little mischievous in Charli's smile as she'd invited Hadlee. Really, it seemed odd to be meeting Felix's family and friends already. She wasn't even quite sure what she and Felix were, though he had admitted they were dating. Sort of.

They'd kissed, they'd had dinner together, and they cast a lot of meaningful looks across the boat, but everything was still extremely new and meeting everyone felt serious.

"You okay?" Felix asked as he parked the truck in a parking lot near the boardwalk.

Hadlee nodded jerkily. "Yeah. Just..." She scrunched her nose as she looked at him. "Are you sure I should be here? I don't want to pull you away from your family. You said Charli just got back from her honeymoon, so shouldn't I...go back to the inn?"

He chuckled and pulled off his seatbelt. "Charli won't let me walk away with my legs intact tonight if you don't come." He gave Hadlee a sheepish look. "I've never brought a woman to our bonfire before."

"Which is exactly why I shouldn't be here," she pressed. "I..." Hadlee searched for the correct words that wouldn't hurt his feelings but would still get her point across. "Truth is, I'm not quite sure where you and I stand." *Honesty is the best policy, right?* "I know you started spending time with me at first because you were trying to protect me, but I'm assuming that our kisses have had nothing to do with that?" She left her question open-ended, hoping it would encourage him to fill in.

Felix pushed a hand through his thick, dark hair. "Yeah..."

That wasn't reassuring at all. His hesitation made Hadlee panic and she tried to backtrack. "I'm not asking us to, you know, determine the relationship right now, or anything, I get that anything between us is brand new, but I guess I just...was worried your friends are going to assume there's more between us than there is."

Felix had gone back to his stoic, brooding face and Hadlee could not, for the life of her, figure out what he was thinking. Now she felt herself swinging a one-eighty and she worried she had pulled back too much so that he didn't know that she did have feelings for him.

"I mean...there is something between us...right?" She wrung her hands together, her mouth continuing to move without her permission. "It's new, it's very new...I realize that, but I just...I don't go around just kissing men willy nilly, I promise. So, I would hope that because I let you do that, maybe you do actually have feelings for me too, even though I know those feelings are small and just beginning. How could they be anything else? After all, we've only known each other a few weeks, right? How could they be anything else?" Hadlee stopped her word-vomit when a large, warm hand landed on her mouth.

"Hadlee..."

She nodded, her movements still stiff and jerky.

A half-smile pulled at his lips. "I get it. And yeah, my friends will probably think we're deeper into this relationship than we are, but their assumptions don't really matter. We're getting to know each other. Obviously we're enjoying each other enough to keep spending time together and even have some intimate moments like kissing, but we'll just take it one day at a time...okay?" His dark eyebrows raised high as he waited for her to answer.

Since his hand was still stopping her from speaking, Hadlee simply nodded. A bit of her tension eased at his simple explanation of things, but another part of her was slightly disappointed that he seemed to be taking everything so casually.

Maybe it was her inexperience with dating, but Felix brought out feelings in her that Hadlee had never felt before. She'd had a couple of boyfriends, but so much of her time was spent in the lab and working to achieve her professorship that she hadn't left much room in her life for relationships. *It's early,* she reminded herself. *You can't expect someone to declare undying love for you when you've only been together a few times. This isn't a Hallmark movie!*

Felix's smile grew as he removed his hand. "Come on. I know things are awkward, but you'll love my friends." He frowned. "Except for Benny. You're not allowed to have any soft feelings for him at all."

Hadlee laughed softly, her anxiety becoming even more subdued. "I'll do my best to rein in any fluffy emotions heading his way."

"Good." Felix leaned in and gave her a short peck, which only left Hadlee wanting more. "Come on. You'll feel better if we just get it over with."

She nodded and climbed out of her side of the truck, walking around to take Felix's hand. Together they walked onto the beach and headed to the north. Not far ahead, Hadlee could see a fire burning and a small crowd of people. "That must be them?"

Felix chuckled and squeezed her hand. "You take on the vast dangers of the ocean, but you're terrified of people?"

She glared at him. "My life has been spent communicating with fish. They're much easier than people."

"So you're the fish whisperer? Maybe I should take you on my next fishing trip. You can coax those puppies right into the boat, no line needed."

Hadlee snorted. "Wouldn't that take all the fun out of it? I thought holding the line was part of the enjoyment?"

He shrugged. "There are days when it would be worth it."

"Well, I hate to break it to you, but I can't actually *talk* to the fish. I just study them and read between the lines."

"Lame," he teased.

Hadlee laughed softly. "I suppose it is."

"Don't worry," he whispered as they came within hearing distance of the group. "You're anything but lame and everyone else will think so as well."

Before Hadlee could respond, they were standing in front of a dozen or more people, all of whom were now staring directly at her. That earlier anxiety ratcheted up and Hadlee stumbled back a step, only staying upright because Felix was still holding her hand. "Uh, hi," she said softly, giving a small, awkward wave.

Felix tugged her forward, dropping her hand to wrap his arm around her back, effectively stopping Hadlee from running away from all the attention. "Hey, guys. This is Dr. Hadlee Ford." He nodded at Genni and Cooper. "I know some of you have met her already, but just in case you haven't, she's the one studying the crabs this summer from my boat."

"Oh, we've met," Bennett said, emerging from the crowd, his eyes dancing with amusement. Walking forward, he bowed to Hadlee, reminiscent of the night they both ate dinner at Felix's. "Welcome, Fish Doctor, to our humble fire. Might I get you a plate?"

Hadlee couldn't help but laugh, especially when Felix nearly growled like a wild animal. "Thanks," she said in response to Bennett. "But I'm not hungry yet."

Bennett put his hands in the air. "Don' fillet me!" he exclaimed, the words aimed at Felix. "Can I help it if she's pulled me in hook, line and sinker?"

FELIX WAS GOING TO kill him. Did the man never stop? Felix had never noticed how absolutely annoying Benny could be. *Why is this coming up now? He didn't used to drive me crazy, but now that Hadlee's around, I just want him to back off.*

With a mental headshake, Felix got himself back under control. These protective feelings were ridiculous. Hadlee wasn't his. Yes, he liked her, for more than just her looks, but he still had a lot to learn and he wasn't in a hurry to jump into a fully committed relationship...no matter how good a kisser she was. But still, he shouldn't be feeling so possessive. Especially in regards to Benny, who wasn't serious in his actions.

Ken groaned. "Benny, if you start up with your horrible puns, I'm gonna take the food and leave."

"Ah...you're just a little guppy," Benny said, turning to address Ken.

Ken went to stand from his chair, and Benny laughed before going back to his seat, not the least bit concerned about being beat up.

"Oh my word..." Hadlee said through her laughter. "Is it always like this?"

Felix shook his head. "No. Benny behaves himself most of the time."

"Hadlee," Charli said, rushing forward. "I'm so glad you made it." She took Hadlee's hand and pulled her out of Felix's embrace and toward the rest of the women in the group.

He let her go, but it was a struggle. He was already growing too used to having her near and felt colder with her gone. *Too early,* he reminded himself. *It's too early to feel that way.*

A slap on his shoulder had him lurching forward before he caught himself. Felix turned his glare on Cooper. "Did you need something?"

Cooper grinned. His long hair was pulled back in a ponytail tonight. "She's awful cute, Cap."

Felix rolled his eyes. "Anything besides that."

Cooper chuckled. "I just thought I'd let you know that she's a really good person." He sobered and lowered his voice. "I heard there's been some trouble in town with some of the old guys, but Hadlee is sweet, polite, doesn't like to cause trouble or work for us at the inn, and has more patience in her pinky than I've ever had in my entire body."

"What makes you say that?" Felix asked as his eyes darted to mark sure their topic of conversation was all right before turning back to Cooper.

"One of the guys on her team is a total doofus," Cooper said with a snort. "You think Benny gets you riled up...this guy is worse."

"Luke," Felix muttered.

Cooper laughed. "I forgot you would have already met him." He took a drink of his soda. "That guy knows how to push everyone's buttons, but Hadlee just smiles through it all. When she puts her foot down, it's like a firm but loving mother moment." Cooper shook his head. "Anyway, my point is...if you like her, you should go for it. She's a keeper."

"Aren't you married?" Felix asked wryly.

Cooper slapped Felix's back again, though he tried not to show just how hard it was. "Happily," Cooper said. "But just for the record, Hadlee wouldn't be my type anyway." He winked. "She likes fish too much."

"Not another one," Ken said as he joined the men. "I met her the other night." He pointed his remarks to Cooper. "But we weren't talking about fish."

A bunch of squeals had all the men's heads jerking up, followed by grunts and eyerolls when they realized the women were all just excited about something.

"Are you telling me the good doctor is as obsessed with scaly fins as you are?" Ken asked, nudging Felix's side.

Felix shoved his friend to the side. "She's a marine biologist," he defended. "What do you think?"

"I think...my mom might have been right in this case," Benny inserted.

Felix huffed. "This ought to be good." His thoughts flashed to Benny and Mel's mother, who now lived down in California as a homeless hippy. Most of her conversations centered on being free of Big Brother and living as one with nature. Needless to say, Felix didn't pay much attention to Mrs. Frasier's teachings.

Benny leaned in as if imparting a great secret. "She always said when you find someone with the same level of weird as yourself, don't let them go."

"Watch it," Jensen snapped, punching Benny's shoulder. "Are you telling me you think your sister and I are weird?"

Felix chuckled as the group then began to argue and joke about everyone else's level of weirdness. Normally he would have been just as invested as the rest of his friends, but he kept finding his eyes wandering to the women, who were still chatting and surrounding Hadlee. Felix frowned, unsure if the group was interrogating her or welcoming her.

"Dude...keep the drooling to a minimum, huh?" Cooper said with a laugh.

Felix jerked his gaze away, realizing that every man there was giving him a knowing look. His neck suddenly felt hot enough to fry a fish on and he rubbed it uncomfortably. "I think I'll, uh, go break that up before they scare her off."

"Good idea," Ken said sagely. "We wouldn't want her to run away before your fish fetishes have a chance to get to know each other."

"You guys suck," Felix grumbled, but a small smile played on his lips as the men continued to razz him behind his back. Cautiously, he approached the ladies, trying to figure out how to interrupt without getting clawed.

"Hello, Captain," Caro said as she noticed his approach. The local sweets shop owner put her hand on her hip and turned as he arrived. "Come to claim something?"

Felix gave her a glare, which only made Caro smile wider. "I thought I should rescue her before you scare her away with your excitement."

Caro rolled her eyes. "Men. They just can't handle a little female fun."

"And you think she's safe with all you Neanderthals?" Charli shot out.

Felix glared at his sister. "Probably more so than with you."

Hadlee let out a small laugh, her fingers covering her lips. She worked her way through the group of women. "Excuse me," she said softly over and over until she stood in front of Felix. "Were you worried about me?" Her gray eyes were glittering in the firelight and the shadows danced on the angle and lines of her face.

Felix clenched his hands into fists to keep from tracing the movement of the light on her skin. "I think it was *you* who was worried," he said with a huff. "I practically had to carry you across the sand."

Her smile grew and his heart seemed to skip a beat. "Thank you for that," she said softly. Looking over her shoulder, Hadlee smiled at the group of women before coming back to Felix. "I hate to admit it, but you were right. They aren't as scary as I thought they would be."

"Ooh, don't tell him that." Caro groaned, coming up to slip her arm through Hadlee's. "Anytime you tell a man he's right, you'll never hear the end of it. Somehow, saying they were right once translates into you're right forever."

Felix took the excuse to grab Hadlee's hand and pull her away. "Aaand this is what I was afraid of. They're filling your head with all sorts of stupid stuff."

"Don't worry!" Caro called after them. "We'll work on corrupting her some more later."

CHAPTER 16

Hadlee snuggled a little more comfortably into her seat. The night was getting cool, but she was far from ready to head back to the inn. This group was everything she would ever hope for in friends or more importantly, a family. She had never felt so accepted and welcomed, not even from her own sisters and father.

She had been too much like a mother to her younger sisters, which meant she had been an authority figure, not someone they brought into their social lives. Her father was too wrapped up in work, and despite the fact that she was following in his footsteps, he still had little time for her. As was evidenced by his attitude toward her work. His loyalty was with his colleagues, not her. It seemed that no matter how hard she worked, she never came away with an assurance of his pride, let alone his respect.

A warm hand landed on her knee. "Are you cold?"

Hadlee couldn't help but smile at Felix's concerned gaze. "I'm fine," she said, working to withhold a shiver.

He scowled, but unlike when they'd first met, it didn't intimidate or make Hadlee upset. She was growing used to his broody personality and was realizing that it wasn't ego or cockiness that caused his behavior. He was a more serious personality and was also a protector. His sense of humor wasn't light and happy-go-lucky like Benny's was. No, Felix took life at face value and took care of those around him, just as he was trying to do right now as he shucked the sweatshirt he was wearing.

"Here," he said in his low, growly tone, thrusting the shirt at her.

"I'll be okay—" Hadlee started, but she snapped her mouth closed. *Let him take care of you.* The words were odd, but they were also a revelation. This was how he showed he cared. "Thank you," she said, hoping he could hear the sincerity in her voice.

Felix nodded before turning his attention back to the group, who were still going strong with their bantering and storytelling.

Hadlee pulled the oversized shirt over her head. It was already warm from his body heat and the smell of campfire smoke.Plus, Felix's unique musky scent made pulling on the shirt one of the most strangely intimate experiences Hadlee had ever had. She felt her face flush and hoped desperately that everyone else would assume it was because of the fire.

"How long are you going to be in town?"

When the group went quiet, Hadlee broke free from her haze and blinked a few times. "I'm sorry, was someone talking to me?"

Bennett snickered, but Melody slapped his shoulder before leaning forward slightly. "I was just wondering how long you're in town," she said sweetly. Her large blue eyes were bright and full of an invitation for friendship.

Hadlee wasn't sure she had ever met someone as friendly as Melody and it made her laugh to think that Melody and Bennett were siblings. They couldn't have been more different. "I've got another month," she said. "I need the data to cover a large enough span of time that the information can't be based simply on a certain week in May, you know?"

Melody nodded. "Cool." She tilted her head, her long blonde hair flowing in the breeze. "So what got you into marine biology to begin with? And did you always want to teach?"

"What is this? The Spanish Inquisition?" Felix asked.

Hadlee reached over to pat his hand. "It's fine," she assured him. "I don't mind telling everyone a few things about me." She straightened in her seat. "I have to admit that I didn't really know what I wanted to be when I grew up, and spent a lot of my time raising my three younger sisters." Her heart still pinched when she thought of losing her mother, though it had been many years ago. "Because of that, I knew that when it was time for college, I needed to stay closer to home." She shrugged. "My dad is a professor, so I just began taking classes in his field of study and stuck with it. I had always liked fish, so it seemed natural." She smiled. "Now I'm a professor like he is, which kept me at home, allowing me to help my sisters graduate and move on with their lives, and it has also let me be around to help take care of my dad."

Melody's full lips were pulled into a slight pout. "But...do you love what you do?"

Hadlee nodded. "Yeah. I enjoy it. Who wouldn't enjoy being around fish and nature all day? And figuring out new ways to help them?"

Melody's frown eased. "Well, good. I'd be sad if you only did it because your father did."

The words brought an unexpected spark of shame to Hadlee, but she pushed it aside quickly. The feelings of being an imposter weren't new to her and she had learned not to listen to them. It didn't really matter why she was doing what she was doing. The fact was, she was making a difference and that was enough.

Caro yawned loudly. "Well, I'm bushed," she said, stretching her arms in the air. "I'm gonna pack up and go home." Her eyes turned to the man who ran the cookie truck, Jack. Hadlee had learned the two were engaged and Caro offered him an inviting smile.

"Right." Jack jumped to his feet. "I think I'll turn in too."

Ken snorted, but covered it with a cough when Caro turned a glare his way.

"Come on, babe," Cooper said, tugging on Genni's hand. "We better get back to the inn." As they gathered their chairs, Cooper looked to Hadlee. "Do you want a ride back?"

"Uh..." Hadlee turned a questioning look at Felix.

"I've got her," Felix said.

She tried to hold in her smile, but it was a struggle. Truthfully, Hadlee wasn't ready to leave Felix's side yet, but she didn't want to be too forward about it. Her weird ramblings in the truck had already helped her meet her embarrassment quota for the evening, so she wasn't about to make the first move to stick around a little longer. "Thanks anyway," she said to Cooper and Genni.

"We'll see you in a bit, then," Genni offered, giving Felix a stern look, which Felix returned.

"I'll put out the fire," Ken said, standing up to grab a bucket sitting behind his chair.

"I should help carry the food," Hadlee said, standing up.

"I'll get the chairs," Felix offered. "Just meet me at the truck when you're done."

Hadlee nodded and went about helping take down their buffet. It was about fifteen minutes later that she finally met up with Felix at the truck. He stood with his arms folded, leaning his shoulder into the passenger side door, and his dark silhouette took Hadlee's breath away.

Having her entire body react to simply seeing the strong ship captain brought yet another revelation for the night. *I'm falling for him. I'm falling for a grumpy, protective, handsome, broody captain.* She sighed. *Now to figure out if it's a good thing or not.*

THE SLIGHT SWING OF Hadlee's hips had Felix hypnotized as she walked in his direction. He'd been struggling to take his eyes off her all evening and his protective instincts had gone haywire every time she'd been more than a few feet from him. The entire situation was amazingly stupid. She was completely safe here, so why were his emotions acting as if they were hopped up on caffeine or something?

"Hey, Captain," she said softly, coming to a stop about a foot from where he waited.

A half-smile tugged on his lips at the sight of her in his sweatshirt. It was too big for her, but something about seeing her in his clothes was satisfying to his male ego. "Hey, Fish Doctor."

Hadlee closed her eyes and shook her head. "Bennett seems to have a thing with nicknames," she said with a laugh.

Felix shrugged and let his arms fall to his side as he straightened from the vehicle. "You ready to go?"

She gave him a small smile and nodded, but Felix could have sworn he saw a spark of disappointment in her look.

Maybe she's ready to say goodnight as much as I am. Which was not at all, if he was being honest with himself.

He opened the door and helped her inside, his body coming alive automatically as he touched her hand and waist to get her settled. Flexing his still tingling fingers, Felix walked around and jumped into the driver's seat. As much as he wanted to spend more time with her, he wasn't sure it was a good idea. Every time he touched Hadlee, he found himself wanting more.

He stuck the keys in the ignition, then paused as a thought from earlier came floating through his mind. "Can I ask you a question?"

Hadlee turned her head in the dark. "Sure. What's up?"

He put his arm on the steering wheel and turned in her direction. "Do you, or do you not, like being a marine biologist?"

"I do."

He nodded, still thinking about her earlier words. Something about them wasn't quite right and he was trying to pinpoint it. "Do you, or do you not, like being a professor?"

When she hesitated, Felix knew he'd figured it out. "I do...for the most part," she hedged.

"If you could do anything in the world, what would it be?" He wasn't sure why he was pushing this. It wasn't like Hadlee had ever come across as hating her job and she'd just admitted that she mostly enjoyed it, but he couldn't seem to help wanting to know more than she told other people. There was something she was holding back and he wanted to know what it was.

"I...hmmm." Hadlee faced the windshield, looking into the night. "I don't know that anyone's ever asked me that before."

Felix let go of his keys and leaned back in his seat. "Never? Not even your dad?"

A sarcastic chuckle came from Hadlee. "Definitely not my dad."

Her words were soft, but they still punched Felix in the gut. "You said he was busy with work," Felix pushed. "You meant it, didn't you? Like, *really* busy with work."

She tucked a piece of hair behind her ear and nodded. Felix was grateful for the street light, which gave him just enough light to see her movements. "Yeah. I meant it literally. When Mom was alive, Dad was home for family dinners and stuff, though he wasn't necessarily the type to get down on the floor and play with us." She grinned his direction. "He did read us a lot of books though, but his textbook stories didn't always go over very well."

Felix snorted and draped his right arm across the back of the bench seat. Even in the dark he could see that she was tense and struggling to tell her story. It sounded like she'd never had anyone to tell her side to, and he wanted to encourage without hurting. He let his fingers play with her hair, eventually moving to the back of her neck, massaging the tight muscles there.

Hadlee let out a long breath and shivered under his ministrations. "Are you sure you want to hear all this?" she asked. "I've never been one to have a pity party."

"This isn't a pity party," Felix said, his voice slightly huskier than normal. "This is me getting to know you better."

That same sarcastic laugh echoed through the same. "By what? Hearing all my dark secrets?"

"Yep."

Hadlee shrugged. "All right, but don't worry, I'm not expecting sympathy or anything. All in all, I've had a good life, even if it was missing a few things." She sighed and leaned into his fingers a little more. "When Mom died, Dad seemed to fold into himself as he went into mourning. Instead of coming home at night, he left his office open at all hours and turned his attention to his students... I couldn't decide if he wanted away from us girls, or if teaching was a way of keeping himself busy."

"Does it matter?" Felix growled. "He left his four daughters alone. No father should have done that."

She sighed. "I suppose not, but that's the way it was. Since I was the oldest, I became the mother. My sisters aren't quite as...studious? I'm not sure that's the right word, but they weren't quite as academically driven as myself, so it wasn't the easiest task to take care of my own studies as well as help them make it through school." Her teeth flashed in the dark. "But you know what? We made it. My sisters are happy and healthy and that's all that matters."

"And you?"

"I'm the same."

"But are you really?" Felix let go of her neck and undid her seatbelt. With a little tug, he pulled Hadlee over next to him. A bench seat was the best part of having an old truck and he tucked her into his side. "Why did you become a professor, Hadlee?" he whispered into her hair as his arms tightened around her.

Hadlee was breathing heavily and she shook her head. "I already told you."

Felix slowly shook his own head. "But I don't think that was really it."

Hadlee leaned back enough to look at his face. "And what do you think the reason is?" she snapped. Immediately her eyes closed and she dropped her forehead to his chin. "I'm sorry, Felix. I didn't mean to be rude."

Felix shifted so her face was tucked into his neck. "If that was rude, you shouldn't be hanging out with me." He rubbed her back, trying to help ease her anxiety again. He knew he was breaking her barriers, but from his outside perspective, he could see something she seemed to be missing, and it felt important. "But to answer your question..." He took a deep breath for courage. "I think you became a professor because you were trying to find a way to connect to your father. Your sisters took off for their own lives and your father had his. You couldn't follow your siblings, but you could follow your dad."

She huffed. "You sound like a psychologist."

He snorted. "Definitely not, but...you lost some of your happiness tonight when you were talking about your job and why you did it, and it made me curious." Felix kissed her temple. "I'm sorry your family can't see what a treasure they have. It's their loss."

A shaky breath made Felix's arms tighten even more. "That's very kind of you," she whispered. "Thank you. But it's not like it's your problem."

But I want it to be. Felix froze for a second before going back to rubbing her back. Why was he digging? Why did he want her to see her life for what it was? Why did he want her to realize how wonderful she was? Why, why, why?

Because you're falling in love with her.

His back began to ache from the tension radiating through his body. He could lie to himself and try to deny the thought, but the last several weeks had been building up to this moment. No matter how much he had looked forward to being free after Charli was taken care of, this small woman in his arms was reeling him in without even trying.

He understood her perspective of raising her siblings, since Felix had taken on a similar role when his parents died, but Charli hadn't walked away without a second glance. Their relationship had only grown stronger in adulthood and he was grateful for it. Hadlee had been left on her own, desperate enough for attention that she'd taken on a career just to be in her father's line of sight.

Now Felix found himself wanting to give her that attention. He wanted to heal her broken heart, and he wanted to do it by keeping her with him.

He shook his head, confused, but resigned to what was happening. He hadn't planned on these feelings, but he couldn't deny how much it had brightened his life either. *It's too soon to tell her though. Let's get through the next few weeks and then we'll see where we stand. She might walk away at the end easy as pie.*

He kissed her temple again, ignoring the stab of pain that thought brought, but he forced himself to be realistic about the situation. *Guess that means I need to savor each moment though, huh?*

His lips traveled from her temple to her cheek, then down to the edge of her mouth. "Your family are idiots," he muttered as his lips lingered on her skin.

She laughed breathlessly. "No, they're not, don't be mean."

Felix grinned. "I'm not. But someone has to speak the truth." He began toying with her lips, first kissing the upper, then the lower. "And I'm going to prove it to you," he murmured against her mouth.

"Mmm..." she hummed, her hand gripping his shirt. "And how will you do that?"

"Like this." No more words were needed as Felix used everything in his arsenal to show Hadlee just how special he thought she was. Everything within the standards of him still being a gentleman, that is. He'd been raised to respect a woman and no matter how much Hadlee called to him, he would keep himself in check, though he'd never been tempted quite like he was with her.

He had no idea how much time passed before he forced himself to let her go, just as much for her sake as his own. Letting her off at the inn should have been easy after their interlude in the truck. He should have been sated and content, but it was the exact opposite.

The more she gave, the more he wanted, and Felix found sleep slow in coming as he counted the minutes until he would see her the next day.

CHAPTER 17

Another week passed in easy camaraderie, though Hadlee's mind continued to bring up her conversation with Felix in his truck. While his attention and touches had been amazing, it was the secrets she'd revealed that kept marching through her head.

I like being a marine biologist. I do.

But somehow, now that she'd been forced to realize it wasn't her dream...she felt lost. It had never occurred to her that she might have a different path in life. One where she wasn't fighting for her father's attention or against an entire board of men who didn't want her around.

But if I DID shift to another career, would I have any attention at all?

The question stung. Mostly because Hadlee wasn't sure of the answer. While her sisters seemed content with the paths they were taking, Hadlee knew for a fact that they rarely visited with their father. They were too caught up in school, marriage, and careers, though they kept in touch once in a while.

Meanwhile, Hadlee still lived in the house she'd grown up in and worked at her father's knee. She might be an adult now, but in some ways she'd never grown up, never taken that leap of faith to fly from the nest.

The idea was more than a little frightening. She'd thought she was content, if not exactly happy, doing her research and taking care of her only living parent. Now, all of that was in question and it made Hadlee's head spin.

"Hadlee?"

She shook her head and blinked several times. "I'm sorry. What?"

Felix smirked at her. "I was just asking if you thought you had all you needed for the day? Or if you wanted to set out a few more traps."

She tucked a chunk of hair behind her ear and gave a soft laugh. "Sorry. I suppose I've got a lot on my mind."

Without a word, Felix gently pulled her into his chest and let her rest against him.

His quiet support was one of the things Hadlee loved the most. Felix rarely required an explanation or forced her to defend herself. The more they got to know each other, the more he simply offered himself as a solid foundation for her to build on. It was a new and wonderful experience.

"Our team is probably watching us," she murmured into his shirt.

Felix grunted, his body shaking slightly. "Who cares?"

Her smile was hidden from him, but it was there all the same and she found herself relaxing even more into his hold, her arms wrapping around his torso, siphoning every bit of warmth that he offered.

"You still haven't answered the question though," Felix pointed out.

She sighed. "I think we've got enough for today. Besides, it's late in the afternoon. By the time we wait on more traps, it'll be near dusk."

"Sounds good." He pulled away, but grabbed her hand. "Let's drive *Morwenna* into the harbor." He started shouting orders as he led Hadlee up into the wheelhouse. It had become routine for her to stand between him and the wheel as they navigated their way home. Once settled in the correct direction, Felix dropped his mouth near her ear. "What are you doing tonight?"

A rash of goosebumps ran down her neck as he spoke, but Hadlee tried not to show too much of a reaction. "Just dinner at the inn." She glanced in what she hoped was a coy way over her shoulder. "What about you?"

He straightened and smiled out into the horizon. "I was hoping to take a pretty girl to dinner."

"Girl?" Hadlee sniffed, feigning indifference. "You must be talking about *Morwenna*. I'm sure she'd be happy for your company." His chuckle shook against her back.

"She wasn't the *woman* I had in mind."

"Oh? Who was it, then?"

He stepped impossibly closer to her, bringing their bodies into full alignment, as the ship slowly rose up and down with the waves of the ocean. "A woman with chocolate-colored hair and light gray eyes that make her appear as an angel, with porcelain skin so soft it doesn't feel real."

Hadlee was breathing heavily by the time he was done. Their flirting session had just taken a serious turn and it only pulled her heart in deeper.

When he spoke next, it was a whisper in her ear. "And one who doesn't mind eating fish as often as I do."

His tease broke the spell and Hadlee laughed breathlessly. "She sounds like something special."

He squeezed her side slightly. "Oh, she is." He paused. "So...what do you think?"

"About?"

"Dinner?"

She smiled. "I'd love to go." Turning over her shoulder, she continued, "But I might not order fish."

"Sacrilege," he muttered, causing her to laugh again. "But I suppose I'll survive."

Her smile lasted the rest of the way into town, cleaning the boat and eventually arriving back at the inn. Glancing at the clock, Hadlee knew she had just enough time for a shower before meeting Felix, but there was something she felt compelled to do first.

Grabbing her phone, she sat on her bed and punched in the number for her father.

"Dr. Ford," he said gruffly, obviously not having seen his caller I.Dd.

"Hey, Dad," Hadlee said, trying to infuse her tone with cheer. "How are you?"

"Hadlee," her father greeted. "Is your research coming to any early conclusions?"

She sighed and pulled on a string from her jeans. "Yeah. Things are looking more and more like the young crabs are not developing the same shells as the older ones. But that doesn't mean they won't as they get old. There's definitely still some variables to any conclusions I end up with. Further research would need to be done to really nail down any issues."

Her father grunted, but didn't speak.

Good job, Hadlee. It looks like your research is going to be useful, Hadlee.

His lack of response irked her much more than usual and gave Hadlee the courage she needed to push forward. "Dad...what would you think if I quit my job and took up something else?" The line was quiet for so long that Hadlee was concerned the call had been dropped. "Dad?"

"This is the trouble with women in this field," he muttered. His tone sounded distracted, as if he wasn't really speaking to her, but Hadlee was listening anyway. "Their attention spans just aren't made for the long term."

"Excuse me?" she asked, shocked at such a rude comment. "How can you say that? I've spent *years* studying to become a professor and years more building my tenure. That was way out of line."

Her father cleared his throat and softened his tone. "Hadlee, sweetheart, you've done good work while you were here. But the truth is, you just aren't ever going to be as capable as the men in this field. Women like you don't have the drive or staying power in order to succeed. So, if you want to do something else, you go right ahead. After your last debacle, it's not like the board will miss you."

Her jaw clenched and vision swam with unshed tears. How could she have been so fooled by this man? Did he ever love her? He was her father! Didn't that mean he was automatically supposed to support her? Why in the world did she spend so much time seeking his approval when he obviously didn't care one iota?

"Would the board care if Christian left?"

"Now, honey, that's different and you know it." He sighed and she could imagine him rubbing his forehead. "You shouldn't take what I'm saying personally."

Hadlee huffed. "Oh, really? Then please tell me how I'm supposed to take it?"

"Now, see? I've upset you and that wasn't my intent."

Hadlee pulled the phone away from her ear as he continued talking, and stared at the screen. For once, she had nothing more to say and with her heart in shatters, she also had no more reason to listen.

It only took one click to shut her father up. For a split second, it felt good to walk away, but the heartache that was left behind didn't stay quiet for long. Letting herself fall back into the bedspread, Hadlee allowed the tears to flow.

She'd give herself five minutes to mourn what she'd apparently never had, and then she would get up and move on. Her father might not want her, the college might not want her, but on the other side of a town, a fisherman did. And his opinion was quickly coming to mean more than anybody else's.

THE SMELL OF COLOGNE stunk up Felix's cab and he grimaced as he pulled up to the inn. "Stupid stuff. Don't know why I put it on." Charli had given it to him for Christmas and he'd never worn it, but for some strange reason, Felix had wanted to impress Hadlee. And that had led to him wanting to smell like something other than *Morwenna* and fish carcasses.

He pulled up to the inn and got out, leaving the door of the cab open in order to help air it out and marched up to the front door. His knock was quickly answered and Genni gave him an easy grin.

"Hey, Cap." She looked him over and whistled. "Don't you clean up good?"

"Watch it," Cooper said, coming up behind her and wrapping an arm around her waist. "I might get jealous."

Genni grinned over her shoulder at him. "Don't worry, babe. He can't compare to you."

Felix rolled his eyes. "Thank heavens," he muttered.

Genni laughed and opened the door wider. "Come on in. I'll walk up and get Hadlee."

"No need," came the sweet voice Felix was waiting for. "I'm here."

His eyes shot to the staircase and every other part of the inn faded into the background. Dressed in a pencil skirt, flowy blouse and heels, Hadlee carefully maneuvered her way down the stairs. The outfit was dressier than anything Felix had ever seen the scientist in and he suddenly was very grateful he had worn the cologne. She was a vision with her hair curled and flowing free and the soft green of the blouse bringing out the color of her eyes. Felix walked to the bottom of the stairs just as she arrived and held out his hand to help her down the last step. "You look amazing," he said through his thick tongue.

What has this woman done to me?

"You don't look so bad yourself," she said softly, staring into his eyes.

"I'd grab a jacket if I were you," Genni offered, breaking the staring contest between the two. "It looks like the wind is picking up."

Hadlee stepped around Felix and headed toward the coat rack near the door. "Thanks, Gen. I appreciate it."

"Let me help you with that," Felix said, stepping up behind her to hold the coat. Her smile of gratitude was enough to speed up his heart rate. *I'm in so deep I'm never getting out at this point.* "Ready?"

She nodded and Felix took her hand, leading her to the truck.

"You left the door open," she observed. "I hope your battery didn't die."

"Would be better than riding in a stinky truck," he muttered.

"What?"

"Nothing," Felix said, putting on an extra wide smile. He helped her into the cab, sniffing a few times to make sure the airing out had helped before moving around to his own side.

"Where are we going?" Hadlee asked as she buckled herself up.

"The Ocean House," he said, pulling out of the driveway. "It's one town over, but the nicest place we have nearby."

"I'm glad I dressed up, then," she said. "What's their specialty?"

Felix grinned and Hadlee laughed.

"Let me guess? Seafood?"

"We *are* on the coast," he said.

"Good point."

The ride wasn't short, but they filled the time with easy chatter. The table was tucked in the corner just like Felix had requested, but the best part was the view. The ocean side of the restaurant was all glass and sat on a rock overhang to the water. The small table Felix had requested was the prime location for a couple looking for atmosphere and view combined.

"So gorgeous," Hadlee gushed as soon as their hostess left.

Felix smiled as he watched her take it all in. While the restaurant would put a decent dent in his pocketbook, watching Hadlee enjoy it made it all worth it. "Just like you," he said softly.

Her cheeks flushed as her eyes met his. "You're such a flatterer," she said.

Felix shrugged. "I'm only telling the truth." He picked up his menu.

"Have you been here before?" she asked.

He nodded. "Once or twice."

She scooted her chair around so they were sitting side by side instead of across from each other. "Okay...tell me what's good."

The next hour-and-a-half sped by as they ate, laughed, and held hands all while enjoying the crashing of the waves on the shoreline and sinking of the sun. Felix could hardly believe that it was already time to take her home, since they were headed out on the water again tomorrow.

"Do you think we'll be able to sail the rest of the week?" Hadlee asked as they stood from the table. "I saw there might be a storm coming up."

He nodded. "Storms change directions quickly out on the water, so we'll just keep track of it. I've been keeping an eye on the Weather Channel, so if it hits us, we'll just wait it out."

The drive home was slower since Felix kept his usually lead foot elevated a bit more than usual. Hadlee was sitting in the middle with his arm around her and nothing in the world could have made him hurry to end their time together.

It was amazing how much he found himself looking forward to the possibilities of their future. He knew at some point they would have to address her job and the fact that she lived a few hours away, but right now, she was here, with him, and he was going to enjoy every moment of it. The future he had previously imagined, the one where he had no one to take care of or be responsible for, now seemed bleak and lonely compared to what he was currently experiencing. He couldn't imagine being alone for the rest of his life.

"Are you full?" he asked as they came back into the city limits of Seaside Bay.

"Hm?"

"We didn't order dessert," Felix explained. "Did you want to stop at Caro's for a quick bite?"

"She's open this late?" Hadlee asked, surprised.

Felix nodded. "Yeah. Her hours have been wonky lately because of construction, so she's open later in the evening."

"Is she remodeling?"

"Yeah. You remember that she and Jack are engaged?" Felix waited for her to nod. "Well, they're moving his cookie business in with her storefront, so they're doing some work to make the layout function better."

"Gotcha. Is her stuff good?" Hadlee inquired.

"Best chocolates I've ever had," Felix responded honestly. Caro was a wonder in the kitchen and her fiancé baked cookies in a way that made a person believe in magic. Felix could only imagine the skills their children would have in the kitchen.

"Sounds good to me," she said, snuggling deeper into his shoulder. "I've never been one to turn down a piece of chocolate."

He smiled and kissed the top of her head before pulling into a parking spot. "We'll have to walk a block, but it looks like downtown is busy tonight." The street parking was fairly full, which was unusual on a weeknight. Must have been a good tourism week.

Hand in hand, they headed down the sidewalk until they reached Sassy Sweets. A small bell rang as Felix pulled open the door and they were greeted by Chloe, Caro's teenage assistant.

"Mmm...you were right," Hadlee gushed as they walked out. She licked a spot of chocolate from her lip. "That is divine."

Felix chuckled low as she studied the content of the small pink box in her hands.

"What next?"

Felix grabbed a caramel and popped it in his mouth, enjoying the melting sugar on his tongue.

"Felix."

He stopped, quickly grabbing Hadlee's arm and tucking her into his side. "Harry." Felix frowned and his brows furrowed as he studied the group of men who were blocking their way on the sidewalk. "Can I help you?"

Harry wasn't looking at Felix. He was glaring at Hadlee. "We warned you," he said. "And now we're hearing that your findings are exactly what we were worried about."

Hadlee stepped away from Felix slightly, standing tall as if to show she wasn't afraid, though Felix could feel her shaking. "What are you talking about? I haven't published anything about my research yet."

Harry shook his head slowly. "You know what we're talking about. You're about ready to tell the world that the crabs are dying and it just isn't true!" His voice had grown into a full shout toward the end of his rant.

"Hey," Felix responded, pulling Handlee behind him and putting a hand out. "Let's just all calm down."

"We don't need to be calm," George said from behind Harry. "She's doing exactly what we said she'd do. If we let her publish her research, we'll all go under."

"I don't know where you've been getting your information, but it's wrong," Felix said firmly. He stepped forward, letting his muscles tighten. He knew it wasn't quite a fair fight since he was at least thirty years younger than the youngest of the men, but right now he didn't care. He only wanted to intimidate them out of taking physical action and protect Hadlee.

"She's lying to you," Harry tried to argue, but Felix took another step and the man snapped his mouth shut. "Felix. Our fight isn't with you."

"As long as you're trying to frighten this woman, then it most certainly is with me."

Harry shook his head and backed up, the other men following his lead. "You're wrong, son." His gnarled finger pointed over Felix's shoulder. "Don't say we didn't warn you when she brings down you and everything you've ever known."

"Leave," Felix said tightly.

Harry shook his head sadly. "We're not going down without a fight," he said, but turning around, he did leave, taking the other men in the opposite direction.

Felix turned and immediately swept Hadlee into his arms. She was shaking so hard her teeth were chattering. "It's okay," he said. "I've got you."

"Who's telling them this?" she asked, her voice thick. "I don't understand why everybody is so against me. Even if my findings come out negative, it would take years more of study to figure out if the effects were long-lasting or if the crabs learn to adapt on their own. I'm just a small fish in a big pond, but somehow they don't believe me."

"I don't know," Felix said, rubbing her back. "I'm as lost as you are." His mind whirled as to who would want to shut Hadlee down and the only thing he could think of didn't quite make sense. "Would..." He paused, unsure if he should continue. "Is there any chance your dad has a contact in town?"

Hadlee jerked out of his arms. "What?" she gasped.

He shook his head. "Forget it. I shouldn't have said anything. It was just my random thoughts coming out without being thoroughly vetted."

She chewed her lip, not looking convinced, but nodded and let him take her back to the truck. Unfortunately, the night didn't end on the high it had begun. After a chaste goodnight kiss, Felix sent her inside the inn, wishing he had a better excuse to keep her out longer, but knowing she needed a break. Her shock hadn't quite diminished from their incident and he figured a good night's rest was probably the best thing he could do for her right now. Tomorrow on the boat he'd talk to her again and they'd see if they couldn't figure out what was going on.

CHAPTER 18

The morning had been slightly tense between Hadlee and Felix and she wasn't quite sure how to break the ice. Their evening last night had ended on a sour note and Hadlee had to admit she was still in a dark place. First her father, then the men of Seaside Bay. What was it about her that made everyone think she was worthless?

Even Felix had been derogatory toward her when she'd first arrived, though he had obviously changed his tune after getting to know her, which she was grateful for, but his soft touches and nearness weren't helping her feel any better today. He was probably picking up on her attitude, which was why things were off between them.

She also wasn't quite ready to apologize. She wasn't sure she *should* apologize. Her head was torn between standing her ground and demanding that people start treating her with respect, and groveling at everyone's feet until they realized she wasn't here to hurt anyone.

To top it off...Felix's question about her father wouldn't leave her mind. He'd backtracked last night, but the damage was already done. Could her father be behind the trouble? He'd made it clear yesterday that he would never be proud of her work no matter what she did, and he didn't even seem to have much respect for females in general. She wasn't sure where his ideas had come from—her oldest memories never brought up any visuals of him treating her mother in a sexist fashion—but somewhere over the years, he'd become the man she hung up on last night.

Hadlee shook her head and finished recording her data.

"Ready for another load?" Ethan asked.

Hadlee's head jerked up. She glanced at the bucket of crabs she still needed to study and shrugged. "There's only a few left, so I suppose so."

Ethan grinned. "The next trap is only about ten seconds away."

Hadlee smiled back automatically, but she didn't feel the usual emotion behind it. "Great. Let's get collecting." She followed Ethan to the side of the boat as they came up on the flag. Reaching out the hook, he expertly grabbed the pole and brought it to the deck. "What the…?"

Hadlee frowned and stepped up to the side so she could see better. "What's wrong? Oh…"

Ethan was holding a partial rope in his hands, glaring at the water.

"Did it break?" Hadlee asked, looking from his hands to the water and back.

Ethan's jaw was tight as he shook his head. "CAP!" he shouted over his shoulder.

Thundering footsteps came down the steps from the wheelhouse and soon Felix was standing at their side. "Are you kidding me?" he growled.

Hadlee was still confused. "How can a rope just break like that? Did another boat run over it?"

Felix snorted and took the rope from his employee's hand. "It didn't break. It was cut."

"No…" Hadlee breathed. Gingerly, she took the rope from Felix's hand as if afraid it would strike at her like a snake. Studying the end, she could see he was right. The end of the rope was neat and clean, obviously having been cut off with a knife. "Who would do that?"

"Stupid old men who don't want you here," Felix grumbled.

She stiffened. "Do you really think they would ruin your stuff?"

Felix sighed and took off his sunglasses before pinching the bridge of his nose. "I don't know, but I can't think of who else would do this."

"Is there a problem?" Joshua asked as he and Chrissy walked up to the group.

"Josh, I'm sorry to ask you to do this, but I need you to swim down and retrieve the trap. The rope isn't attached any more."

The large man frowned and stared at the rope. "Was it cut?"

Chrissy gasped. "What?"

Hadlee nodded. "It looks like it."

Joshua shook his head before turning and walking purposefully toward the stairs that led downstairs where he would change into his wetsuit.

Hadlee tapped her foot as she continued to play with the rope. "I just don't understand," she murmured to herself. The animosity of the town was so over the top. Why did they think they had information that was in direct contrast to what she was telling them? A warm hand landed on her lower back.

"Don't worry about it," Felix said. We'll get this figured out."

Hadlee immediately turned into him. "Please don't do anything rash. I'm sorry that whoever did this was probably trying to stop me, and in so doing they broke your stuff. I'll pay for it." She plowed on when he opened his mouth. "Why don't we just finish up for the day and when we get back to land, we'll report it to your friend. What was his name? Captain...Wamsley?"

Felix huffed. "Yeah. We can do that, but I make no promises that I won't confront Harry and his goons."

Knowing that was as good as she was going to get, she rested a hand on his chest. "Thank you."

Joshua, followed by Luke, arrived in their diving gear. "Thought it might take a few minutes to locate the trap if it floated around at all, so we should get the tanks."

"They shouldn't have gone anywhere," Felix said. "But it never hurts to be prepared." He yelled for the rest of his crew. "Julian!" The first mate came hurrying from the back and everyone went to work getting the men ready for a dive.

Like Felix thought, it only took minutes for the men to bring the trap to the surface, as it hadn't really shifted from its spot.

"There's nothing in it." Joshua gasped once his mouthpiece was out. Holding onto the edge of the boat, he handed what rope was left over to Julian, who began to pull it in. "Someone opened it."

Felix cursed softly and Hadlee slumped into the boat railing. "They're really serious about stopping me." She shook her head, shaking her loose hair out of her face. Looking up to Felix, she asked, "What can I do to convince them I'm not a threat?"

"No idea," He grunted as they put the trap away. Once done, he came back to help pull the men into the boat. "Hang on and I'll get us to the next trap."

A heavy sinking feeling sat in Hadlee's stomach as they ended up finding all the traps in the same situation as the first. Cut ropes and open cages. Whoever wanted to stop her had spent much of their day chasing down Felix's flags. They were dedicated, she had to give them that, but their actions were far more harmful than anything Hadlee had done or would do thus far.

When they were finally docked, Hadlee sent her crew home. Staying to clean up had become a nightly thing and though her team sometimes stuck around, tonight she wanted a chance to speak to Felix alone. Not to mention they would need to go to the police station when they were done.

She automatically headed to grab the mo, knowing that would be her job since no one else enjoyed it. Feigning complete focus, Hadlee kept her head down, but her peripheral vision was set on Felix. The tightness of his shoulders and clenched jaw gave away his mood. The problem was, Hadlee wasn't sure if he was mad at her, or the situation.

With their awkward morning, this only made things more strained between them and she hoped they could clear the air soon. Right now, Felix was the only bright spot in her life and she wasn't ready to let go of that just yet.

FURY SWIRLED THROUGH Felix stronger than a category I hurricane. How dare anyone sabotage his equipment over something as stupid as Hadlee's research. He shook his head as he finished writing his logs for the day. "Why won't those old men listen to reason?" he muttered as he straightened up his small desk area.

"Captain?" Julian's voice was tentative. He'd worked with Felix long enough to know when Felix was in a bad mood. When Felix looked up, Julian continued, "I think we're done out here. Anything else you would like me to do?"

Felix shook his head. "No. Thank you. You can go."

The first mate hesitated and Felix waited him out. "You do know that Hadlee's still out here, right?"

Felix let out a long breath. "Yeah."

"Okay. Just wanted to make sure." Still looking slightly hesitant, Julian finally turned around and left.

Felix waited a few more minutes before standing up from his seat and heading out onto the main deck. He wasn't sure what to feel right now. He was ticked at the men for what they were doing. He was also worried for Hadlee, but a small part of him was frustrated with her as well. He knew it wasn't right, but he was starting to wonder why she didn't just back off from her research. There were obviously things going on behind the scenes he didn't understand, but was any of it truly worth risking herself and her team over?

Part of him hoped that Hadlee had given up on him and headed home, but another part of him was relieved to see she was sitting on a bench, swinging her feet and staring at the water. "Hey," he grunted, taking the seat next to her.

She eyed him sideways. "Hey."

Felix let the silence envelop them as their shoulders brushed, sending heat through his chest that began to calm the storm inside of him. The small voice inside his mind that wished Hadlee hadn't waited was frustrated that she had so much power over him. It was everything he hadn't wanted, to have to answer to another person and to be free of any entanglements.

"I'm sorry."

He frowned before turning her way. "What?"

Hadlee sighed and twisted on the bench so she was looking at him directly. Her knees brushed against his thigh, sending the internal heat even higher. "I said I'm sorry."

"For what?" Felix made a face, confused at her apology. If anything, he should be apologizing for being so stand-offish today, but Hadlee certainly hadn't done anything wrong.

"It's my fault that your traps are all messed up," she said softly, the anguish in her voice nearly tangible. "If I hadn't come, you wouldn't have to replace anything and you wouldn't—"

"Stop right there," Felix said curtly. "None of this is your fault. You didn't cut the ropes, and you didn't ask for those jerks to interfere with your life."

She shook her head, obviously not listening to him. "They wouldn't have bothered you if it weren't for me."

Felix shrugged and took her hand. His desire to protect and hold her close immediately came rushing to the forefront. The closer he got to her, the more he wanted. Most of him didn't want her to feel bad about the traps, or about the trouble the men were causing. Logically he knew his other feelings were wrong, but they still simmered in the background, even if he was working to ignore them. *She's worth it,* he tried to remind himself. *She didn't ask for this, and those men aren't willing to listen.* "It's just rope," he said, trying to downplay her anxiety.

"I *know* it's just rope, but it's rope that you shouldn't have to replace." She straightened and gripped his hand with her extra one. "I know I already told you I would pay for things, but I mean it. It's covered."

"Hadlee." Felix groaned. "Let it go. It's not a big deal." He needed them to move onto something else before his feelings became even more muddled than they already were.

"It is a big deal, and I think we should talk to your friend, Captain Wamsley."

Felix considered it. He wasn't sure that was the best way to go, but Ken was already involved, since he'd been informed about the last confrontation. "We can do that, I guess."

Hadlee jumped to her feet. "Yes. Let's do that. I want this stopped. I still don't understand why they're so against me, but I refuse to let them put you in the middle. If they break something else of yours, I'm not going to be so nice about it."

He chuckled as she pulled him to his feet and they left the boat. Since her crew had already left, they climbed into his truck and Felix drove them the couple of miles to the police station. Felix walked around to help her down and together they walked inside.

"Cap!" Officer Derrick Windsor called out as they walked through the door. His smile was wide as he stood up to shake Felix's hand. "And who's this beauty?" Derrick winked at Hadlee.

"Dr. Ford," Felix answered for her, tugging her slightly closer through their combined hands. Derrick was married, but that didn't mean Felix was okay with him flirting with his girlfriend.

Derrick's eyebrow went up. "Doctor, huh?" He turned to Hadlee. "Nice to meet you, Dr. Ford. I've heard a lot about you."

Hadlee smiled. "First of all, it's just Hadlee. Second, I'm afraid to ask what you've heard."

He shrugged and straightened. "Nothing I would worry about if I were you."

His eyes darted to Felix and Felix could tell Derrick was lying. But why? "Is Ken in?"

Officer Windsor nodded. "You're lucky. I think he was headed home in a few minutes." The officer grabbed the phone and punched a button. "Hey, Cap. Felix and his pretty Dr. Ford are here."

Felix rolled his eyes while Hadlee gave a soft laugh.

"Yeah. Okay. On it, Sir." Derrick put the receiver down. "Head on back. He's waiting for you."

Felix nodded. "Thanks." Keeping his hold on Hadlee's hand, he headed down the hall. The police station wasn't large, but Felix already knew where he was going. Sometimes being friends with the police captain had its perks.

"Captain," Ken said solemnly as they came through the door. "Dr. Ford."

"Hadlee, please," she said with a soft smile. "I think we've already been through this."

Ken smiled. "Fair enough." He waved at a couple of chairs that were facing his desk. "Have a seat."

Felix sat Hadlee into her seat before settling into his own. He was slightly disgusted with himself that he had the urge to push their chairs together so he could continue holding her hand. Instead, he forced himself to be okay with the separation. It wasn't like she was leaving or that she wasn't still within a couple of feet of him. It had to just be his protective instincts on overdrive, especially after the day they'd had.

Right now he wasn't particularly in the mood to pander to his stupid hormones. Contrary feelings concerning Hadlee and the whole situation were still churning in the background and Felix couldn't quite get them out of his head.

Ken leaned back, folding his thick arms over his equally thick chest. "So, what brings you two here?" He raised an eyebrow. "I'm guessing this isn't a social visit."

Felix turned to Hadlee, wondering which of them should speak.

"Someone cut Felix's trap lines today."

Okay, apparently Hadlee was going to be the voice for their visit. Felix settled back and tried to appear carefree. He didn't mind them talking to Ken, but he really didn't want Hadlee taking the blame. *But it IS her fault.* Felix pushed the voice back, but it didn't disappear, just stayed with the rest of the conflicting emotions. He could feel his temper growing and it was starting to become uncomfortable. But really...why was this project such a big deal, to either side? Since the men were being jerks, Hadlee should consider just setting it aside, or maybe going somewhere else.

Ken frowned. "What?"

It only took Hadlee about five minutes to explain what they'd discovered today, including how the ropes were all clean lines, indicating it had to be done with a knife.

Ken turned to Felix. "You're sure about this?"

Felix nodded. "She's right. They were definitely cut," he said tightly.

"Any ideas who?"

Felix turned to Hadlee and she shrugged. "We only have guesses. I'm assuming it's the same men who keep trying to run me out of town."

Ken pinched his lips together before opening his laptop. "Give me just a sec. I want to fill out an actual report on this."

Felix huffed a quiet breath, but let his friend continue. It sounded like it might be a longer evening than they'd expected.

CHAPTER 19

Captain Wamsley tapped a pen against his desk. "You're sure you guys didn't see anyone out on the water with you?"

Hadlee shook her head. Her fingers were beginning to ache from squeezing them together so tightly. Felix was still angry and she wasn't sure what more she could do to help him calm down. *I'm surprised he held my hand. It feels like he hates me right now.*

She really needed some kind of sign that Felix wasn't blaming her for everything. She'd tried to apologize and he'd said it wasn't her fault, but the scowl on his face had only deepened, and that told her he wasn't really letting things go.

"I don't think there's much I can do right now," Captain Wamsley murmured, reading his computer screen. "Although I agree that Harry and his idiot friends are more than likely to blame, without any kind of concrete evidence, there's little I can do."

"I know," Hadlee said softly. She flexed her fingers, trying to bring blood flow back to the tips. "I just thought we should let you know what was going on. If something happens later and we end up finding who did this, I want to make sure Felix receives recompense for the broken equipment. Not that I'm not already paying him for the ropes," she hurried to say. "I am, after all, at fault. But still, if somebody eventually owns up to it, he needs to be taken care of." She snapped her mouth shut, turning off her babble. It was a sign as to how frazzled she was that she couldn't stop herself from overtalking.

Captain Wamsley nodded, kindly not saying anything about her overshare. "Of course. I'm glad you told me."

"It wasn't your fault," Felix said in a dark, low tone. He turned his dark gaze toward her, stealing her breath. "We already went over this."

"I know but—"

Felix shook his head harshly. "Enough, Hadlee. We don't need to get into it again."

Hadlee quieted down and slunk back into her seat. She'd known from the beginning that Felix could be a little rough, but right now her nerves were on edge and his snap hurt more than it normally would have. Her chest caved in slightly as she tried to make herself invisible in her chair. Suddenly, she didn't want to be there anymore. They'd told Captain Wamsley what he needed to do. She'd apologized profusely to Felix and had told him that she would cover the cost of repairs, which she would do out of her own pocket if the college refused to pay for it.

Now she just wanted to go home. Felix was still mad and instead of seeking comfort from him, Hadlee wanted away. She wanted time to process and figure out if things were right between her and Felix. She knew she was in love with him, but today it was easy to tell that he wasn't feeling that way about her. Maybe he never would.

She shook her head. That didn't matter right now. She just wanted time to think and be alone. Hopefully by tomorrow morning, things will have settled between them.

Hadlee stood up. "If there isn't anything else you need, I'm going to head back to the inn."

Captain Wamsley shook his head. "No. I think that's good enough. Be sure and let me know if there's anything though, okay?" He raised both eyebrows and tilted his chin down. "And be careful out there. If these guys are willing to break someone else's equipment, then they might escalate to physical violence. We already know they don't mind intimidating you, but now they've taken things a step farther, and we should be on our guard."

"I will, thank you." Hadlee gave him a brittle smile, hoping he couldn't see how fake it was. "Goodnight." She nodded her head and turned to walk out the door. Felix's body was immediately noticeable behind her. She could always feel him near, and if she didn't know him well, his large presence would frighten her.

After saying goodnight to the nice officer at the front desk, Hadlee went outside and took a deep breath of the cool, night air. The salty tang was refreshing after feeling cooped up in the office.

"Come on," Felix said gruffly, heading toward the truck.

Hadlee bit back a sharp retort. She didn't like confrontation, but at the moment, she wasn't willing to continue in his company either. "I think I'll walk home," she said, forcing another smile. "But thank you for the offer."

Felix's shocked look was oddly satisfying as he stared at her. "You can't be serious."

Hadlee jerked back slightly at his tone. "I think the walk will do me some good," she answered carefully. *And it will give me a break from you. No matter that I'm falling in love with you, I'm too frazzled to handle your anger at the moment.*

He stormed back in her direction. "Don't you have any sense of self-preservation?"

"What are you talking about?" Hadlee asked, backing up. Logically, she knew Felix would never hurt her, but that didn't make him less frightening at the moment.

"Harry and those other guys are after you," Felix growled in that low tone of his. "They've already cornered you before, they went so far as to cut the lines to my traps, and you think you're going to be safe walking home, in the dark I might add, by yourself?"

When he put it that way, Hadlee felt foolish that she had even mentioned walking home, but the realization didn't alleviate her need for distance. "I see," she said, keeping her voice soft. Taking a deep breath, she folded her hands primly in front of her. "Thank you for explaining your concerns. Would you be willing to drive me home? I would greatly appreciate it."

Felix stared at her a moment longer, as if unsure what to make of her meek attitude. Then he nodded. "Of course. I was planning on it."

Silent, Hadlee followed him to the truck and thanked him for his assistance in holding the door.

Felix climbed in his side and started the truck, but didn't put it into drive.

Hadlee's anxiety continued to climb the longer they stayed still. She just wanted to be alone. Why wasn't he moving?

"I'm sorry," he said gruffly.

Slowly, Hadlee turned her head. "You're sorry? For what?" While she knew what she would be sorry for if she were acting the way Felix was, she wasn't sure this kind of roughness was unusual for him.

He sighed and fell back in his seat. "I'm sorry I've been a jerk."

Hadlee nodded graciously. "It's all right. I know it's been a rough day."

Felix shook his head. "No, you don't get it." He turned toward her. The light from the police station made his face visible in the evening light. "I...haven't handled things well today, and I'm sorry." He took off his hat and pushed a hand through his hair before throwing the hat on the dashboard. "It wasn't supposed to be this way."

"I know," Hadlee soothed. "I don't think any of us could have imagined that—"

"No. I mean this." He waved a hand between them. "Us."

Hadlee frowned. What was he saying? And why did it feel like he wasn't happy about their relationship? Wasn't it him who kept telling her how special she was? Had he been lying? "I...don't understand."

"Of course you don't," he grumbled.

The pain that hit Hadlee's chest stole her breath. She still wasn't quite sure what he was talking about, but whatever it was, it wasn't good. Her need for space was stifling her. "You know what?" she whispered, unable to speak any louder through the lump in her throat. "I think I'll take my chances on the street."

"HADLEE." FELIX GROANED, throwing his head back against the seat. "Come on." He huffed and grabbed the steering wheel. "I'll just take you home."

"No thank you," she said, opening the door despite the vehicle running.

His frustration soared at her stubbornness. Hadn't they already been through this? It wasn't safe for her to walk alone in the dark. "It isn't safe."

She didn't answer, just continued to get out.

Felix snapped. "It wasn't supposed to be this way!" he shouted, hitting the steering wheel.

"You already said that," Hadlee shot back. She immediately closed her mouth as if she hadn't meant to respond to him. "I'm sorry. I'm just going to go."

Despite his anger, Felix's protective side refused to leave him be. Slamming open his door, he marched around to her side. "You weren't supposed to be you," he grumbled as he glared at her, hoping she would just submit to being driven home.

Hadlee threw up her arms. "I don't know what you want from me, Felix. I thought you and I were friends. I thought we were becoming more than friends. But after today, I'm confused. Do you regret our time together? Do you regret kissing me? Okay! Just say so! But right now I can't really handle your anger along with my own stress."

He shook his head. The words were on the tip of his tongue, but he knew they would hurt her. He knew they were the wrong thing to say. His emotions were a boiling volcano and he knew himself well enough to know that he was about to blow.

Resentment at the situation was choking him. Worry for Hadlee mixed with frustration that she didn't even seem to consider dropping her research felt like a chain around his neck, weighing him down until he couldn't handle it anymore. He tried to swallow the words…the accusations…to hold them back, but that little part of him that resented being tied down before he was ready seemed to be stronger than usual tonight, and they came out anyway. "After my sister got married, I was supposed to be free."

Hadlee stopped walking and slowly turned back to him.

"I've taken care of her most of my adult life. The part of my life when I should have been able to enjoy dating and friends and no real responsibilities." Blowing out a breath, he paced away and pushed a hand through his hair. *STOP!* his heart screamed, but his mind didn't listen. Now that he had started, the words flowed like molten lava, burning with every syllable. "I didn't want a relationship." He looked right at her. "I wanted freedom. But then, Mitch, good old Mitch, had to get a hold of me and call in a favor."

Hadlee's bottom lip was trembling, and her eyes were watery, but she stood tall. She took everything he said and never bowed to his anger, though he could see she was struggling under the weight.

"I dreaded being tied to your research all winter." A harsh laugh escaped him. "And then you had to be…" He waved at her. "You. You had to be kind and intelligent and sweet…and beautiful." Felix shook his head. "And like a fool, I fell for it all. A woman with no self-preservation and who's so caught up in her work, she's willing to risk everything for it. And when those goons in town wouldn't leave you alone, I stepped in to protect you just like I used to do for my sister."

He stepped closer to Hadlee. "But you're not my sister." *And my feelings are anything but brotherly.*

That last thought fell short of escaping. Of all the words he should have spoken, they were probably the least likely to tear her down, and yet they were the ones that stuck like glue to his dry throat.

The silence between them grew heavy and oppressive. Felix felt as if he were being choked and he was afraid to open his mouth. Afraid he would say more he shouldn't or that he would say something too revealing of his feelings and give her hope they might still have a future. Because in this moment of highly charged emotions, Felix realized with startling clarity that they didn't.

It would never work between them. She wanted something he simply couldn't give her and wasn't sure if he ever could. It didn't matter that he thought he loved her, he could never be what she needed. The gentle, loving boyfriend and eventual husband she deserved was not him. He never should have given into his attraction. That had to be all it was. Attraction. Lust. Desire. If he truly loved her, he wouldn't know so easily that they could never be together. It had all been a mistake.

He straightened his shoulders and his intent must have shown in his face because a small sob broke free from Hadlee. It was the first sound she had made since he'd begun his tirade, and the tiny noise pierced his heart in a way he hadn't expected. It made what he needed to do next feel like he was swimming in a riptide.

Before he could speak, Hadlee stepped up and put a hand on his chest. "I'm sorry," she whispered thickly. "I'm sorry I was such a burden. I had no idea what you felt like you were giving up to take me around on the water this summer. I never would have asked that of you."

She was shaking and Felix had to clench his fists to keep from wrapping his arms around her. Those protective instincts were roaring again.

Hesitantly, she leaned up on tiptoe and left a barely there kiss on his cheek. "Thank you for all you did." Stepping back, Hadlee nodded, then turned and walked away with her head held high. The dignity in her walk caught Felix off guard.

You don't deserve her.

With each step that took her farther away from him, his anger drained until she was gone, and so was the indignant voice that had led his behavior for the last few minutes.

"Happy?"

Felix spun, his heart nearly jumping through his throat. "What?" he croaked.

Ken stood against the wall of the building, leaning casually as if he hadn't a care in the world, but by the set of his jaw, Felix could tell his friend was upset. Standing up, Ken walked over and got in Felix's face. "I think this is the second time I've ever been ashamed to be your friend," Ken said in a low tone.

Felix reared back, his anger immediately simmering again. "What is that supposed to mean?"

"What did that woman ever do to you?" Ken asked. "She didn't ask you to protect her. She didn't ask you to take her out. She didn't even ask you to take her out on your boat. Yet you did it all and then at the first sign of trouble, you tuck tail and run."

Felix's fist landed on Ken's jaw before he recognized it had even moved. He froze after realizing what he had done. Not only had he hit a friend, but Ken was still on duty. He could bring Felix in under assault charges with a snap of his fingers.

Ken worked his jaw a little. "Feel better?"

"Not really," Felix said tightly.

Ken nodded. "My guess is in the morning you'll feel worse." Ken headed to his patrol car. "And you'll deserve every moment of it."

Felix didn't move as his friend pulled out and headed in the same direction Hadlee was walking. A flash of jealousy tried to make itself known, but Felix pushed it down. He wasn't jealous. It all stemmed back to that stupid lust he felt for Hadlee.

The cold breeze began to penetrate his clothes and a shiver rocked his body. He waffled back and forth on what he should do, but in the end, there was only one choice. Hadlee had known he was going to break up with her and had taken the situation graciously. He'd be a fool to mess that up now. Ken would see her home.

In the morning, Felix would be in control enough to handle taking her out on the boat. He would simply stay in the wheelhouse the whole time and let Julian and Ethan handle everything on deck. In a few weeks, she would go back to her lab and Felix could forget she ever existed. Or at least try.

CHAPTER 20

Morning came way too early for Hadlee. She had stayed up late crying and feeling bad for herself, only to fall into a deep sleep less than two hours before her alarm went off. She cringed when she looked in the mirror, glad that she was the first one up from her team. A hot shower would help ease her tight muscles and a cold rag would be absolutely essential for her red, puffy eyes.

Despite her ragged appearance, however, she was grateful to be past the grieving she had gone through last night. While her heart was still sore and she couldn't figure out what it was about her that seemed to repel all the men in her life, she was determined not to let them win.

Her father didn't care about all she had sacrificed in order to be close to him. Her colleagues refused to take her seriously. And now the one man who she thought saw something more had proven that he was nothing but a liar. Even the great Captain Felix Mendez didn't want her in his life. His freedom was worth more than she was.

"They might not see something worthwhile," she whispered to herself, "but I won't let them stop me. Maybe I'm not meant to have relationships. Maybe I don't have anything to offer that they find of worth, but that doesn't mean I'm worthless."

She took a ragged breath and let the hot water sluice down her back. Her head hung to her chest, hair plastered to her face and shoulders. "Those men don't define me," she continued. "I can still report my research and make a difference in how we take care of our wildlife and shorelines."

The water shut off and her skin immediately broke out in goose-bumps. She grabbed a towel and vigorously rubbed her wet body until it was red and warm. "I can contribute to science even if I can't contribute anywhere else."

Try as she might, the words felt hollow. She wanted desperately to believe in herself, but it was hard. It seemed like everything was falling apart all at once. "Baby steps," she told herself, winding her hair into a wet knot. Her energy today was going to go somewhere other than fixing her messy locks. Besides, it wasn't like there was anyone she was trying to impress.

"One step at a time." Taking a deep breath, she came out of the bathroom in a burst of steam and went back to her room with her chin held high. Gathering her things, she hurried down the stairs to grab some breakfast. She had work to do this morning and no one, not moody ex-boyfriends, or old professors or uncaring fathers, was going to stop her from moving forward. Her progress might be slow, but it was still going to be progress.

And for now...that would be enough.

An hour later, Hadlee had managed to avoid most of the questions at breakfast about not only her appearance but why she needed to run an errand at the docks without her team. Genni, in particular, had been highly suspicious of Hadlee's motives, but had simply stood by with a confused look on her face, rather than pressing the matter, for which Hadlee was grateful.

The sun shone bright that morning, the light mist on the water quickly dissipating as she approached the docks. Her eyes automatically landed on the *Morwenna*, which was docked at the far end of the harbor. The pain from last night threatened to bring her to her knees once more, but Hadlee stiffened her spine and turned away from the temptation. Putting on her sunglasses, she slowly walked along the wooden dock, searching for signs of life in the boats. There were several crowds where people were obviously headed out for early morning fishing tours and Hadlee steered clear of them, looking for a ship captain or sailor who was by himself.

She needed a decent-sized boat, but not something massive. The *Morwenna* had been perfect.

Stop. It's time to let it go.

She forced her feet to keep moving, a plastic smile on her face. Movement on a small vessel caught her eye. The boat itself was too small for her purposes, but maybe the owner would at least have some suggestions of whom she might approach.

"Excuse me!" Hadlee waved when the man looked up at her with a furrowed brow. "Could I ask you a few questions?"

He appeared slightly past middle age with a ponytail of hair in the back and a shiny hairless top. His skin was wrinkled and deeply tan, signs of someone who spent a lot of time out in the sun. "You talking to me?" he asked in a gruff voice.

His grunting reminded Hadlee of Felix, and she once again had to shove her wandering thoughts back to the task at hand. "Yes."

The man stood and walked closer to the dock, holding onto a pole as he studied her. "What do you need?"

"I'm looking for some suggestions," she said as pleasantly as she could manage. "I'm looking for a boat that I can hire to take me and my research team out on the water for us to do some work. It pays well and will be for about three weeks."

The man scratched his stubbly chin. "And you think mine would..." He trailed off as if waiting for her to finish for him.

"No, I'm sorry," she explained. "I'm afraid your boat is very nice, but a little too small for what we need. I was hoping, however, that you might know of someone who would be interested in the work."

He made a face, but didn't brush her off, for which Hadlee was grateful. "Wait a minute," he muttered, his eyes narrowing. "What did you say your name was?"

Hadlee froze. *Uh-oh.* She tried to study him from behind her sunglasses, searching her brain for memories of seeing him before, but nothing came to mind. "I'm, uh, Dr. Hadlee Ford," she answered, stepping back and preparing to flee if necessary. Hiring a ship looked like it might be harder than she'd expected. She had no idea how far the hate for her and her work had spread through the fishermen in the town.

He tilted his head. "You're that science lady." It was a statement, not a question.

Hadlee nodded anyway. "I am." She stuck her chin in the air. If she was going to convince herself that she was worthwhile, this was definitely a time for that kind of confidence.

The man shook his head. "I can't help you." He turned his back to her and Hadlee opened her mouth to call him back, then stopped.

Just be grateful he didn't threaten you, she told herself before moving on. An hour later, she was still trying to get anyone to talk to her and she was growing slightly frantic. It was closing in on the time that she was supposed to have met Felix and she worried she would run into him if she stuck around too much longer.

"You're looking for a ship?" The young man she was talking to scrunched his face.

"Yes," Hadlee said, her fingers twisting into a knot. She'd decided to try and speak to the youngest person she could find, hoping they weren't as against her and her research as the older men seemed to be. Unfortunately, it also appeared that the young man knew less of the captains and ship owners than the others did.

"Well..." He sighed and looked around. "I don't really know of anyone you could hire for that long, but you might be able to rent your own boat."

Hadlee paused. She hadn't thought of that. She had a little experience running a boat, but only a smaller one than Felix's. Her little bit of experience at Felix's hands wasn't enough to qualify her to take out that kind of boat. But maybe she could handle something smaller. "Where would I find something to rent?" she asked.

"Head across the street and you'll find the rental shop. They'll know what's available."

"Thank you," Hadlee said, her anxiety starting to ebb. "You've been a great help."

FELIX GLANCED AT HIS watch for the hundredth time in the last ten minutes. "Where is she?" he muttered. He marched out of the wheelhouse and stormed the deck. "Have you seen anyone?" he asked Ethan, who was lounging in the shade of an awning.

Ethan jumped to his feet and shoved his phone in his back pocket. "Uh, no, sir. I haven't."

Felix ground his teeth together. He had planned to stay out of Hadlee's way today, and for the rest of their time together, but now he needed answers. Punching her number into his phone, he waited while it rang. Growling a curse under his breath, he hung up when he got her voicemail. He tried another number, this time getting an answer.

"Hey, Felix, how are you?" Genni's quiet tones were soothing to the frustration welling inside of him.

"Hey, Genni. I'm looking for Hadlee. She's not answering her phone. Is she still at the inn?" There was a pause and Felix's heart began to pound in worry.

"She's not here," Genni said carefully. "None of them are. Hadlee left early this morning, then came back and got everyone else. Are you sure they aren't there at the dock?"

Felix pinched his lips together. "No. They're not here. At least not at my slip." He sighed. "Thanks, Genni. I'll look around. Maybe she got caught talking to someone."

"That would make sense. She's a total sweetheart and I know several people in town have mentioned how nice she is."

Felix nodded. "Thanks. Talk to you later." He put the phone back in his pocket and his hands on his hips. What was he going to do now? Hadlee had to be up to something if she came and went twice already this morning...but what? And why didn't she have the decency to let him know her plans?

"Captain Mendez?"

His head snapped up at the familiar voice. *Finally.* Felix went to greet Joshua, but stopped and frowned when he noticed the young man was alone. "Joshua," Felix said calmly. Felix walked to the edge of the boat so he could talk without having to shout. "Where is everyone? You're late."

Joshua raised an eyebrow and folded his arms over his chest. He was a big man and Felix had a feeling that Joshua wasn't happy with him at the moment. *Did Hadlee tell everyone we broke up? Really? How is that any of their business?*

"I came to get our equipment," the researcher said firmly. "I just need permission to come aboard."

"You're getting your equipment?" Ethan skidded to a halt behind Felix's shoulder. "Why? Aren't you coming out with us anymore?"

Joshua held Felix's eyes as he shook his head. "No. We've found other accommodations."

Just what is going on here? Felix narrowed his gaze and tilted his head. "What's going on, Josh?"

The college student held his hands out to the side. "Just following orders. Now, can I come aboard or not?"

"Not." Felix stepped up and walked over the small plank to the dock. "Take me to Hadlee."

"No."

Felix jerked a little. "What?"

Joshua shook his head. "I said no...sir. I was sent to retrieve our equipment. You have no right to keep it from us."

"Where is Hadlee?" Felix stepped forward and dropped his voice. He wasn't trying to intimidate Joshua, but something was going on and Felix felt as if he didn't have all the answers.

"She's with the rest of the team," Joshua said just as softly. "And I was sent to gather our equipment. If she had wanted you to know where she was, she would have come herself."

"I'll find her myself, then." Felix spun on his heel and marched off. She couldn't be too far. If Joshua was expected to carry their stuff, then Hadlee wouldn't have camped out a long distance from his boat.

"Stop," Joshua said, coming up right behind Felix.

Felix ignored him and kept walking.

"Captain Mendez," Joshua said more firmly. This time he grabbed Felix's arm.

Felix spun, his fist clenched, but he stopped himself. He'd been out of control last night, but he wouldn't be that way this morning. That woman had him in knots and it wasn't right. He needed to get things cleared between them once and for all, then he could finally settle his stupid hormones and set the last few weeks behind them. "Your director had a contract with me and is currently breaking it. Now...you can either take me to her, or I can take this up with the police captain and he can hunt her down. Which will it be?"

If looks could kill, Felix would be in Davy Jones's locker. Luckily, Joshua could be as angry as he wanted, but it wouldn't do a thing to hurt Felix. Finally, the young man nodded curtly and walked around Felix, heading down the dock.

It only took a few minutes to find a rental boat parking in a slot nearest the land. Hadlee, Chrissy, and Luke were busy organizing things like coolers and a few cases of water.

"What's going on here?" Felix asked, standing above them on the dock.

Hadlee gasped and snapped her head in his direction. Her shocked face quickly dissipated and she looked...resigned? Something about her sadness poked at Felix's defenses, bringing those pesky feelings back to the surface again. The very ones he had worked so hard to bury last night.

"Captain Mendez," she said calmly. "How are you this morning?"

"Let's cut to the chase, Hadlee," Felix said. "What are you doing here, in this?" He pointed to the boat. It was meant more for a fun day on the water pulling tubes or skiing rather than the work Hadlee and her team were supposed to be doing. It would be difficult for them to handle all their work within such a small space, though Felix figured they could do it. *But why do it? When she has a contract for the* Morwenna, *why rent this piece of junk?*

Hadlee sighed and twisted her ponytail. Walking to the side of the boat, she held out a hand and Felix went to grab it, but Joshua was already there. The knowledge that she hadn't been reaching for him stung, though he couldn't blame her for not wanting his help. Touching her probably wouldn't help his chaotic emotions either.

"Please walk with me," Hadlee said softly as she walked away from the boat.

They were twenty or so feet away when Felix stopped her. "Explain."

Hadlee turned to him and straightened her shoulders. "You made yourself clear last night that I was a burden in more ways than one, Captain Mendez. I took your words to be that you wished to be made free from any and all obligations." She shrugged. "So, I released you. I've found us another boat which we can use and you can go back to the life you've been craving."

"We had a contract."

"We did." She nodded.

"And you're breaking it."

"Actually, I believe you did that last night. You made it plain that you wanted nothing to do with any of us."

"Geez, Hadlee." He groaned, pushing a hand through his hair. "I still figured I'd finish out our contract. I wasn't telling you that I wouldn't take you out on the boat."

"Forgive me if I misunderstood how much pressure you've been under by having to deal with me all summer," she said testily. As soon as the words slipped out, she paused and deflated. "I'm sorry. I shouldn't have said that. Captain Mendez—"

"Felix."

She slowly shook her head. "I think it's best if I stick with your formal name. Now, I haven't told the college that I've switched boats, so you'll still get paid your full amount. Thank you for all your help, but you are now free of responsibility. I do, however, need the equipment we brought with us and I asked Joshua to retrieve it, so if you would please allow him aboard, I would appreciate it."

Felix had no words as she walked back and then climbed into the boat. Joshua came over to stand by his side, looking expectantly at Felix.

Not knowing what else to do at this point, Felix silently let the young man follow him, gather their gear, and leave. Felix also sent Julian and Ethan home, while he sat in his small office corner and stared at the water.

Hadlee's stoicism and resignation bothered him. It felt as if he had broken something precious and beautiful. The voice that had spilled all his frustrations last night was silent as the rest of his mind mourned. He wasn't even quite sure what he was mourning. Hadlee's affection? The contentment he had felt in her presence? The possible future filled with her special brand of sweetness?

Whatever it was, it left a gaping hole in his heart and for the first time since last night, his anger was quiet enough that Felix began to think that he'd made a very grave mistake.

CHAPTER 21

Hadlee held back a groan when she and Chrissy bumped into each other yet again. Her neck was burning from the sun, she was tired of working in such a cramped area, and they still had two weeks to go in these conditions.

"Sorry," Chrissy said as she readjusted herself to be out of the way.

"No worries," Hadlee said. "It was my fault." She tried for a smile, though it probably looked as wrong as it felt. "We're all just doing the best we can."

Chrissy nodded and went back to work.

Hadlee was grateful her TA didn't say anything else. All three of her workers had spent the last week asking multiple questions about why they were in a new boat and what had happened between her and Captain Mendez, but Hadlee had refused to answer. Vague explanations didn't go very far when one was working with curious scientists.

They had given up pressing her in the last couple of days, however, for which Hadlee was grateful. Her strength was waning with each passing day and so was her patience. If they made it through the next couple of weeks without killing each other, it would be a miracle.

"Not again." Luke groaned.

Hadlee looked up. "Something happen?"

Luke snorted and threw up his hands. "The line is cut."

She frowned. "What?" Standing up, Hadlee walked over to the corner of the boat where Luke was reaching in with a hook to grab the crab trap. Along with the boat, they'd rented a few to set out to continue their research. It wasn't as good as the dozen that Captain Mendez had, but at least it allowed them to keep working. "Are you sure?"

Luke gave her a wry look. "I think I know a broken rope when I see one."

Joshua came up behind her. "Let me see the hook."

Luke huffed and handed it over before stepping back with his arms folded over his chest.

Hadlee followed suit and stepped back to let Joshua have room to work. After a couple of tries, it was clear to see that Luke was right. The rope was not there.

"I'll grab my suit," Luke grumbled, twisting his shoulders in order to work his way past the crowd.

Hadlee plopped down on the bench, practically melting in the muggy air. She wiped her forehead, cringing at the amount of sweat on her hand. "I can't believe they did it again," she murmured. "How did they know which ones were ours?"

Joshua joined her, taking a swig of his water bottle. "I don't know. Someone had to have been watching us." He shook his head. "What I don't get is why they keep believing we're trying to shut them down, even though you've told them over and over again that we're not."

Hadlee shook her head as well. "I don't know. For some reason, they refuse to believe me."

He rubbed his hand over his hair. "It doesn't make sense."

Hadlee didn't answer. There was nothing she could see that would make it better. If the saboteurs were back up to their old tricks, there was little she could do, though she did plan to bring it up to Captain Wamsley when they docked in a couple of hours. Her job was already hard enough as it was. She didn't need the fishermen of the town making it worse at the moment.

"Think I need the tank?" Luke asked as he zipped up his wetsuit.

Joshua looked over the side. "It's not that deep, so probably not."

Luke nodded. "Be back in a sec." Sitting on the edge of the boat, he tugged on his fins, then fell backward into the water.

As the bubbles from his drop disappeared, a wind slapped Hadlee in the face, causing her hair to fly into her eyes. "Whoa," she muttered, re-pulling her hair into a ponytail. "Where did that come from?"

"Oh!" Chrissy gasped, frantically trying to grab some papers as they were picked up in the strong breeze.

"Ah, geez." Hadlee jumped to her feet and rushed over to help. She breathed a sigh of relief as a cool feeling swept over her back and neck. A cloud must have passed in front of the sun, giving them all a slight reprieve.

"Hadlee?"

She looked back at Joshua. "Yeah?"

"I think we're in trouble." He pointedly looked in the distance and Hadlee realized things had gotten very dark.

She glanced at the sky and her mouth went slack. Dark angry clouds were rushing over the horizon, coming directly toward them.

A splash caught everyone's attention. "Can't find the rope," Luke gasped, treading water. "Hang on, I'll look again."

"No, wait!" Hadlee pinched her lips when Luke was gone before she could stop him.

"He'll only be a minute," Chrissy said in her soft tone. "As soon as he's back, we'll get him in and head out."

Her voice was calm, but Hadlee could see Chrissy's worry in her wide eyes. "You're right," Hadlee said in a calmer tone than she felt. She was the one in charge here and needed to keep a cool head. "Let's start to close things up so we can get moving as soon as Luke gets back up here."

Joshua began dumping specimens overboard while Chrissy and Hadlee gathered up all the paperwork. The wind was only gaining speed and the job was more difficult than it should have been.

"Guys!"

Hadlee practically leapt to the side of the boat where Luke was floating.

"Here." He tried handing her the rope.

"Forget the trap," Hadlee said. She ushered Joshua over. "We have a storm coming. We've got to go now."

Luke pulled his goggles over his head and glanced at the sky. "Yikes. Get me out of this water." He swam to the back of the boat and Joshua helped him get seated before taking off his flippers and coming onto the deck.

"Secure the supplies!" Hadlee shouted as the strong breeze became a true wind. It was beginning to wail and the boat rocked as the waves began to grow stronger. "Joshua! Get the engine going. We need to move toward shore."

Joshua pushed his way past the rest of the crew and went to the dash.

Turning her attention away from him, Hadlee went back to helping Luke, then Chrissy get everything put away. They had just tucked the last of the papers away when raindrops began to hit her face. "Joshua!" she said. "Why aren't we moving?"

"It won't start!" he shouted back. Fear was palpable in his voice, causing Hadlee to turn to look at him.

"What!" she screeched. Her carefully cultivated cool was gone. She rushed to his side. "What do you mean, it won't start?"

Joshua demonstrated by turning the key, which sputtered only a second before dying. "I mean...It. Won't. Start."

"How is that possible?" she whispered hoarsely. Hadlee frantically began to study the dash, reading all the gauges, before coming to a screeching halt. "The gas," she whispered, almost inaudibly.

"What?" Joshua leaned over her shoulder.

Hadlee pointed to the gas gauge, unable to speak.

Joshua cursed and rubbed the top of his head. "How are we out of gas? It doesn't make sense. Shouldn't they have filled it this morning?"

Hadlee nodded. "They should have." She pinched her lips together. "Somehow, I'm guessing this has something to do with the same people who cut our ropes."

The boat shifted and they both had to hold onto the dash to keep from falling over.

"Whoever did this better hope I never find them," Joshua said through clenched teeth. "Because I'm going to kill them."

Only if we aren't killed first, Hadlee thought, but refused to say that out loud. Her thoughts were immediately followed by a prayer. She had three people in her stewardship and right now, she was going to need all the help she could get.

FELIX AWOKE FROM HIS nap with a snort when the front door slammed open.

"Felix Edward Mendez!"

"Charli." He groaned, flopping back on the couch. "What are you doing here?" Felix grumbled, rubbing his eyes.

"Kicking my brother's butt," she snapped, marching in and standing in front of him with her hands on her hips.

"Oh, is that all?" Felix rolled his eyes and grabbed the couch pillow. "Maybe you could wait until I'm done sleeping, huh?" He paused when a crack of thunder broke nearly overhead. "Whoa. When did that blow in?"

"Forecast said it was supposed to miss us," Charli said, her voice more solemn. "But here it is." She glared at him. "And the one you let get away is out in it."

Felix frowned, taking a moment to let her words penetrate. Once they did, he jumped to his feet. "Hadlee is out in this?"

Charli raised a single eyebrow. "Yes. Her boat hasn't come back in." Charli shook her head. "I'm surprised you care after throwing her away."

"I didn't throw her away," he growled, marching to the closet to grab his raincoat.

"That's not what I heard."

"I don't really care what you heard, Char," Felix said. "You weren't there." *But she's right.* He'd spent the last week regretting everything. Humility was truly a bitter pill to swallow, but the recognition that he was also a straight up bully was another. It was the main reason he hadn't tried to go talk to Hadlee again.

He was a coward and he didn't deserve her at all.

When the ropes had been cut, he'd become a mess. Every fear and frustration he'd from the situation had come bubbling into words and each one had been directed right at Hadlee. He could still see her stoic face as he declared that he wasn't supposed to fall for her. She'd taken his rant with grace, the same way she did everything, and then calmly walked away, even though Felix had just taken her heart and done his best to grind it into shark bait.

What was worse was how his memory kept reminding him of how hurt she was about her father's dismissive behavior, and that of her colleagues at work. They treated her as if she was worth nothing. Felix had done his best to counteract their treatment, but in one swift moment, he'd ruined it all.

And it had cost him any chance at a happy future he'd had.

"No...but Ken was."

Felix paused, then slowly turned around. "I know," he said softly. "I was wrong, okay? You want me to say it? I'm an idiot. A jerk. And other words that our mom would wash out my mouth for, but right now, none of that matters. Hadlee's in danger and I need to help."

Charli shook her head and huffed. "Ken asked me to come get you, since you weren't answering your phone, but I'll be honest. I don't think you'll be of any help. I hope Hadlee slaps your face when she sees you again."

"I'd take it," Felix grumbled, pulling on his coat. "At least that would mean she's safe and close by."

Charli rolled her eyes and shook her head. "Come on, you sorry piece of chum. Ken's waiting at the harbor."

Felix tapped his foot impatiently as Charli drove. The rain was starting to come down quite heavily now and the storm was in full swing. Lightning flashed often in the distance and the thunder rumbled in response. He tried to pay attention to how quickly the noise came after the lightning, but his mind was racing too rapidly for him to think straight.

"Just a word of warning," Charli said. "No killing anyone when we get there."

Felix frowned as she paused and pulled into the parking lot. "What do you mean?"

Charli pointed through the windshield.

Felix followed her finger and his frown turned into a scowl. Harry, George, and a few other fishermen were gathered around Ken's large frame. Everyone appeared to be talking as their arms were waving wildly through the air. Knowing immediately that the men had something to do with Hadlee's lack of return to the dock, Felix leapt out of the SUV.

"Careful, Felix," Charli called after him. "It was your temper that got you in this problem in the first place."

Her words hit home and Felix's stomping faltered. Closing his eyes, he took in a deep breath, pulled his hood over his head, and then continued walking up to the group.

"It was that professor!" Harry shouted. "He's the one who told us she was trouble."

Ken shook his head. "What I still don't get is why you listened!" Ken shouted back. "You took the word of a man you didn't know over the word of the woman who was right in front of you."

Harry hung his head. "I know," he said, his voice barely audible over the wind. "He was Cole's nephew, but we never meant for it to go this far."

"What's going on?" Felix said. His voice was rough, though he was doing his best to stay in control. His anger must have been evident since all heads snapped in his direction.

"Thank heavens," Ken breathed. He slapped a hand on Felix's shoulder. "Hadlee and her team are still out on the water in that dinky little thing they rented."

"Charli told me that. What I don't understand is what Harry had to do with it."

Harry deflated even more. "We cut the lines on her traps," he said. "It was meant to slow down her work."

"And?" Ken prompted.

"And we drained the gas from her boat."

Felix's eyes bugged out. "She's out of gas! In this storm! What were you thinking?" he shouted.

Harry winced. "The storm was supposed to miss us. We knew someone would eventually find her, but we wanted to send a warning."

"So you left a woman and three college kids out in the middle of the ocean with no way to get back in. Wow, Harry. That's something to be really proud of."

"I'm sorry!" Harry shouted back. "We shouldn't have done it. But we had no idea the storm was coming and that professor convinced us that it was us or her. Who do you think we're going to pick?"

"I think you should have taken the time to find out the truth," Felix ground out. "Just which professor was it that convinced you all to possibly kill a group of innocent people?" If it was Hadlee's father like he'd suspected previously, Felix knew he would do something he would ultimately regret. That man didn't deserve his daughter.

Harry's shoulders drooped. "Uh...Christian Sumner. He's Cole's nephew."

Felix grit his teeth. That was the bozo whom the board kept using to threaten Hadlee into submission. If given the opportunity, Felix would see that man disgraced and fired. He dismissed the other men and turned to Ken. "I'm gonna take *Morwenna* out. Does anyone know where her last location was?"

Ken shook his head. "They said the traps were a couple miles south, but I have no way of knowing if she was near the traps when she ran out of gas."

"It's a place to start," Felix muttered. "Have you called the Coast Guard?"

Ken nodded. "Yeah. They're working on it." He frowned. "I called you down here so you knew what was going on, not because I wanted you to go out. I don't need two lost boats right now."

Felix shook him off. "She needs me," he said. "I already lost her once. I can't do it again."

"It's not a good idea," Ken warned.

"No...but it's the only one I've got."

CHAPTER 22

"**H**ANG ON!" Hadlee screamed as the boat tipped dangerously to the side once more.

The crew held tighter to the areas of the boat they were already burrowed in. Each person had done their best to find a space where they could hunker down and ride out the storm, but with each rogue wave, Hadlee grew more and more worried that it wasn't going to be enough. She had no idea how far they'd drifted off course and with the storm, her phone wasn't working, so she doubted anyone had any way of finding them. The only thing in their favor at the moment was the fact that they all had lifejackets, but if they were knocked into the ocean, she wasn't sure they would be enough.

Not to mention I've probably lost all my research.

The loose papers had become less important when their lives were on the line, so Hadlee had quit trying to save them in favor of keeping her team safe. Her computer was tucked into one of the bench seats, but everything was so wet at this point that she doubted it had survived either, but only time would tell.

"We've got to do something," Joshua shouted over the wind.

Hadlee clenched her jaw. She agreed, but what could they do? "I'm out of ideas," she admitted.

Joshua nodded. His calm demeanor was one she was extremely grateful for at the moment, especially since every single one of her TA's was probably thinking about how this smacked reminiscent of her last research trip. She'd been caught in a storm, although less frightening than this one, with a boat full of workers.

Just like today, the storm had come on suddenly and hadn't been on the forecast that morning. Unlike today, Hadlee had been in a large boat, one that was able to handle the storm well enough until they got into shore. It hadn't been pretty, but no one had been in any true danger, though a few of the researchers had been shaken by the experience.

And here she was again. She didn't know how they had missed the fact that the gas was low, but whether it was her own negligence or the mistake of the people who rented her the boat, it wouldn't matter to her constituents. She knew without a shadow of a doubt that the board would more than likely fire her when she got back.

With a mental force Hadlee didn't realize she still had in her current state of exhaustion, Hadlee pushed the worries aside. She didn't have time to worry about her research, her career, or even her future. Right now she needed to focus on keeping her team alive and getting them out of this situation.

"Has everyone tried their phones?" Hadlee asked. She had checked her own, but she realized she hadn't asked the whole team to check their signals.

"No signal!" Luke shouted from his corner.

"Same here," Chrissy screamed.

Hadlee met Joshua's dark eyes and he shook his head, indicating his was the same way. She blew out a long breath. "Okay." She chewed her bottom lip and tried to think of another way. Their little boat didn't have radio access, so that wasn't helpful. "OARS!" she cried. "Has anyone looked for emergency oars?"

"HANG ON!" Luke cried.

Hadlee turned her head away from the water as it came sloshing over the side, choking her for a second as her whole head was enveloped in the wave. She sputtered, gasping as the water retreated. "Well?" she called out.

"I didn't look," Joshua said. When no one else responded, Hadlee assumed no one had.

"Okay, let's check the benches," she said. "It's the best bet we have for emergency supplies."

A scrambled search, filled with slipping and sliding and cursing, began as everyone tore apart the benches looking for anything that might help them in the situation.

"Found two!" Luke yelled triumphantly, holding one in the air.

"DROP!" Joshua's deep voice bellowed.

Luke hit the deck, still clutching the oar, and Chrissy screamed when his body slid from one side of the boat to the other.

Joshua grabbed Luke's leg and held on until the wave had settled for the moment. Hadlee whispered a prayer of thanksgiving that they'd made it through yet another wave.

"Over here," she called to Luke, asking for the oars. She held them to her chest as if they were the greatest treasure in the world. A strong shiver rocked her body and Hadlee was reminded of how cold she was at the moment. If she wasn't careful, she would become hypothermic. A quick glance at Chrissy showed her small body shaking even harder than Hadlee. *Dear Lord, help us get out of this. I don't care about my job or myself. But help me save my team.*

After riding out another wave, Hadlee handed Joshua one oar and she took the other. "Let's do the best we can to paddle between waves and try to at least get closer to shore."

"Which way is shore?" Luke asked, voicing the question Hadlee didn't want to address.

The truth was, she didn't know. They were so lost at the moment, she had no idea which way would actually help them find help.

"The wind was blowing south," Joshua said, wiping water from his face. "Unless it changed direction, land should be to the east." He pointed to the right side of the boat and Hadlee was so relieved she could have kissed him. *Yeah...kissing has already gotten you in enough trouble,* she scolded. *Just get to work.*

                    LAURA ANN

The next ten minutes were filled with shouts as they tried to move the boat in between wave hits, but it was proving impossible. Two small oars were just not enough against the wild ocean. Even if they weren't being swallowed by a storm, they would have made very little progress, but with the waves as strong as they were and with them having to stop every couple of minutes to hold on, it just wasn't working.

"We aren't getting anywhere," Hadlee said, depression sinking into her gut like a ship anchor.

Joshua let out a string of expletives and threw the oar onto the floor of the boat. It was the first real sign of outrage he had shown, and it let Hadlee know everyone was losing hope.

"What's that?" Luke asked, shading his eyes from the rain. "A LIGHT!" he screamed. "It's a light!"

Hadlee turned and got a faceful of water for her efforts. Once she could breathe again, she squinted into the dark, her heart pounding even harder than before. "HEY!" she screamed, waving her arms in the air. Logically, she knew whatever was behind the light wouldn't be able to see her, but the temptation to try was too strong. "OVER HERE!" she screamed so loudly her throat felt raw.

Her team joined her and soon Joshua and Luke were also shouting and waving their arms.

A loud noise, like a gun, had all three of them ducking to the deck just as another wave swept over them. The boat tilted heavily again and it was at least thirty seconds before Hadlee could pick her head up enough to try and see what had made the noise. Her first concern was that some part of the boat had broken, but instead, she found Chrissy huddled against the dash of the boat, a smoking flare gun in her hands.

Chrissy was shaking so hard Hadlee could hear her teeth chattering. "I found it in the bench," she said, right before her eyes rolled back in her head and her tiny body crumpled.

"CHRIS!" Luke scrambled across the deck and grabbed the woman, holding her gently in his arms. "She's breathing," he called out. "Just fainted."

"Hold her close," Hadlee said. "She's too cold."

Luke nodded and brought her into his chest.

"Give me the gun." Joshua reached out and took it, studying it. "We should look for another flare."

Hadlee nodded and together they ransacked the benches once more. *Please, please, please...*she begged. *Let us find just one more thing...*

FELIX'S KNUCKLES WERE white as he held onto the wheel, trying to keep the boat under control in the heavy waves of the storm. He was heading south, trying to stay the same distance from the shoreline as he had taken her on when they were working together. He was hoping she followed a similar pattern to their previous outings. In fact, he was counting on it. It was the only thing he had to go on.

His radio was tuned into the Coast Guard and he was hoping to hear some good news. There was no way he could sit on the sidelines and do nothing, but he was fully aware that their equipment had a better chance of finding Hadlee than he did.

"See anything?" Ken shouted as he slipped in the door of the wheelhouse.

Felix shook his head. He was grateful to have a friend with him, but it just meant one more person who was in danger because of him. This whole situation was his fault. Yes, Harry was responsible for the fact that her boat didn't have enough gas, but if Felix hadn't been so horrible to her, if he hadn't let his fears control his tongue, if he had given into the fact that he had fallen in love instead of shattering the best thing that had ever happened to him, then Hadlee wouldn't be out in a too small vessel in the middle of a vicious storm where the lives of herself and her team were all in danger.

"Don't worry," Ken said, squeezing Felix's shoulder. "We'll find her. Someone will."

Felix nodded, but couldn't bring himself to speak. He hadn't cried since he was a little boy, but right now, he was afraid if he opened his mouth, every emotion he was holding back would come spilling out faster than the waves beating the deck. A crashing came from below and he winced. Who knew how many things were going to be broken by the time he got back to the harbor?

"Crap," Ken shouted as the boat tilted dangerously, then rocked back and forth as it righted itself from the rogue wave. "How do you do this all the time without getting seasick?" he asked from the corner he was using to stay upright.

Felix's legs were planted wide, and for the most part, he was able to keep his position, though there were times it was difficult. That last wave had probably swept anything that was moderately loose off the deck. "Practice." Ge grunted. Though he wasn't out in storms often, Felix had spent enough time on the water to have developed a good set of sea legs and a stomach of iron. It was a necessity for anyone wanting to make their living on the sea. Adapt or die.

"We have a sighting," a voice crackled over the radio. Felix snapped to attention, listening to the mumbled coordinates.

"Where are they?" Ken asked breathlessly.

"We're going in that direction already," Felix said. "We should be there in about three minutes." He refused to let himself feel relief yet. One, he wasn't sure the boat they'd spotted was actually Hadlee and two, even if it was, no one knew what kind of shape the team would be in by the time they were rescued.

The boat rocked again and Ken cursed some more as his shoulder was thrown into the wall. "I'm going to blame you for the bumps and bruises that will be covering my body," he grumbled.

"Fair," Felix said, his mind only partly on what Ken was talking about. He was too busy peering into the dark and wishing he had Superman vision. *There.* Up ahead, it looked like lights, though with all the rain, it was hard to tell for sure.

"I think I see them," Ken said, coming back up behind Felix.

"Me too." The men were silent as the *Morwenna* worked her way closer. The radio crackled again and it took a few repeats before Felix realized they were talking to him.

"Who are you? Do you need help?"

Felix picked up the radio. "This is Captain Felix Mendez of the *Morwenna*. We're searching for a lost boat from Seaside Bay and heard you found a rescue." He waited impatiently for the reply. His heart felt as if it would pound through his ribcage and sweat was trickling down his back despite the fact that it was a cold night on the water.

"You should turn back and let the professionals handle this," the man said on the other line.

"Did you pick up a Dr. Hadlee Ford?" Felix persisted.

"Are you family?"

Felix grit his teeth and was about to say something snappy back, but Ken grabbed the handheld. "This is Captain Kenneth Wamsley, Seaside Police. I'm the one who called in the missing boat and crew. Can I get a report on your find?"

"Captain, you should know better than to venture out into weather like this."

"I know, sir, but there are extenuating circumstances." Ken gave Felix an apologetic look.

"The boat has four people on it," the man on the other line finally responded. "That's all I can tell you."

"It's her," Felix murmured, holding his ground through yet another wave.

Ken frowned but nodded. "Can you confirm anything else for me? Their families will be worried if I don't have any other news."

"One woman has been identified as the one you are looking for. The rest will have to wait."

"Thank you, sir."

"Do you need an escort back to Seaside?" The man sounded frustrated and Felix couldn't blame him, but if the Coast Guard thought they were leaving now that he knew Hadlee was in that boat, they had another thing coming.

Felix adamantly shook his head and he and Ken had a staredown before Ken finally shook his head in resignation. "No. We'll be following you into shore. Where's the nearest harbor?"

"We're just north of Florence, and our station is located there. We'll keep an eye on you."

"Thanks," Felix muttered, ramping up his engine to get moving again in the shifting water. His engine grew loud as he turned in the churning water in order to follow the larger Coast Guard into shore.

The next thirty minutes were tense. Though he was able to follow, it was the unknown that kept Felix on edge. The rain was starting to die down, but the swells were still strong. It was the possible condition of Hadlee and her team, however, not the water, that had Felix wishing they could hurry.

Was she hypothermic? In shock? Had anyone been hurt or thrown overboard? The Coast Guard said there were four people, but that didn't mean there weren't injuries or illnesses to consider.

Ken must have noticed Felix's anxiety because he once again squeezed his friend's shoulder. "They've got her. She'll be fine now. Probably just needs some hot tea and a warm bath."

"One can only hope," Felix managed to respond. He planned to be there to make sure she was okay, but past that point, he didn't know what to do. Would Hadlee even want to see him? Would she be angry he had come? Angry he had broken up with her? Would she curse him out and send him packing? Would she be willing to hear his apology and subsequent begging?

And he was willing to beg. Even if it was only for the chance to see she was okay, Felix would get down on his knees and do whatever groveling it took to get that information. Anything else was going to be left in Hadlee's probably very wet and cold hands.

CHAPTER 23

Another shiver rocked Hadlee's body, but she refused to sit down just yet. She needed to make sure her TA's were taken care of before she could even think about taking time for herself.

"Please, miss," the medical assistant said, rushing after her. "You need to sit down."

"In a minute," Hadlee slurred. She wavered on her feet and the assistant helped stabilize her. "My team," she whispered, gripping the table in front of her.

"The other passengers are fine," the assistant assured her. "The only one we need to take care of is you." She pulled on Hadlee's arm and Hadlee had no energy to resist. They stumbled their way back to the cot Hadlee was supposed to be sitting on and Hadlee fell into it. "Here we go." The assistant wrapped a blanket around Hadlee's shoulders. "Go ahead and let's lie down."

Hadlee's muscles slowly began to melt into the firm surface and her heavy eyes began to close.

"Hang on," the assistant said. "I need to take your vitals." The room began to spin and the floor heaved. The assistant threw out her arms and held onto the wall until the boat settled again.

"I'm gonna hurl," Luke moaned from his own cot.

The assistant's head jerked in that direction. "Hang on!" she shouted, rushing over to grab a basin before Luke lost what precious little was in his stomach.

Hadlee's eyelids grew heavier and heavier until she could no longer keep them open. The blanket on her wasn't enough to keep off the chill since her clothes were still wet and her body shook so hard, her cot was shaking with her. Curling onto her side, Hadlee tucked her knees into her chest and tried to create a little body heat, but it was as if there was none left to generate.

Without her permission, her mind drifted to a time when she was overly warm, and with it came the face of a man who stole her breath. Felix's very presence, whether he was touching her or not, had always warmed her from the inside out. He radiated heat like a furness and on more than one chilly evening, he had shared that heat with her when they were cuddling on the couch, or simply holding hands and talking.

The familiar pain nearly crushed her chest and Hadlee gasped at the intensity of it. She was so cold at the moment it was a miracle she could feel anything at all, but apparently heartache didn't care if you were battling hypothermia or not.

The pain couldn't have come at a worse time. Her body and mind were too fatigued to fight the memories and soon her mind's eye was flooded with them. Felix standing straight and tall at the wheel of his boat. Him offering a strong hand. His smirk or smile when he enjoyed something. The deep rumbling laughter that seemed to fit his broody personality. The softness in his eyes when he leaned in to kiss her...

It was too much. Hadlee's eyes filled with tears and she had to fight for her breath, which was coming in hard gasps. She'd worked so hard to be too busy this last week to think on all that she had lost, but now it was coming back with a vengeance.

What's worse is that I not only lost Felix, I've more than likely lost everything.

Would there be anyone waiting for her when she finally got off this boat? Or at the hospital they were probably being transferred to? Would her father care that she had almost lost her life? Or would he blame it on her foolish behavior?

Her mind refused to quiet and Hadlee found herself feeling out of control as she did her best to hide her sobs and shaking. Now that her TA's were being taken care of, Hadlee had a fleeting thought that she really had nothing else to live for. Her career was shot, her family was distant, and the man she loved had thrown her away in exchange for his freedom. *Why even try anymore? Maybe it's time I realized just how worthless I really am. Everyone around me has been telling me that for years. Why haven't I listened?*

Squeezing her eyes tight, she held on through the shaking and the tipping of the boat. As she slipped into deep unconsciousness, her last clear thought was that if God wanted to go ahead and take her now, she wouldn't argue with him. *I just hope heaven is warm...*

A consistent high-pitched beep broke into Hadlee's broken dreams and pulled her into wakefulness. Her eyes were still like bricks, so she didn't open them to see where she was, but judging by the smells and sounds, she had obviously been moved into a hospital. It made sense after the disaster of a research trip she'd just had.

The next thing she noticed was that she was weighed down by a comforting weight and her body was no longer shaking. It was a welcome feeling. Apparently warmth did exist and somehow the medical care providers had been able to bring her temperature back up to normal ranges.

Her third thought was the one that finally broke through the haze of full wakefulness as she wondered what had happened to Chrissy, Luke, and Josh. With a jolt, her eyes opened and she tried to sit up.

"Whoa!" came a deep voice from her right.

The voice was vaguely familiar, but Hadlee's mind was set on one thing, so she didn't worry about it. "Chrissy," she breathed, still struggling to get up. "Where are Luke and Josh?"

"Shhh..." the deep voice continued. The person's large hands pressed down on her shoulders. "They're fine, Hadlee. Everyone is fine. You're the last one to wake up. Your crew was cold, wet, and bordering on hypothermia, but everyone is fine and already on their feet."

She quit fighting and sunk back into the bed. "That's good," she whispered, drained of energy from the scant moments of struggle. Blinking heavily, she focused her eyes on her informant and another gasp slipped through. "Felix," she breathed. "What are you doing here?"

He winced at her question and Hadlee immediately felt guilty. She hadn't meant to be rude, but when a person was sitting at your hospital bed, it probably wasn't kosher to question their presence. She automatically opened her mouth to apologize, but stopped herself. *No. It was a valid question. He made himself clear the other day and I don't understand why he would be here. Or why the hospital would call him.*

"You're awake!" a perky nurse said, walking through the door. "Welcome back." The pretty woman sauntered over with a wide smile. She began looking through the machines that Hadlee was hooked up to and pushing buttons. "You were out for quite a while," the brunette said with a laugh. "Did you have a nice nap?"

Hadlee was positive the nurse was trying to start a friendly, teasing conversation, but she definitely wasn't in the mood. "How long was I asleep?" she asked before clearing her throat. She could really use a drink, but as she watched the nurse wink at Felix, Hadlee wanted nothing more than for the woman to be gone. Jealousy she had no right to feel was slithering up her spine and it was difficult to push back. She'd take dehydration any day if it meant getting the woman out of her room.

"Here," Felix said softly, holding a straw to her lips.

Hadlee turned her eyes to his, and opened her mouth at his prodding. If her arms had any strength, she would have taken the plastic mug from him, but even trying to lift them resulted in her whole body shaking. Apparently, cold oceans and crazy thunderstorms were energy suckers. "Thank you," Hadlee whispered once done. The cool liquid was exactly what she needed, but it was the look in Felix's eyes that called to her. She couldn't quite tell what he was thinking, but whatever it was, it was pulling her in like a whirlpool in the middle of the ocean.

"About ten hours." The nurse interrupted their moment with her answer to Hadlee's question. "Once your temperature was under control and you were still sleeping, the doctors felt like they should let you wake naturally." She smiled again. "Sometimes all our bodies need is a blanket and a nap. I'm envious." With another wink, the woman walked out the door.

FELIX BARELY NOTICED when the nurse left the room. He couldn't seem to drag his eyes from Hadlee's pale face. Purple half-moons were under her eyes and green veins could be seen through the skin on her arms as if her entire body had become translucent from the trauma of the last twenty-four hours.

Hadlee's soft gray eyes came back to his once they were alone and the question she asked earlier hung in the air between them. He supposed he owed her an explanation...and an apology...but he wasn't sure how to break the barrier. He had barely slept, sitting on the hard couch in the corner as she lay unconscious in the bed. Her small body looked broken, though she had only come out with a few bruises and cuts from the ordeal.

"How did you know I was here?" she asked softly.

Felix cleared his throat and rubbed the back of his neck. "I, uh, was looking for you."

Her eyes widened. "What do you mean? You weren't out in the storm, were you?"

He hesitated, but ultimately nodded. Lying to both himself and her was what had gotten Felix into this tough spot, and he vowed he wouldn't do it again.

"Why?" she breathed. "Why would you do that?"

How much could he tell her? What would she be willing to hear? There were several answers of varying degrees, though all were true. He didn't want to scare her by sharing too much, but he didn't want to lose her further by not sharing enough. He shrugged. "What would any man do when the woman he loves was in danger?"

Crap.

He hadn't meant to be quite so telling, and the pregnant pause between them was exactly why. She wasn't ready to hear what he had to say. It would have been smarter to work up to it.

"I don't understand." Her voice trembled and he watched her grip the blanket in a tight fist.

Felix blew out a breath and grabbed a chair, setting it next to the bed. This was going to be a long...overdue...chat. "Maybe we need to go back a little."

She nodded jerkily.

"George, Harry, and a couple other fishermen came to Ken when the storm came up because they knew you were in trouble," he explained.

Hadlee's jaw grew tight. "They're why I ran out of gas, aren't they?"

Felix nodded regretfully. "They siphoned it out before you left for the morning, hoping to keep you from completing your work."

Hadlee turned away from him, but Felix still saw the single tear that slipped down her cheek. He started to move toward her, but forced himself back down. He hadn't earned the right to touch her, and at this point, he wasn't sure if he ever would.

"Well, they did it," she said hoarsely. "Everything was lost in the storm, so their goal was accomplished."

Felix didn't have any answer to that, though he found himself mourning for all her work. This might not have been her dream job, but he knew Hadlee well enough to know that it still meant something to her. She was the type to put her heart into everything she did and that included trying to help the stupid baby crabs off the coast. "Once Ken understood what was going on, he called me." Felix made a face. "Well, he tried to reach me, but, uh, my phone was off. So he called Charli, who came over and told me what was going on."

Hadlee continued staring at the far wall, but nodded to let him know she was listening.

Hoping to break through her wall, he decided to share how Charli had basically cussed him out. "Charli took me to task for being such an idiot and then together we rushed down to the docks."

Hadlee scoffed. "I'm sorry to be such another burden to you, Captain Mendez."

Shoot. That was NOT what I meant. "Hadlee." He waited until she glanced sideways at him. "Charli didn't have to convince me to help. Her job was to wake me up, but even that was ultimately unnecessary." He sighed. "I've been drowning in misery for the past week and the names she called me were nothing compared to what I was calling myself."

Hadlee turned her head more fully and scrunched her eyebrows together.

Felix leaned forward, resting a hand on the side of her bed, and continued. "Anyway, Ken told me what was going on and I immediately headed for the *Morwenna*."

"So...what? You felt guilty?" She shook her head. "That wasn't necessary. Did the *Morwenna* get damaged at all? It's my fault you were out there, so I'll pay for it."

Felix pinched his lips together. She wasn't getting it. "It doesn't matter, Hadlee. I don't care if the boat made it to shore in pieces. None of it is worth more than you are."

She leaned back as much as it was possible, as if trying to get away from him.

Felix leaned in. He wasn't willing to let her misinterpret his words. "I owe you much more than just trying to find you in a storm, Hadlee. But I need to start with an apology."

"No," she whispered. "That isn't necessary."

"I'm sorry." He wasn't going to listen to her protests. He had hurt her. He got it. If her pain had been anything close to his this past week, then it was a wonder she hadn't already asked for him to be kicked out of her room. "I'm sorry I let my fears overrun my good sense. I'm sorry I said a bunch of lies, trying to convince you and myself that they were true. I'm sorry I said you were a mistake. I'm sorry I degraded everything that had happened between us." He swallowed, trying to clear the lump in his throat. "And most of all...I'm sorry I made it seem like anything in my life, my freedom or my career, was worth more than you were."

Hadlee blinked rapidly and turned toward the ceiling, obviously fighting a strong emotion. She didn't speak to him and Felix stopped as well. Right now the ball was in her court. He'd given her an offering, and it would be up to her as to whether or not it was accepted.

"I...I need some time," she finally whispered, still not looking at him.

Despite knowing he didn't deserve anything more, the words still hurt. "I understand," he said. "I'll burrow myself in the corner."

"I'd rather you let me have some time to myself," she said.

Felix shook his head and stood up so he could look her in the eye. "I thought you were dead, Hadlee," he said. "I can't leave just yet, even if you choose not to ever forgive me. I'll sit back and not talk if that's what you want, but unless you call security, I can't leave yet. Please don't ask it of me."

Her chest was heaving as they stared at each other. The chemistry they had shared earlier sparked through the air and Felix felt his breath catch. The need to kiss her was almost more than he could bear, but he kept himself under control...barely. He had a long way to go before he could ask for something so precious again.

Pale lips opened and Felix waited with baited breath to see what she was going to say, but the entrance of her doctor made the energy fizzle like a balloon losing its helium. It only took three words to shatter everything they had been working towards. "How's our patient?"

CHAPTER 24

"Fine," Hadlee croaked, turning toward her new visitor. "Thank you."

The older doctor smiled and tapped at the table in his hands. "Let's just take a look at those vitals, huh?"

Hadlee waited quietly as he took her pulse and shined a light in her eyes, then checked her charts. "When can I go home?" she asked as he finished up.

The doctor's lips pursed as he read through her file. "Other than the fact that you're still somewhat dehydrated and will probably be exhausted for the next couple of days, I don't see anything that's keeping you here."

Hadlee let out a sigh of relief. "Great. Thank you."

The doctor glanced toward Felix. "Are you the one taking care of her when she's released?"

"Oh, no—"

"Of course," Felix said, sitting up straight in his seat. His dark eyes gave her a significant look to not argue before going back to the doctor.

Anger began to simmer. Hadlee wasn't quite sure what to think of Felix's apparent change of heart, but she did know one thing. She needed a little distance in order to think about things. She didn't like being cornered into accepting his help or forgiving him. She knew she wouldn't be able to hold a grudge forever—she absolutely *would* forgive him—but that didn't mean she had to trust him again, and it definitely didn't mean she had to be willing to re-enter a relationship with him. "No," she said firmly, turning to the surprised doctor. "I've got a room at a bed and breakfast. I can rest there for a few days before going home."

Soft blue eyes darted back and forth between Hadlee and Felix, but ultimately the doctor nodded. "As long as you have a ride there, then that should be just fine."

Hadlee nodded back. "It'll be taken care of, thank you."

The doctor gave her a kindly smile before turning to leave. "Excuse me," he said softly as he bumped into someone at the door.

It wasn't until the doctor was in the hallway that Hadlee was able to see who the doctor had run into. "Dad!"

Caleb Ford shuffled in, looking older than Hadlee had remembered him. "Oh, Haddie," he said, coming up to her bedside. Dark circles were under his eyes and his hair looked like his fingers had been his only comb for several weeks. "What happened, hon?"

Her eyes filled with tears at his concern. She hadn't known what her dad would do when they met again, and she certainly hadn't expected him to drive over to see her. Apparently she hadn't given her father enough credit, and that made her feel sick with guilt. "I'm sorry, Dad," she said. "It was an accident." She left off the fact that it was sabotage. If he was worried about her, then knowing the town had been trying to shut her down wouldn't be helpful.

Her father waved her words away. "I know, I know. I heard all about it." He sighed, the wrinkles on his brow growing deeper. "How are you feeling?"

She tilted her head back and forth. "Tired, but okay. I'm guessing I'm going to be sore for a while though."

He nodded with pursed lips, his fingers tapping on the side of her bed. She recognized the look on his face. He had something to say and Hadlee wasn't going to like it. Her earlier wariness began to come back. "That's good," he murmured, his eyes not meeting hers. "Good."

"What is it?"

"Hm?" His craggy face came up.

"What do you need to tell me?"

Caleb sucked in a breath through his teeth, looking at the wall before coming back to her own gaze. "I didn't want to say it quite yet..."

"Just tell me." Hadlee braced herself. It wasn't until she remembered that Felix was sitting in the corner quietly that she regretted pushing for answers. Maybe this was a conversation that was better had at home.

"The college board and department have already met about your...situation."

Hadlee clenched her teeth. She'd been expecting this, but that didn't make it any easier to say.

"Your judgment has been found...wanting," her dad continued. "They've terminated not only your research project, but your employment."

"I see," Hadlee said tightly. "And tell me, Dad...how did you vote?"

The resigned look on his face told Hadlee everything she needed to know. What a fool she was to think that his concerned look when he came in meant that he had changed his mind about her. Whoever said that facing death brought out people's true feelings obviously had never had a near death experience.

"Right." Her shaking hands smoothed her blanket as she refused to meet his eyes. She was too afraid of crying in front of him.

"Now, sweetheart, you know we've talked about how you're just not cut out for this type of work. We both knew you'd never last long."

"Leave." Felix's voice was dark and low, and it took both Hadlee and her father off guard.

"Who're you?" her dad asked, taking the glasses from his head to balance them on his nose in order to see better. "I've never seen you before."

"Captain Felix Mendez," Felix said tightly. "I captain the *Morwenna*, the ship Hadlee has been working on all summer."

Her father raised an eyebrow. "I see. And what right does that give you to tell me, her father, to leave?"

"Being a ship captain doesn't give me any authority," Felix said. "But let me make a couple of things clear. I'm the man who loves your daughter. And despite the fact that you've done a bang-up job of making her feel worthless, I'm also the man who is working to repair the damage."

Hadlee's breath whooshed out of her. She'd never heard anyone speak to her father that way before. As a long-time professor, he was always treated with deference and she had no idea how he would handle this kind of hostility.

"Now listen here," her father began.

"No. You listen." Felix's thighs were right up against her bed and he leaned forward, looming over her even though his attention was on her father. "From the moment your daughter arrived in my town, I knew she was something special. It was part of why I was so frustrated with her presence. I had planned to live the rest of my life footloose and fancy free, and seeing her threatened all that."

"What does this have to do with anything?" Her father tilted his head back to look better at Felix through his glasses.

"Patience, doctor," Felix said sarcastically. "Sometimes you have to listen to some research before you can make a clean judgment."

Hadlee's father huffed, but to her surprise, he nodded, obviously waiting for Felix to continue. She also turned to Felix. He had already told her he was sorry, but there was something about the story he was telling now that had her attention. During a time when she'd never felt so alone, having someone on her side was more welcome than she wanted to admit...even if it was the man that she wasn't sure she could ever take back, no matter what her heart wanted.

FELIX WAS LIVID, THOUGH he wasn't sure he had the right to be. Everything he was accusing Dr. Ford of, Felix himself had done as well. He knew he was being a hypocrite, but at least he was trying to fix what he'd done.

"Every wall I put up between us was slowly worn away by Hadlee's work ethic and consistently kind nature." He couldn't help but look down at her even while he was talking to her father. She needed to see that everything he spoke was the truth. "Brick by brick, she pulled me into her circle and let me into her life." He paused then, the emotions overcoming him. It was a new sensation for Felix. He rarely got emotional and when he did, it certainly wasn't with soft feelings.

"Get to the point, Captain," Dr. Ford said gruffly. "You claim to love my daughter, yet why was she out in a storm where she could have been seriously injured, let alone killed?"

"Dad!" Hadlee scolded. "It wasn't Felix's fault."

"It's okay," Felix said, rubbing her arm with his fingertips. He wanted to sigh at the contact, but they had company, and that would just be weird with her only living parent in the room. He looked back at Dr. Ford. "For most of the summer, your daughter was cruelly bullied by several of the older fishermen in our town."

"What?" Dr. Ford's arms fell to his sides.

"A Professor Summers from your college used a couple of contacts he had to spread rumors that Hadlee was here to shut down the crabbing industry with her research. You can imagine how threatened the men felt in our town who have spent their entire lives supporting their families from our fishing industry."

The doctor nodded, still looking stunned. Hadlee also looked surprised.

"Christian did that? He's the one who was talking to Harry?"

Felix's shoulders fell slightly. "Harry told us about it when he admitted to siphoning your gas. Apparently Christian is the nephew of Cole Summers, one of the men you met at the beach."

"Siphoning gas?" Dr. Ford growled. "Now what are you talking about?"

"The closer I grew to your daughter, the more she let me into her own life. Like telling me the board of your department treats her like a second-class citizen." Felix felt his nostrils flare. "And how her own father doesn't take her seriously, despite the fact that she raised three younger sisters, got her own college degree, ran your household, became a professor, and was very close to becoming the youngest Associate Professor you have at the college. All while you brushed her efforts off to the side and told her she wasn't cut out for the profession."

Dr. Ford opened his mouth, then snapped it shut.

That's right. You've got no defense, do you? "Now...I'll admit that I made my own mistakes." Felix relaxed his aggressive stance. It was time to come clean to both of them. "The more I fell in love with Hadlee, the more scared I grew." He blew out a breath. "I raised my own sister during her teenage years and she just recently got married. I was supposed to finally be free. I'd spent most of my adult life taking care of her and didn't want anything to do with being tied down to another person." He looked down again. "But Hadlee pulled at my heart in a way I'd never felt before."

He shook his head. "One night after the men of the town made me realize how little I was able to protect her, I snapped. I let my fears overcome my good sense, and in a few sharp words, I threw away everything we had because I was scared. I wasn't willing to take the risk of giving up myself in order to gain her."

Slowly, so she had time to pull away, Felix picked up her hand and cradled it in his own. "All that night, I worked to convince myself that I had made the right choice. That hurting her now was better than hurting her later. That we would both eventually be happier apart than we would be together. But I was wrong." He looked back at Dr. Ford, who was still standing silently, though his brows were now furrowed. "Then I spent the next week sinking farther and farther into depression while Hadlee behaved like the queen she is and put her work and teammates ahead of her own needs and hurt. While I lazed on my couch, she rented another boat and went about her work. The couple of interactions I had with her during that time, she was poised and kind despite how horribly I treated her."

"I'm failing to see how this has anything to do with the storm," Dr. Ford finally said, tucking his hands in his pockets. "While your story has been enlightening, it doesn't answer some of the key questions I had to begin with."

"I'm getting to that," Felix said wearily. This was proving to be more taxing than he'd thought. Who knew emotions could wear someone out? "Yesterday, Hadlee went out on the boat as usual. A storm had been on the radar, but the forecast showed that it would swing south, so no one took it seriously. However, what Hadlee didn't know was that those same men who had been giving her trouble had siphoned gas from her boat, hoping to send another message when she got stuck out on the water for a few hours. They figured it wouldn't last long, knowing the rental company would realize she hadn't come in as the sun went down. But they hoped it would scare her into wanting to stop the project."

Hadlee's bottom lip began to shake and she placed it between her teeth. The hand Felix still held gripped his back.

"No one could have predicted that the storm would come ashore rather than taking the path the weather forecast said," Felix said in a softer tone.

"So you're telling me that her life and that of her research team was put in jeopardy because Professor Summers spread a few rumors?" Dr. Ford looked livid.

It's about time, Felix thought, though he refrained from saying so. He shrugged. "More or less. That's how it began anyway." He straightened his shoulders. "But that's not the important part of this story," Felix continued. "The important part is that Hadlee has been thrown aside once again and none of it is her fault." His muscles began to tighten once more. "She is a wonderful, beautiful, intelligent, and most importantly, kind woman and doesn't deserve the disdain you and your colleagues have given her."

"It sounds like you need to add yourself to that mix," Dr. Ford snapped back.

"I did," Felix defended. "But at least I'm trying to apologize. I've seen my mistake and I'm trying to fix it. I have yet to see the same from you."

"Felix," Hadlee breathed. "You two need to stop this."

"And you can be sure that if she ever decides to let me back into her life, I'll see to it personally that she never sheds another tear thinking that she isn't worthwhile," Felix pressed on. "It will become my mission in life to prove to her just how amazing she is, whether or not anyone else sees it."

"Felix," she whispered again, only this time, the word held a different tone. It was softer and warmer and was absolute music to Felix's ears.

He pulled her hand up to his lips, pressing them to the skin on the back of her fingers. "I hadn't really planned to say all that in front of your dad, but..." He shrugged. "It seemed like the best way to get everything out in the open."

Hadlee was looking at him like he was her hero and it made Felix want to puff up like a peacock, though he worked to resist the urge. As they stared at each other, however, the familiar chemistry began to shimmer through the air, igniting their breaths and unconsciously pulling them closer together. Unlike earlier, when their attraction was wrought with tension, this moment felt much more welcome. She wasn't hiding her tears or holding herself back. She'd heard every word he said and Felix felt as if he had laid himself bare. If seeing him in all his imperfect glory wasn't enough to make her sail into the sunset, then he knew without a shadow of a doubt that falling in love with her was the wisest thing he'd ever done.

"I think you're pretty amazing as well," she said softly. A small, tired smile played on her lips and Felix focused on the movement. As if in a trance, he began to lean down, but a clearing throat paused his movements.

"He's still here, isn't he?" he asked, not backing up, but not pursuing his original line of intent.

She smiled wider and nodded. "Yes."

"If I kiss you, will he leave?"

She laughed softly. "I don't know if it will work that way."

Dr. Ford sighed long and loud. Felix didn't have to look up to see that the professor was not exactly happy with this turn of events. "I have a few calls to make," he huffed.

When his footsteps disappeared, Felix leaned close enough that he was sharing Hadlee's air. Closing his eyes, he breathed her in, knowing he would never feel satiated. He would never get enough of her, and finally, he was okay with that. "I'm sorry," he whispered, his lips brushing hers.

"I forgive you," she said, reaching up to meet his mouth, but Felix held back just a little longer.

"I really mean it, Hadlee," he pressed. "Everything I just spilled to your dad was the truth. I was an idiot, a jerk, a bully. I'm so sorry and I'll do everything I can—"

She let go of his hand and reached up to grip his shirt, stopping his continued apology. "Felix."

"Yes?"

"If you don't kiss me, you're going to be even more sorry than you already are."

He smiled, then closed his eyes and laughed. "Yes, ma'am," he said, giving her a small peck. "I definitely don't want any more guilt than I already have." With that, he took her mouth fully, but held back from getting too aggressive. She was still pale and weak, and would need plenty of rest before she was fully recovered.

With her permission, he planned to see she got everything she needed in order to be back to one hundred percent. And then...all bets would be off.

CHAPTER 25

"I'm *fine*, Felix," Hadlee said for what felt like the fiftieth time. She caught his hands to stop him from fluffing her pillows yet again. "Really. I'm fine."

Felix gave her a sheepish grin and put his hands in the air, then backed up from the bed. "Sorry. Just trying to—"

"Felix," she said softly. "I get it. You've apologized too many times, and I've told you I forgive you. So please...let it go."

He sat down on the edge of her bed and took her hand, playing with her fingers. The touch sent tiny electric sparks up Hadlee's arm. She had a feeling that his touch was better for her recovery than anything else the doctor could recommend. He made her feel alive and it brought into sharp contrast the last thoughts she had on the boat before they were rescued. She'd been ready to give up. It had felt like there was nothing left to live for, and she had been willing to give herself over to the darkness, but now she was grateful God had seen fit to keep her around a little longer.

Watching Felix stand up to her father and demand his apology had made her feel equal parts horror and admiration. No one argued with Dr. Caleb Ford. Hadlee, herself, had been walking on tiptoe around him for most of her life. Hanging up on him had been the most rebellious thing she'd ever done.

Thoughts of her dad brought a frown to face. He'd awkwardly left when Felix was waiting to kiss her, but he'd never come back. She had no idea what was going on with her father or the college board at the moment.

"Hey..." Felix's warm fingers pressed against the wrinkles on her forehead. "What's wrong?"

"Hm? Oh." Hadlee shook her head. "Nothing."

"Nope. That won't work." He leaned over until his face was right in front of hers. "No more pushing your feelings under the rug. Your thoughts are worth hearing."

She laughed softly, leaning back into the tower of pillows Felix had built. "If I told you every thought that went through my head, you'd be torn between being bored to death and running for the hills."

"Never."

Hadlee laughed again. "I was just thinking about Dad, wondering why he didn't come back." She frowned. "And I'm wondering if he bothered to tell the board about Christian. It's not like the law can touch him. All he did was talk to people. There's no crime in that."

Felix scowled and this time it was Hadlee who tried to smooth out the wrinkles. "Don't be offended, but I don't care where your dad went. If he wasn't willing to apologize, he has no business being around."

"He's my dad."

"And he's a jerk."

Hadlee rolled her eyes and slapped her hands on the comforter. "So are lots of people, but that doesn't mean I'll never talk to them again."

With a groan, Felix shifted back so he was leaning shoulder to shoulder with her against the pillows. "Okay, but only if I'm there to set everyone straight."

"You can't go around being a bully to every not nice person in my life, Felix."

"I can try."

Hadlee smiled and let her head drop to his shoulder. "You're impossible."

"And you're wonderful."

"I know. You've told me enough times," she teased, glancing up from under her lashes.

His shoulder softened slightly as he bent down to kiss the top of her head. "And I'll keep telling you until you're sick of me."

Never. She didn't say the word out loud, not quite ready to plan that far into the future, but she was grateful he was there now. It had taken several hours for her to get checked out of the hospital and by the time he'd driven her back to the inn, it had been dinner time. Felix had been hovering like a mother hen ever since. He'd have spoon fed her dinner last night if she'd let him. He'd shown up first thing this morning to help her, though she planned to stay in bed most of the day.

Chrissy, Joshua, and Luke were all doing the same thing as they lounged around, claiming they felt fine, just tired. Genni had also been a godsend as she brought meals up to their rooms and checked in every half-hour or so.

Hadlee had never felt so cared for and it was an amazing feeling. She'd resigned herself to having nothing and suddenly she had almost everything. The only thing that could make her situation better was to have her job...and her father...back.

"What's up with the *Morwenna*?" Hadlee asked as she pulled on a loose string on the comforter.

Felix sighed. "I'm not sure. I hired someone to tow her back to our port."

Sadness enveloped Hadlee and she raised her head to look up at his face. "Was she badly damaged?"

Felix shrugged, his eyes downcast. "Not...badly...I don't think. Most of the damage was probably superficial."

"I'm so sorry," she whispered. Pulling on the trust that he was working to build between them, she took his hand and pressed it between her own. "You were coming after me. I'll pay for the damages."

"Don't start, Hadlee," Felix said, softening his words with a kiss to the end of her nose. "We've been through this and it's not worth talking about again. I chose to go out and the damages are mine. I don't regret them for a moment. The only thing I regret is how I treated you and forcing you to go out in that tin can to do your research." He pinched his lips together. "Speaking of which, what are you going to do about your project?"

"Oh...that." She fell back against the pillows. She'd been putting off worrying about her equipment and research. It hurt to think about, but surprisingly enough...not as much as she expected it to. Earlier in the summer, Felix had opened her eyes to the fact that being a professor wasn't her dream job.

But what is?

This is where things got painful. With no job and no future, she had no idea what she wanted to do with her life. After being thrown out of her program, there was no college in the country that would take her on. But what else could she do? She'd spent her entire adult life grooming herself to become a full professor and now that path wasn't feasible.

"Yeah...that," Felix said with a smile. "Let's talk about the elephant in the room."

"Elephant might not be the right word...maybe a sturgeon?" Hadlee offered.

He chuckled as intended and wrapped an arm around her shoulders. "Any ideas on what you might want to do?" His fingers played a rhythm against her shoulder. "It might be a little premature of me to say, but I wouldn't mind if you found something that kept you closer to Seaside Bay."

"You wouldn't mind that, huh?" she asked, unable to stop the smile from stretching across her face. Leaning to the side, she cuddled into his chest. "Well, don't worry," she said softly. "I wouldn't mind that either."

HER LAST WORDS WERE soft and murmured, and Felix could feel that her weight was growing heavier. She was obviously falling asleep, and as much as he wanted to stick around and let her nap on him all day, he had a few errands he needed to run.

It took him fifteen minutes before he worked up the motivation to gently set her in the pillows and walk out of the room. He was careful to close it as quietly as possible, but nearly ruined it when he turned around to see Genni right behind him. "Geez, Gen." Felix blew out a breath. "I just got her to sleep."

Genni rolled her eyes. "You make her sound like a baby."

He shrugged. "I've decided it's my duty to take care of her."

"She's a grown woman, Felix. You can't run her life." Genni gave him a significant look.

"Maybe not, but nothing says I can't try." He grinned when she shook her head. "All joking aside, she really is asleep. Did you need something?"

Genni shook her head again. "Nope. I was just making the rounds, checking on everyone."

Nodding, Felix tilted his head toward the stairs. He walked right behind Genni as they went down the stairs and met up in the kitchen. "I appreciate you taking care of them all so well," he said as Genni went to the fridge and grabbed a couple of water bottles. He caught the one she tossed his way.

"It's my job," she said nonchalantly. "Well...sort of. I didn't really sign up to take on a bunch of invalids, but it's not a big deal."

"It is," Felix insisted, "and I'm grateful to you."

Genni gave him a soft smile. "I take it things are better between the two of you?"

The water bottle twisted in his hands. "Yeah...I'm not sure how, but she says she forgives me for being a dolt."

"You deserve to be forgiven."

Felix laughed without humor. "No. I don't, but she did anyway." He shrugged. "That's just how Hadlee is. Sweet to the core. I don't deserve her at all." Genni's feet came into his line of sight and he looked up at her.

"Everyone deserves to be forgiven," she said softly. "If Cooper and I weren't willing to forgive each other, we'd have never gotten together, never gotten *back* together, and wouldn't still be married." She smiled. "We all make mistakes, sometimes really stupid mistakes, but just like she has every right to forgive you, you had every right to be worried about pursuing a relationship with her." A lone eyebrow rose high on Genni's forehead. "Don't downplay your importance in your mission to make sure she knows hers."

"How do you know so much about what happened?" he asked. He thought their relationship was mostly between them and now her father.

Genni's grin became mischievous. "I live in an old house with thin walls." She leaned in. "And a really small town."

Felix smiled back. "Sounds like a recipe for gossip."

"Or simply being well-informed." Genni shrugged and took a drink of her water. After screwing the lid back on, she looked at him again. "What are you going to do now?"

Felix made a face. "I need to head down to the docks and see if *Morwenna* is in yet."

"She was being towed?"

He nodded. "Yeah."

"Is the engine down?" Genni tilted her head, her concern evident.

"No." Felix shook his head. "The engine should be fine, but I'll give it a onceover when I can. A bunch of the stuff on deck got messed up in the storm though. I'll have to see what's missing and what needs to be repaired."

"How bad do you think?"

He shrugged. "I'm not sure, but it doesn't matter. I'd do it again in a heartbeat."

"You're lucky you didn't get in trouble with the Coast Guard," Genni pointed out.

"Maybe. But still…I couldn't sit around waiting." He shook his head adamantly. "It wasn't an option."

"I get it." She sighed. "Well…better get going, then. I'm sure she'll wake up in not too long, and since you've been glued to her side every waking moment, I'm guessing you won't want to be gone too long."

He gave her a sheepish grin. "Sorry."

"Don't be. I think it's sweet." Genni laughed. "Mostly I'm just happy to see you happy, and we all think Hadlee is something special."

"She is," Felix assured his friend. "More than I can ever say." He held up the water in a salute. "Thanks. I'll be back soon."

Genni saw him off and Felix jumped into his truck and slowly drove to the harbor. He was a little nervous about seeing his pride and joy. His boat had been everything to him, but in a moment's decision, he'd sacrificed it all to go after the woman he loved. He didn't regret it, but he wasn't looking forward to seeing the aftermath either. No matter how much he loved Hadlee, seeing *Morwenna* in bad shape was going to hurt.

The docks came into view and Felix could see a crowd gathered around his slip. "They must have just gotten here," he murmured. Ken's large stature could easily be picked out of the crowd, but Felix could also see Benny's blond head, his sister Mel's long ponytail, and even Charli's dark skin among a larger crowd of people.

He frowned, unsure why everyone was hanging around. It wasn't like there would be much to see right now. He could see the towboat just leaving the harbor, so there was no good reason for them to be standing around.

Climbing out of his truck, Felix slowly walked over. Ken spotted him approaching and tilted his chin at him.

"What's up?"

Felix gave a thrust back. "Hey. What's going on here?" He pointedly looked at the crowd. "Why is everyone standing around the docks?"

Ken smirked and folded his arms over his chest. "They're here for you."

"What?"

"We came to help," Charli said, stepping away from the group. As usual, Bronson, her husband and Felix's brother-in-law, was right behind her.

"We heard *Morwenna* was damaged, so we're here to help clean up and do any repairs we can," Bronson said, his hand resting on Charli's back.

Felix was stunned and for a few moments, words were completely lost to him. "I...don't understand," he said. His voice was shaky as if he couldn't quite control his thoughts and Benny came up to slap him on the back.

"Heya, Cap. You've got a huge crew for the day. Put us to work."

"I don't even know what needs to be done," Felix said in a daze. "I haven't seen her since the storm."

"Well, then." Charli stepped sideways and swept her arm out, indicating he should go aboard.

With heavy steps, Felix moved forward. He nodded and tried to smile at the crowd that had arrived. Harry and a few of the other fishermen were standing by, offering solemn nods as Felix went past. He acknowledged them, but wasn't ready to stop and chat. Instead, he continued to the small bridge that connected his boat to the wooden dock.

Julian and Ethan were already aboard, but they were waiting by the rail for Felix to arrive. Julian saluted. "Ready for your inspection, Captain."

Normally Felix would have rolled his eyes at the old-fashioned formality, but today he was still trying to process that most of his friends and a good chunk of the town had shown up to support him. It was still surreal. "Thank you," Felix said softly, stepping down from the bridge.

Taking a deep breath, he began to walk around the deck. Things didn't look good. It was going to take time and money to fix the boat back up to her former glory, but as his eyes went back, yet again, to the crowd, he thought that maybe, just maybe, it would all turn out all right.

CHAPTER 26

Hadlee covered her mouth as she yawned and stretched from her nap. Blinking sleepily, she glanced toward the window and realized with a start that the sun was farther across the sky than she would have expected. She had slept a good portion of the day. That was completely unlike her. She rarely took naps, let alone wasted an entire day.

Glancing around the room, she wasn't surprised to see that Felix had left. Sticking around while she was sleeping would have been horribly boring. Deciding she would feel better if she got up and moved around, Hadlee pulled back the covers and stood on slightly shaky legs. "So ridiculous," she muttered, frustrated that one scary experience had taken so much out of her body. "The storm's over," she scolded. "Get ahold of yourself."

She only held onto the wall a couple of times as she padded down the hallway to the bathroom. It was time to get herself cleaned up. As much as she was flattered by Felix's very attentive behavior, a few minutes to herself would not go amiss. And Hadlee knew she would feel much improved once she was clean and fresh.

Thirty minutes later, she fluffed her dry hair and decided to check on her team. She hadn't seen them since first thing that morning. She knocked softly on Chrissy's door, but there was no answer. "Chrissy?"

"They're all downstairs."

Hadlee jumped and put a hand to her chest. "Oh my gosh, Genni. You startled me."

Genni smiled. "Sorry. We heard the water shut off a bit ago and I wanted to come check on you." She looked Hadlee up and down.

"I'm glad to see you're looking no worse for wear. How're you feeling?"

Hadlee stretched her neck from side to side and rolled her shoulders. "Stiff. Sore." She smiled. "But alive."

"And that's the most important one of all," Genni assured her. Waving her arm, she beckoned Hadlee forward. "Can you make it downstairs? I think you'll feel better after you eat a good meal. You still look a little shaky."

"A meal would be great. Thank you." She walked just ahead of Genni, slowly working her way down the stairs. "You've gone above and beyond, Genni. Thank you so much for everything."

"Psssht." Gennis blew off the compliment. "Between you and Felix, I'm gonna get a big head by the time this is all over from your thank you's."

"He thanked you?" Hadlee stopped at the bottom of the stairs and waited for Genni to walk beside her.

"He thanked me enough for the next year combined."

Hadlee laughed softly. "That was nice of him."

"Felix has always been nice," Genni said carefully. "But a little rough around the edges." She hooked her arm through Hadlee's and began walking her to the dining room. "However, after chatting with him this morning, I have a feeling that you're rubbing those edges a little smoother than they were before."

Heat infused Hadlee's cheeks, but she didn't know what to say in response. She wasn't sure she was the reason Felix was shifting, but it was a nice sentiment. "I'm sure I'm not the one helping him," she tried to hedge.

"I'm sure you are." Genni pushed open the dining room door. "Look who woke up!"

"Hadlee!" Chrissy stood up and walked around to give Hadlee a hug, followed quickly by Luke and Joshua.

Hadlee's eyes filled with tears at the love from her crew. They might drive her crazy sometimes, but they were the closest thing she had to family. After a long moment, Hadlee pulled back. "Is everyone okay?" She met each individual set of eyes and breathed in relief when each person nodded in response to her question. Chewing on her lip, she pulled back slightly. "I need to apologize to all of you," she began.

"Don't do it," Joshua said in his deep tone. His dark brows were furrowed. "This wasn't your fault. We all know that."

"Captain Wamsley told us everything," Luke said, folding his arms over his chest. "You had no way of knowing those men would sabotage the boat."

"He also mentioned that he'd eventually need to talk to you about charges against them," Chrissy said softly.

Hadlee nodded, but didn't speak. She hadn't considered that she would have to talk to the law. She wasn't afraid of Captain Wamsley, but she wasn't sure what to do about Harry and his friends. She'd forgiven them once before, but what was the right thing to do now?

"I hope they're stuck behind bars for a long time," Joshua muttered. His anger flashed through his nearly black eyes and it made Hadlee sad. She hadn't meant to introduce any of her young helpers to such an ugly part of life.

"Remember that they were manipulated by someone else," Hadlee began. "It wasn't really their fault."

"They made their choices," Joshua argued. "And it included risking all our lives with their stupidity." He turned and went back to his place at the table and Hadlee didn't have an argument to his words.

Deciding instead to leave him to his stewing, she found an empty seat at the table and sat down.

"Coming in hot!" Genni called out as she came back in the dining room door.

Hadlee hadn't even known her host had left, but the steaming plate in her hand was a welcome sight. "This smells fabulous," she said, eyeing the fried chicken and mashed potatoes. "Thank you."

"Eat hearty," Genni said as she walked back to the door to leave.

"Genni?"

"Yeah?"

"Did Felix say where he was going?" The flush in her cheeks reappeared as she asked the question, but he'd been so adamant that he wasn't going anywhere, and yet she hadn't seen him since waking up.

"He's down at the docks, working on fixing up *Morwenna*."

Hadlee perked up. "She got back today?"

Genni nodded.

"Do you know how bad the damage was?"

Her host shook her head. "No. I haven't heard from him, though I know a bunch of the town was planning to surprise him by coming to help."

A slow smile pulled on Hadlee's lips. Felix had some of the best friends Hadlee had ever seen. "Okay. Thanks."

As soon as Genni was gone, Luke gave Hadlee a look. "What are you planning?"

Hadlee finished chewing her bite. "As soon as I'm done, I'm going to go help."

"Don't you think it's a little too soon?" Chrissy asked, wringing her hands together.

Putting her hand on Chrissy's small ones, Hadlee smiled reassuringly. "It doesn't matter. Felix risked himself to help save us. The least I can do is help clean up his boat one last time."

Joshua grunted as he ate. "Somehow I doubt this is going to be the last time."

Hadlee laughed softly. He was right. And she didn't care if anyone knew it.

"CAPTAIN?"

Felix looked up to examine the piece of wood that Ethan was holding up. "Garbage," Felix muttered. He sighed. Most of what they'd pulled off the decks had gone into the garbage. He was going to be replacing most of the benches and loose equipment. The only thing that had turned out in his favor was that *Morwenna's* inner core was fine. The engine had come out fine, though Felix planned to give her a good tune-up just to be sure, but the outer part of the boat didn't survive quite as well. "It's all replaceable," he reminded himself. "Hadlee, Chrissy, Luke, and Joshua aren't."

"Hey, Cap." Julian elbowed Felix.

He looked up, then turned when Julian nodded toward the dock. "Hadlee?" His eyes opened wide and his jaw went slack at the sight of her and the very team members he had just been muttering about, standing on the far side of the bridge.

"Permission to come aboard," Hadlee said with a soft smile.

Instead of waving her over, Felix bounded over and met her on the dock. "What are you doing here?" he asked, frowning. "Shouldn't you all be resting?"

"We're fine," Hadlee assured him, resting her hand on his arm. "We want to help."

Felix turned back to the boat. "As you can see, half the town came to help."

"I know," Hadlee said with a smile. "It's fantastic. Just goes to show how much they all love you."

Felix shrugged. "I grew up here. I know a few people."

"Doesn't mean they have to like you," Luke offered. Joshua punched his shoulder and Luke scowled while rubbing the appendage.

Felix chuckled. "True enough." He rubbed the top of his head. "Well, come on and we'll find something you can do."

"No going easy on us," Hadlee warned as they walked to the boat. Reaching back to grab her hand, he winked. "No promises."

Hadlee dropped his gaze, but she was smiling and Felix loved the blush that stole up her cheeks. Over the next few minutes, he helped put Joshua, Luke, and Chrissy to work, but kept Hadlee with himself.

"I want to help," Hadlee demanded, stomping her foot on the deck.

Felix's eyebrows went up, he looked down at her foot, then back up at her. "Feel better?"

"No," she mumbled. "But don't baby me, Felix. Where can I help?"

Grinning, he pulled her into his chest. "You get to help me. Is that all right?" he whispered in her ear.

A shiver stole up her spine and Felix's grin grew wider. "I suppose," she said breathlessly.

"Perfect." He forced himself to step away from her, though it was the last thing he wanted to do, and began walking back to where he'd been before Hadlee had arrived.

"Captain Mendez!"

"Now what?" Felix groaned, throwing his head back.

"It's my dad." Hadlee gasped.

Felix's neck nearly snapped in half when he whipped around to see Dr. Ford. "I didn't expect him," Felix said, glancing down at Hadlee.

She shook her head. "Me either. I haven't heard from him since he left yesterday."

"Do you want to talk to him?"

Hadlee chewed her bottom lip, then looked up at him. "I suppose we should."

"Only if you really want to."

"He's my dad, Felix. No matter how jerky he is, I'm not ready to cut him out of my life."

"If you say so," Felix grumbled. Huffing, he kept a hold of her hand and they walked back to the dock area. "Dr. Ford."

The older man nodded. "Hadlee. Can I speak to you?"

She started to let go of Felix's hand, but he held on tighter. "Want me to go with you?"

She paused then nodded. "Yeah. If you don't mind."

Together they went to where Dr. Ford was waiting. "Hadlee. How are you?" His eyes were the same grayish-green that Hadlee's were and they seemed to study her from head to toe.

At least he looks like he cares, Felix thought sarcastically. He probably needed to ease up, but when the guy left without saying anything to Hadlee, or even calling to check up on her condition, it ticked Felix off. That wasn't how a father should be, but he wasn't sure Professor Ford even recognized what he was doing. Being ignorant wasn't an excuse, but it gave Felix less ammunition to use against the man. Mostly, he just didn't want Hadlee to be hurt. Especially if her father never changed.

"Doing better, thanks," Hadlee said crisply. She was holding Felix's hand tightly, giving away her anxiety, though it wouldn't be visible to her father. "What brings you here?"

Dr. Ford rubbed the back of his neck. "I wanted to check on you again. The hospital told me you were released, but it took some time to figure out where exactly you were." He sent a quick glare in Felix's direction.

"Dad," Hadlee scolded. "I told you months ago that I was in Seaside Bay. It's on the research project itself. Don't look at Felix like this is his fault. I'm an adult, so the hospital didn't need to call you or get your permission."

To his credit, the doctor did look a little set down at her words. "I see," he said carefully. His bushy brows pulled together. "Well…I came here for a purpose."

"I thought you said it was to check on me."

Felix bit back a smile. Hadlee was in a sassy mood and he loved it. She rarely stood up for herself, preferring to stay out of the confrontation, but at the moment, she wasn't letting her father get away with anything.

"It was, it was," Dr. Ford said, stumbling over his words. "But the board also asked me to deliver a message."

"You were talking with the board?" Hadlee frowned. "What for?"

"I needed to tell them about Captain Mendez's accusations."

"Accusations? Really?" Hadlee huffed. "Would you like me to get the police captain over here and have him tell you about the men who confessed what they did? Or maybe you'd like to talk to the men themselves? They're working right over there." Hadlee pointed to the far end of the boat.

Felix grimaced. He hadn't realized she'd seen Harry or the others. He'd purposefully kept her on the opposite side of the boat, but apparently it hadn't been enough. "Ken wants to talk to you about them," he whispered.

"I know," Hadlee said back, glancing up at him. "We can do that later." She grinned. "After they work for a while."

He chuckled. "Have I told you how much I love you?"

Hadlee's inviting look almost made Felix grab her right there, but then she turned back to her father and Felix had to hold himself in check.

"You didn't really answer my question, Dad," she said. "Did you want to hear more proof? Or are you going to take our word for it?"

Her father rubbed his neck again, obviously uncomfortable with the fact that Hadlee was finally standing up for herself. "It doesn't matter, I suppose. We spoke to Christian."

"And?"

"And he admitted he mentioned a few things."

Hadlee rolled her eyes. "You know what? I don't want to stand here and listen to you talk about how he got a lecture and is still keeping his job, but I've still lost mine." She stepped forward and Felix purposefully let go of her hand. She didn't need him at the moment. "I have given my heart and soul to that program, and if those men don't recognize all that I've done, but are willing to keep a man who risked four lives because of jealousy, then I don't want to work there anyway." She started to turn away, but her father stopped her.

"They've got an offer for you."

Hadlee slowly spun back and folded her arms over her chest. "Are you serious?"

Her father nodded.

Hadlee looked back at Felix as if asking his opinion, but Felix kept his face neutral. This was her choice. He didn't want to influence her decision at all, though he secretly hoped she threw it back in their faces. Facing her father again, she nodded regally. "I'm listening."

CHAPTER 27

Clutching a bowl of fruit, Hadlee let Felix help her down from his truck.

"Ready?" he asked with a smile.

"Of course," Hadlee responded. "Your friends are wonderful."

His hand went to her back and he bent down close to her ear. "I think they're your friends, too."

That familiar heat enveloped her and she unconsciously leaned into Felix's side. She was going to miss this if she didn't figure out a direction for her life in the near future. A few days ago, Hadlee had sent her team home now that they were no longer needed, but she herself was stuck in limbo.

Her father had given her an offer from the board, but Hadlee hadn't accepted it right away. She wanted time to think it over. And most of all, she wanted time to figure out if going back to the college was what she actually wanted out of life. She had enjoyed her job for the most part, but the thought of going back was leaving Hadlee feeling...empty. Plus, there might be another offer on the table that Hadlee wanted to explore.

If she went back, she gained financial security, a chance to further her research and the fulfillment of everything she had worked so hard for. However, it wasn't without a cost. Leaving meant she was going back to the very people who didn't treat her with the same respect as her colleagues. It also meant leaving the people, or more specifically, the person, who finally made her feel worthwhile. Felix and his friends had done more to help Hadlee feel welcome than her own family.

"Hadlee! Felix! You made it!"

Hadlee couldn't have stopped smiling if she wanted to. She was sure that given time, she would grow to love them just as much as she already loved Felix. They were his family and they had opened their arms to her without reserve or question. Her own father hadn't even apologized even after Felix's set down.

"Hi, Mel," Hadlee responded.

Mel hurried over and took Hadlee's bowl. "You didn't need to bring anything," she scolded playfully.

Hadlee shrugged. "I wanted to. You guys have been feeding me every time I come."

"That's what's so fun about being a guest," Mel said with a smile. "Everybody takes care of you."

"I think people have been taking care of me for too long," Hadlee responded, tucking a piece of hair behind her ear. The light breeze was just enough to blow her hair annoyingly around her face. The heat of the fire was pulling her in and she pulled Felix closer.

He swung the camp chairs off his shoulder and they set up right in the middle of the group.

"Hadlee," Ken drawled. "Just the girl I wanted to talk to." He leaned forward with his hands on his forearms. "Thought you might want an update on Harry and the boys."

Hadlee laughed softly. "Update away, Captain Wamsley."

"They're being charged with a misdemeanor," he said. "The financial amount wasn't high enough for a felony, which is in their favor."

Felix scoffed and Hadlee gave him a look before turning back to Ken.

"They have a court date next month and they'll probably either have to pay a fine or do some community service."

Hadlee nodded. "Thank you," she said softly. She didn't like sending men to court, but she kept reminding herself that they made a choice. One that could have killed her and her TA's. That might not have been their intent, but it still had been the result.

Ken nodded. "Now...who's hungry?"

"Benny isn't here yet," Mel said. "Eat now before he comes and hoover's the whole table."

"On it!" Ken jumped from his seat.

"Ready to eat?" Felix asked, leaning forward to rise.

"Not yet," Hadlee said. "Go ahead. I'll eat later." He frowned and Hadlee waved him on. "I'm fine. I promise I've been eating enough and I'll eat later." She laughed and shook her head as he finally walked away. His almost smothering attentiveness hadn't waned at all despite the time that was passing. If he didn't calm down soon, she was going to have to say something.

"Pssstt..." Mel slipped into Felix's seat. "Have you made any decisions yet?"

Hadlee ticked her head back and forth. "Maybe. I'm leaning in one direction for sure."

"What direction is that?" Charli appeared on Hadlee's right, putting her own seat down.

"Hey, Charli," Hadlee said. She was getting more comfortable with Felix's sister. Charli was similar to her brother, a little bit rough around the edges, but with a good heart. Hadlee was learning how to handle Charli's strong personality and how to take her sarcasm. Her husband, Bronson, was the more sensitive of the couple and seemed to do a good job in smoothing Charli's bumps.

"Hey," Charli greeted back. "So...explain."

Hadlee looked back at Mel, who shrugged. She turned back to Charli. "Well...I've been offered a job."

The heat from the fire was blocked as Felix stood between Hadlee and the flames. "You're taking the job back at the college?" he asked. His voice was low and there seemed to be a hint of disappointment, which is exactly what Hadlee would have hoped for.

She craned her neck to look up at him. "No. That wasn't the job I was talking about."

He frowned down at her. "What do you mean? You've gotten a second offer? From who?"

"Have a seat," Mel said, jumping to her feet. "Sorry," she mouthed as she walked back to her own chair.

Hadlee shook her head. "Don't worry about it," she assured Mel. "I needed to bring it up anyway."

"How about you just tell everyone?" Ken said as he passed in front of them on his way back to his own chair. The plate in his hands was piled high with food from the buffet. "All of us are curious as to your plans."

Hadlee clasped her hands together. "I haven't made a full decision, but I've been weighing my options and I'm definitely leaning one way." She turned to Felix. "Mel texted me the other day that she had a hot tip on a job."

"A customer was talking about it," Mel explained. "I automatically thought of Hadlee."

"Up north in Waldport, they're in the process of building a new aquarium." Hadlee stopped, waiting to see if Felix could understand why this would be exciting to her.

Slowly, he sat down, his eyes never leaving hers. "They don't happen to need someone with expert fish knowledge to help run it, do they?"

"Someone's hiring the fish doctor?"

Ken groaned, throwing his head back. "Perfect timing, Benny. As usual."

Benny buffed his nails on his shirt. "I know."

"Go on," Charli insisted, ignoring Benny.

Hadlee smiled again. "They're in the process of hiring a full staff. And yes, they're in need of someone with my credentials." She scrunched her nose. "Truth be told, I'm a bit overeducated for the job."

HOPE WAS SWIRLING IN Felix's chest. He'd been wracking his brain trying to figure out how to make it so Hadlee could stay longer, but so far he'd come up with nothing. This, however...seemed promising. "You would be," Felix said, tilting his head to the side. He loved the way the firelight danced on Hadlee's cheeks. Too bad they were in public, or he'd let his fingers do the same. "But the question is, do you or they care?"

She smiled softly. "They offered me a job, if that's what you're asking."

"And?" Benny interrupted.

"Shut up." Ken smacked Benny's arm with the back of his hand.

"At least it wasn't my head," Benny mumbled. "I'm hungry."

"Wait, wait, wait," Charli broke in. "What about the job offer from your dad? Didn't you get one?" Her eyes darted back and forth between Hadlee and Felix. "I thought Felix said you got one from the college?"

Hadlee nodded. "I did. They have come to a consensus that maybe my forced resignation wasn't quite the right move and offered to let me back into the faculty."

"And the guy who tried to ruin you?"

Felix scoffed and leaned back in his seat. His plate teetered on his knee and he had to grab it before it fell. "The guy got away with everything. All they did was give him a scolding."

"Technically he didn't break the law," Ken offered as he wiped his mouth with a napkin. "So they really had very little they could do as recourse."

"Doesn't make it any less horrible," Mel said with a frown. Jensen, her husband, took her hand and laid their combined digits on his thigh.

"Maybe not, but you can't be fired over spreading rumors," Jensen pointed out.

"Not unless you're sued for libel," Charli snapped. She took a deep breath when Bronson put a hand on her back. "Sorry. It just ticks me off. So many people nowadays have no integrity at all." She turned to look at Hadlee. "And somehow, I'm doubting you're going to sue, so the guy really is getting away with it all."

Felix snorted. "Exactly."

Hadlee put up a hand. "I know. But in this case, I don't think a long, drawn out court battle is going to do anyone any favors."

"Back to the jobs," Mel said, an eager smile gracing her face. "What have you decided?"

Felix held his breath. Here, finally, was the moment of truth. He grit his teeth, determined to let Hadlee say her piece, but he wanted to beg and plead for her to stay close. If she didn't want to work at an aquarium, he was sure she could find another job. She could teach anywhere with her credentials, or give sea tours, if that appealed to her. Fact was, Felix didn't care if she worked at all...he just wanted her close. He'd experienced distance from her while she was still in town and he never wanted to do it again.

Soft, gray eyes met his. "I wanted to talk things over with you before I made a decision," she said softly.

The whole group seemed to be just as anxious as Felix. Only the crashing of the waves and the crackling of the fire could be heard while they waited.

"How would *you* feel if I became a permanent resident of Seaside Bay?"

"How would I feel?" he clarified, stunned she had to ask.

Hadlee nodded, tucking a piece of hair behind her ear. "Neither of us have any idea what the future will bring, and I don't want to assume—"

"Hadlee," Felix interrupted. "Nothing would make me happier than having you stay here." He frowned. "Although you said the aquarium is north. Would you stay in Seaside Bay? Or live closer to work?"

She shrugged. "Again, that would all depend on you. I don't mind a commute if it means the rest of my time is better spent here."

He reached out to take her hand and brought it to his lips. It was warm from the heat of the fire and he let his mouth linger against the soft skin. "How can I convince you that your time here will be the best you've ever had?"

She gave a small, contented sigh. "What you're doing right now is a good start."

"Not again." Benny groaned, covering his eyes. "Why does this keep happening?"

Abruptly, Felix jumped to his feet, spilling what was left of his food into the sand. Without bothering to clean it up, he pulled Hadlee with him. "Excuse us," he said to the group. "We need a minute to talk things out."

"Talk...right," Charli said dryly. "That's what we used to call it too."

Felix ignored the snickering and groaning as he took Hadlee away from the light of the fire and closer to the cold ocean. Once they were mostly out of earshot, he pulled Hadlee into his chest and gave her a bruising kiss. He hadn't meant for it to be so aggressive, but it felt as if all his emotions had come bursting to the forefront. Their break-up, the worry over her life, the following days of recovering, the frustration with the college, the worry over losing her again when she left...he couldn't quite hold himself back from kissing her until he felt it all begin to diminish.

His hands were framing her face when he finally was able to think clearly enough to pull himself back. Though their lips separated, he kept his hands against her cheeks. "Did that help make up your mind?" he asked gruffly.

The moon was just bright enough for him to make out the dazed look in her eye and it gave him a burst of pride and hope. "I would think so," she whispered, then cleared her throat. "But some more research definitely wouldn't go amiss."

He chuckled and gave her a light kiss on her bottom lip. "You are a scientist, after all…" He kissed at the edge of her mouth and smiled when she let out a shaky breath. "And I happen to know you're very…" He kissed the bow in her top lip. "Very…" His lips moved back to her bottom lip, where he toyed with it for a moment. "Very thorough in your research."

"Felix Mendez," Hadlee said in a tight whisper. Her hand went to his shirt, where she gripped it tightly. "If you don't stop playing with me and kiss me proper, I'm going to do something drastic, like go back to that stupid college with all those old men who—"

Felix didn't let her finish her threat. He knew she wouldn't do it, but that's not what mattered. He wanted…needed…this reassurance just as much as she did. He'd been hovering over her for days, but worry for her health and safety, plus trying to make up for his stupid mistakes, had been his main motivation. Right now, none of that was driving the affection between them.

Right now he wanted her. Without reservation, without worry for safety, without care for the future. Just him and her in this moment. Everything else could go jump in the ocean…where it belonged.

CHAPTER 28

"Oh my goodness, don't stop," Hadlee said breathlessly when Felix pulled away. As soon as the words slipped from her mouth, she pinched her lips together and dropped her forehead to Felix's chest. "Sorry," she said, still breathing heavily.

He chuckled, making her head bounce. His arms tightened around her and Hadlee sighed comfortably. "If I keep going, I don't think I'll be able to stop," he said against the top of her head.

"I think I can get behind that."

He laughed again. "Hadlee...you make everything better."

"Yeah, well...you made me feel like a million bucks."

"Then my job is almost done."

She picked her head up and leaned back so she could see him. "Almost? What's left?"

Felix turned away for a second, looking out at the water, allowing Hadlee to study his fierce profile. Her eyes went along the bridge of his nose and down the lips that had so recently kept her close. This man's kiss touched places in her she hadn't known were empty. That week they'd spent apart had been miserable and if nothing else, had taught her that work was not enough.

Her research, the goal of becoming an Associate Professor, trying to gain her dad's attention, none of it was enough to fill the spot that Felix's absence had left empty. If she had her way, she'd never leave his side again, but Hadlee's logical side knew it was too soon for that. There was so much up in the air still. She needed to accept that job in the aquarium, she needed to find a place to live, she needed to create a whole new life, and she couldn't depend on Felix for any of that. "Felix?" she asked, trying to pull his brooding attention back her way. "You said your job was *almost* done. What's missing?" His heavy gaze came back and Hadlee immediately felt the weight of it. Something was on his mind.

"Hadlee," he said, his tone husky and all-too appealing. "I...I want to say something, but I'm afraid you're going to think it's too soon."

Her heart began to pick up speed and banged against her chest in wild abandon. Her hands clenched tighter in his shirt and it took all her self-control to keep from pulling him in tighter. "What?" she croaked. "Tell me."

He brought his head down, trailing his nose along her skin. "Have I told you lately how wonderful you are?"

A soft giggle slipped through her lips, but Hadlee was too far gone to care that she sounded like a thirteen-year-old girl. "Not today."

"Let me correct that," Felix continued. "Hadlee...you're amazing."

"I thought I was wonderful," she teased.

Felix kissed the side of her smile. "You're wonderful. You're beautiful. You're a genius... You're everything I could have ever asked for in a woman."

"I even like fish!"

"That's the best part," he said with a laugh before growing stoic again. "But in all seriousness...your arrival completely knocked me off my feet." He pulled back to look her in the face. "I thought I had my whole life before me, one filled with long trips on the water and fishing trips with no deadlines." He sighed. "Just me and the horizon."

"And *Morwenna*," Hadlee couldn't help but insert.

"And *Morwenna*," he agreed. "She was the only woman I thought I needed." He brought his forehead back to hers. "Then you showed up and everything changed. You brought color to my life in a way I didn't know it was missing." His arms tightened around and Hadlee could barely breathe, but she wasn't about to pull away. "When I made the biggest mistake of my life and pushed you away, it all drained away. I was happy before, but with you...I'm content, yet I want to be better. I want to protect you, to take care of you, to see your face light up when you find something new. To listen to you teach and work with others and watch you accomplish all the great things you're destined to do."

Hadlee buried her face in the crook of his neck. He made her sound as if she were truly Wonder Woman. While she felt good about herself when they were together, listening to his words in conjunction with him choosing to be with her took everything to a whole new level.

"If you'll let me, I'd like to be around to do those things for the rest of our lives."

Hadlee stopped breathing. Her jaw was hanging loose as she pulled back to look at his face. "Are you...are you asking me to marry you?" She gasped.

Felix slowly nodded. "I am. I know we've only known each other a couple of months, but I can't imagine moving forward without you. We were apart for only a week and I thought life had ended. You've shown me that having no ties isn't what will fulfill me." His voice dropped and Hadlee could hear the rare emotion trying to break through. "My relationship with you is the best part of my life. Please say you'll marry me and keep me tied to you forever."

"Felix," she said, still trying to catch a full breath. "I would love nothing more than to be your wife." She put a hand up to stop him from kissing her. "But I just have to make sure that you're not asking me this because you feel bad about everything that happened." She swallowed hard. "I don't think my heart could take it if you only proposed out of guilt."

"Absolutely not," Felix said with a fierce tone. "I've thought long and hard about this, Hadlee. It wasn't a rash decision and it wasn't a last-minute one. In fact, I was starting to realize I wanted forever with you before I broke up with you, which only added to my stupid decision to separate." His hand left her back and he caressed her cheekbone with his knuckle. "I love you. I love every bit of you, inside and out, and I want to have the right to show you." He gave her a quick peck. "Please put me out of my misery here. I'm about to have a heart attack waiting for your answer."

Hadlee couldn't resist putting her shaking hand over his heart. She smiled and closed her eyes as she felt the organ pounding just as strongly as hers. "Yes," she whispered.

Felix stiffened. "Say it again," he demanded.

She huffed a soft laugh. "Yes. I would love to marry you."

His kiss was fierce and only slightly more than a peck. "Say it again," he whispered against her lips. "Say it one more time and I'm never going to let you go."

"A million times, yes—" Hadlee didn't quite get to finish before Felix took her mouth once more.

His large warm hands were splayed against her back, pulling her into his broad chest. Though the kiss was wild and chaotic, she felt as if she had never been so safe. The smell of fresh ocean mixed with the male muskiness of Felix to overwhelm her nose, while the heat of his body warmed her from the inside out. Her hands, which were eager to touch and explore, slipped up to the slight stubble over his jaw and chin. The prickly sensation was in direct contrast to his soft lips and sent even more electricity through her overly sensitive body.

Her heart was about to pound out of her chest and she could barely breathe for being so overwrought with all things Felix. If she died right now, in his arms, Hadlee was sure that she wouldn't regret a thing. Only a few days ago, she had been sure that her life was over. Now it seemed as if the future had never looked brighter. Happiness and love were ahead of her, and she was eager to get started.

PULL BACK.

Ignoring the thought, Felix continued to have his fill of Hadlee's willing affection. Actually...he wasn't sure he would ever be sated. He wanted her. He wanted *all* of her and it was hard not to just let things take their natural course.

Now, Felix. She deserves respect, not haste.

He grabbed her upper arms and wrenched himself away, both of them breathing heavily. The last coherent thought in his brain had sounded too much like his mother for him to ignore. She'd raised him to hold certain intimacies of life to a higher standard and would be sorely disappointed if he went against it now. Though he finally understood why she'd spent so much time pounding the morals into his younger brain.

"We should go back and join everybody," he rasped.

Hadlee's eyes were wide and she appeared as shell-shocked as he felt.

I'm an engaged man. The words were foreign, but not unwelcome.

"We should," she agreed, starting to pull back.

"Wait!"

Hadlee gave him a look. "I think we're already pushing a line here, Felix."

He grinned and relaxed his hold. "I just forgot something." Reaching into his pocket, he pulled out a small jewelry box.

"Oh." Hadlee's hands went over her mouth. "You were serious when you said you had thought about it."

He shrugged. "I wasn't sure if the right moment would come up, but I wanted to be prepared for when it did." Opening the box, he slid out the platinum band with four diamonds in a line. "I know a solitaire is more traditional, but when I saw this one, it reminded me

of a shooting star." He slid it onto her ring finger. "And that reminded me of you." Much more gently than their previous kisses had been,
he touched his lips to her forehead. "You're amazing."

"I love it," she breathed. "Thank you."

"Now. We really do need to get back or I'll start celebrating again
and someone will stumble across us, making for a very embarrassing
situation." He stuffed the box back in his pocket and together they
walked hand in hand to the group.

A few more people had arrived while they'd been out "talking."
Caro and her fiancé Jack were sitting around and Rose stood in the
background, holding a large vase of flowers.

The beautiful redhead was smiling widely as they walked up and
Felix gave her a nod and a wink.

"Oh my gosh. You did it?" Rose squealed softly.

Pausing in front of the group, Felix looked down into Hadlee's
eyes. "Everyone, I'd like you to meet the future Mrs. Hadlee
Mendez."

Shouts of congratulations and a large amount of arms gathered
around them, creating a group hug which was as uncomfortable as
it was wonderful. When the crowd finally backed off, Rose slowly
made her way to him and Hadlee.

"Congratulations," she said softly, then handed the vase to
Hadlee.

"Oh, wow," Hadlee breathed. "They're so gorgeous!" Her eyes
flitted up to Felix. "Did you plan this?"

He shrugged. "Like I said, I was hoping for the right opportunity."

"I love flowers," Hadlee gushed, burying her nose in the beautiful
blooms. She smiled at Rose. "You're an artist! There are so many
kinds!"

"Would you like to know what they mean?" Rose offered, clasping her hands in front of her.

Hadlee's eyes widened. "You know that?"

Rose nodded. "I love the language of flowers. I've studied it for years."

"The language of flowers. What a beautiful way to say it. Please…tell me what they mean."

"Okay, so this one? The lavender rose?"

Hadlee nodded.

"It stands for love at first sight."

A few chuckles went around the group, including Hadlee. "That might be stretching it a bit."

Felix gave her a sheepish grin and rested his hand on her back. "Just because I didn't recognize it, doesn't mean it didn't happen."

"The red rose and the yellow iris, here, both represent passionate love." Rose grinned. "As if we needed a reminder of that, huh?"

Hadlee's blush was fully evident in the light of the fire, which brought more smothered laughter among the group.

"What about that white and pink spiky one?" Hadlee tilted her head toward the bloom. "It's very different."

"That's a King Protea," Rose explained, moving it around so the flower was more prominent. "It was a hard one to find. It's the national flower of South Africa. And it stands for wisdom and strength."

"Both of which you have in abundance," Felix whispered against the top of her head.

"Flatterer," she teased. "I think I know what the yellow roses mean," she said, turning her attention back to Rose.

Rose raised her eyebrows.

"Friendship, right?"

Rose nodded. "Friendship and caring," Rose added. "It's not meant in a romantic way, and is one of the only roses that doesn't have a romantic meaning." Her bright blue eyes flicked between

Hadlee and Felix. "But I've always thought that friendship in itself can be romantic between the right people."

Hadlee's smile was blinding. "I agree," she said.

"And lastly we have the peonies."

"They are sooo gorgeous," Hadlee said. "I love peonies."

"Me too," Rose admitted. "And their meaning might be the most appropriate of all, considering the occasion." She smiled. "They stand for romance, prosperity, and a happy marriage."

Hadlee turned her eyes up to Felix. "If you hadn't proposed tonight, what would you have done with the flowers?"

"Not let her tell you the meanings," he automatically responded.

Hadlee laughed softly and wiped the corner of her eye on her sleeve. "This is all happening so fast, and it's so amazing." Felix took the vase so Hadlee could hug Rose. "Thank you so much for all the thought you put into those. They're perfect."

"It was an honor to be invited to participate," Rose said. Stepping back from Hadlee, she smiled at Felix, then backed up. "I better get back to Lilly. She's been having trouble sleeping lately."

Ken came up behind Rose. "What's wrong? Is she sick?"

Now it was Rose's turn to blush as she turned to look at Ken. "N-no, she's fine. Just one of those stages kids go through." She flashed him a smile, then turned to wave at the group. "I'll see you all later."

A chorus of goodbye's followed Rose's silhouette as she left the light of the fire.

"Go after her," Felix said to a very still Ken.

Ken's despair was clear even to Felix and he worried for his friend if he couldn't get over the crush he had on the flower shop owner. *Or convince Rose to give him a chance. Something's got to give soon.*

They watched as a determined look came across Ken's face and he gave a firm nod. "I'll be back in a few." Marching away, he shouted, "Rose! I'll walk you back," before jogging to catch up with her.

There was a quiet moment after Ken left before everyone began talking and chatting once more. Felix took the flowers to the food table and nestled them carefully in the center so they wouldn't fall, then hurried to sit back by Hadlee, where he automatically took her hand in his.

"So…" Benny said with a smirk. "Looks like it all worked out."

Felix scowled. Benny was working up to something.

Benny leaned forward. "Hadlee, would you say you got the best fish in the sea?"

"Don't do it," Felix warned, knowing Benny wasn't going to stop.

Hadlee laughed. "Yes, I would."

"When you came to Seaside Bay, did you expect to sail into the sunset with Felix at your side?" Benny continued.

Hadlee leaned her head onto Felix's shoulder. "How many of these do you have?" she asked.

"Too many," Felix grumbled.

"I'd say you've caught him hook, line, and sinker."

Charli groaned and held her stomach. "I can't take any more," she said. "Someone make him stop."

"You're right," Hadlee said proudly, sticking her chin in the air and turning to look at Felix. "Never in a million years would I have imagined that coming to Seaside Bay would mean finding the catch of a lifetime," she said, winking at him. "But the fact that it was unexpected was exactly what made it so wonderful." She raised up to give him a quick peck, leaving him hungry for more. "I'm definitely not throwing this one back."

Groans and laughter filled the air as they settled down into a pleasant, playful evening. Felix had never felt so content. She was right. She had caught him, and he'd given her a good run for her money. But now that he knew what it was like to be tied up in someone else out of love, he knew that it was the most perfect outcome he could have hoped for.

EPILOGUE

"**Y**ou may now kiss the bride."

"This is my favorite part," Caro whispered in Brooklyn's ear as Felix gathered Hadlee against him and proceeded to kiss the dickens out of her.

Brook laughed as they all clapped. "Hadlee's not going to be able to walk if he doesn't stop."

"It makes my knees weak just watching," Caro said with a wink.

"I'm trying really hard not to be concerned here," Jack, Caro's husband, said as he leaned into their conversation from Caro's other side. "But you're making it hard when you won't stop talking about another man's kiss."

Brook grinned but kept her laughter to herself as Caro started sassing Jack back and generally just being Caro. Brook adored her friend, but man...she could be high-maintenance sometimes.

"Everyone's heading to the reception hall," Caro said, grabbing Brook's wrist. "Come on. I'm dying to see what Hadlee did for dessert."

"You mean, you're dying to see why she didn't ask you to do it?"

Caro grinned over her shoulder. "I only got married a month ago, Brook. When would I have had time to cater Hadlee's wedding?"

Some of the happiness drained from Brook's smile, but she put in a valiant effort to keep from showing it. One by one, she'd been watching all her friends find the love of their lives and pair off, leaving only a few singles in the group. And Brook was one of the only girls left. Benny didn't seem interested in love at all and Ken had his heart set on Rose, who had been married once before and didn't look eager to do it again.

She was happy for her friends. She was! Until a quiet evening by herself rolled around and the suffocating weight of loneliness overtook her. It had gotten so bad that there were times Brook was positive there was something wrong with her. How come everyone else had found their future, but her? She'd been wishing and hoping to find her significant other for ages...well before Caro and Jack ever set eyes on each other, or Felix took Hadlee out on his boat. And yet Brook was the one who was still alone.

Now she sat at a dining table, surrounded by smiling, loving friends and she still felt apart from them. She knew she was loved, and she loved her friends too, but she wanted more than friendly love. Brook wanted forever, romantic, and most of all, passionate love. The kind that took her breath away and made her knees weak. The kind that made every problem in her life seem miniscule because She. Was. Loved.

I've been watching too many Hallmark movies, she scolded herself mentally. *Which is just a reaction to the fact that I spend too much time alone.* A long sigh left her lips before Brook thought to stop it and she froze when all the heads at her table turned in her direction.

"What's wrong?" Caro asked, frowning.

"Nothing," Brook said quickly. She pasted another smile on. "Isn't this hall beautiful?"

"Didn't you help decorate?" Benny said wryly.

Oh my word. Someone kill me now. "Oh, uh, yeah...I guess I did." Brook scrunched her nose. "Sorry. I was just trying to make conversation."

"Hey..." Benny snapped his fingers. "You know that one guy..."

Brook waited, but Benny was frowning and not speaking. "What one guy?"

"You know," Benny said. "The one you've been in love with for like...forever?"

"What?"

"Ooh," Caro said. "Do you mean Grayson Cordova?" She nodded her head knowingly.

Great. As if things can't get any worse, now Benny had to bring up my celebrity crush. How many ways can we say 'Brook is a lonely idiot?'

"Yeah, that one." Benny's face got serious. "Did you hear he got in an accident?"

Her eyes widened and jaw went slack. "What? Where did you hear that?"

"It was all over social media this morning," Benny said. "Some stunt he was doing for his latest movie." He scratched his chin. "Something went wrong, but no one really knows what yet." He shrugged. "All I know is the dude's in the hospital and security isn't letting anyone close enough to get answers."

"Wow, that's sad," Caro said softly. "I hope he's all right." Worried blue eyes went to Brook, but Brook tried to wave her friend's concern away.

"I'm sure he will be. They're usually really careful on those sets." Despite her reassuring words, her mind was racing and suddenly she couldn't wait for the reception and dinner to be over. Brook desperately wanted to go home and check all the news sites to figure out what was going on. She'd been following Grayson Cordova since she was a young teenager and he was a teen heartthrob on a show she had followed religiously. As he got older, he transitioned into doing action movies, and despite the fact that the stories never interested Brook, she'd still watched every single one of them.

Imagining that she was his leading lady who got to steal a kiss was one of her favorite fantasies. After all, who wouldn't want to kiss those full lips and feel his thick biceps? The man was six feet and one inch of total hotness and his image in the media was spotless, which only made Brook more interested.

You'll never find your true love as long as you're in love with a make-believe man.

Her mother had said those words often enough that Brook had them memorized. And the older she got, the more she knew her mother was right. She started to sigh again, but caught herself in time to keep her groaning to herself. Giving herself a mental head shake, Brook forced herself to perk up and move on. Felix and Hadlee's wedding was way more important than her silly crush. Plus, since Brook had no dating life of her own...there would be plenty of time for her to research Grayson and any news on him later tonight when she was home all by her lonesome.

After all, that was something she, unfortunately, had in spades.

READ BROOK'S STORY HERE[1]

---

1. https://www.amazon.com/gp/product/B095KT58CW

Thank you so much for joining me on
Hadlee and Felix's journey!
Not ready to be done with the romance yet?
Don't worry! Brook's story is up next.
Let's see if something (or someone) shows up
To help bring her out of her rut…

If sweet, clean romances are your thing, then I'd love for you to leave me a review! They make a HUGE difference in helping us authors get seen by others who will enjoy our work.

Not quite ready to be done yet?
Want to read the stories for the other
members of the Bulbs, Blossoms and Bouquets group?
Don't miss a story!
<u>Her Unexpected Roommate</u>[2]
<u>Her Unexpected Second Chance</u>[3]
<u>Her Unexpected Partner</u>[4]
<u>Her Unexpected Rival</u>[5]
<u>Her Unexpected Catch</u>[6]
<u>Her Unexpected Star</u>[7]
Her Unexpected Delivery
Her Unexpected Protector

2. https://www.amazon.com/Her-Unexpected-Roommate-Blossoms-Bouquets-ebook/dp/B08PPXK15R

3. https://www.amazon.com/gp/product/B08T63NT34

4. https://www.amazon.com/gp/product/B08WJJ3FQH

5. https://www.amazon.com/gp/product/B08YX11KNY

6. https://www.amazon.com/gp/product/B092TQYFZ7

7. https://www.amazon.com/dp/B095KT58CW

www.ingramcontent.com/pod-product-compliance
Lightning Source LLC
Chambersburg PA
CBHW072031220726
48293CB00016B/653